STAFF PICKS

YELLOW SHOE FICTION

Michael Griffith, Series Editor

ALSO BY GEORGE SINGLETON

STORIES

These People Are Us
The Half-Mammals of Dixie
Why Dogs Chase Cars
Drowning in Gruel
Stray Decorum
Between Wrecks
Calloustown

NOVELS

Novel
Work Shirts for Madmen

NONFICTION

Pep Talks, Warnings, and Screeds

GEORGE SINGLETON

STAFF PICKS

stories

Louisiana State University Press ▌▌ Baton Rouge

Published with the assistance of the Borne Fund

Published by Louisiana State University Press
Copyright © 2019 by George Singleton
All rights reserved
Manufactured in the United States of America
LSU Press Paperback Original
First printing

Designer: Barbara Neely Bourgoyne
Typeface: Sentinel
Printer and binder: Sheridan Books

Library of Congress Cataloging-in-Publication Data
Names: Singleton, George, 1958– author.
Title: Staff picks : stories / George Singleton.
Description: Baton Rouge : Louisiana State University Press, [2019] | Series: Yellow shoe fiction
Identifiers: LCCN 2018034730| ISBN 978-0-8071-7033-5 (pbk. : alk. paper) | ISBN 978-0-8071-7083-0 (pdf) | ISBN 978-0-8071-7084-7 (epub)
Classification: LCC PS3569.I5747 A6 2019 | DDC 813/.54—dc23
LC record available at https://lccn.loc.gov/2018034730

The paper in this book meets the guidelines for permanence and durability of the Committee on Production Guidelines for Book Longevity of the Council on Library Resources. ♾

For John Lane, Deno Trakas, and Scott Gould—
rabid Terrier writer/teachers all

There are certain events of which we have not consciously taken note; they have remained, so to speak, below the threshold of consciousness. They have happened, but they have been absorbed subliminally.

—CARL JUNG

CONTENTS

STAFF PICKS

STAFF PICKS

According to the radio station's rules, contestants were permitted to place their hands anywhere on the RV they felt comfortable. Staff Puckett chose the Winnebago's spare tire, which was sheathed in vinyl emblazoned with the image of Mount Rushmore. Staff had considered visiting the granite sculpture, off and on, for twenty years, and now she vowed to herself that soon she'd make her way northwest on mostly back roads, then stare down those four faces whose stony expressions didn't look much different from her own.

But first she had to win the RV. She'd been one of the nineteen nineteenth callers during WCRS's nineteen-day "19th Nervous Breakdown" marathon. Now she and the other eighteen contestants were gathered in the parking lot of State Line RV World, near the border of Georgia and South Carolina. The rules were simple: Contestants had to remain in contact with the RV. The last one standing got the keys.

A man to Staff's left stuck his hand on the taillight, and a woman with bleached hair reached up high onto the back window, which Staff thought a questionable move. The other sixteen contestants—including a doughy, balding man whose shirt blazed with advertising logos—chose the hood, windshield, door handles, random snatches of stripe.

"Good morning," the balding man said. While he waited in vain for Staff's reply, he gave what seemed to be a sincere smile, and Staff automatically believed that he wouldn't last long.

The bleached-hair woman said, "They say there's going to be good prizes for everyone who makes it toward the end, like camp stoves and whatnot. Like tents and sleeping bags." She said, "My name's Marguerite," but she didn't offer a handshake, knowing better than to take her palm off the window and get disqualified first, probably to receive only a pack of matches or a road atlas of the southeastern United States.

Marguerite wore too-tight blue jeans and a denim shirt she shouldn't've tucked in, Staff thought. Though this woman had youth on her side—she might've been twenty-eight at most—she'd fry in the sun. Staff wore an oversized linen dress from a company called Blue Fish that she'd not selected out of her closet in a decade. It was loose, with enough room to spread her legs should she need to urinate in between the every-four-hours-and-fifteen-minutes breaks for food and porta-potty.

Staff nodded. She didn't smile. She wished she'd brought along earplugs and chosen not to wear deodorant. She said, "Staff."

Staff's mother had named her after a dinner plate, though Staff liked to think she was named after an entire setting, or the factory over in England. Staffordshire Puckett. "She'll have enough problems with your last name, when kids start rhyming," Staff's mother said often to her father. "At least Staffordshire sounds regal." It was only a coincidence that, having been named for a plate, Staff soon developed a flat visage to match her moniker.

The condition wasn't exactly medical, but when she remained unsmiling—most of the time—her expression remained frozen in the countenance a mother rat snake might display while regarding her hatchlings. It didn't help that Staff's forehead appeared abnormally large, or that her neck was shorter than average. At the sight of her, ex-projectionists from movie theaters underwent flashbacks of blank screens when reels snapped apart. Art historians approached to ask if she was related to any of the wide-eyed, flat-faced girls portrayed in famous nineteenth-century portraits. They even had a term now for the look of her so-called resting face. Staff didn't like the term.

Fortunately for Staff, her body from the neck down did not look unlike those seen in 1960s auto-parts pin-up calendars. Staff's measurements came out—even at age thirty-nine—to 34C, 22, 36. Most heterosexual men soon forgot about her deadpan face. Gay men concentrated on her skin tone. All women distrusted her.

"Staph!" said Marguerite. "Like the infection? Steph, or Staph?"

"Yeah, like the infection," Staff said, hoping to cause the woman to release her hand prematurely. Staff sidled a half-step in Marguerite's direction. "My brother's named Mersa."

The man to Staff's left said, "I'm Cy, but they call me Cyclone. Y'all might as well let go of this RV now and go do some women's work. I already won a car this way back two years, and a Westinghouse washing machine for Lorene just six month ago." He wore khaki pants and a white T-shirt that read I'M 1/16th EVIL.

Marguerite said, "I'm Marguerite! I guess we're in charge of the back end of this Winnebago here."

Staff looked over at Cyclone and wished she had a pistol in her pocket. He was exactly the kind of person she hoped to leave behind once she won this RV and hit the road for bigger and better places, a more worldly life. She said, "S-I-G-H, Sigh? Like that?"

Cy narrowed his eyes at her. "Are you okay?"

Staff said, "I'm killer."

She didn't say, "One time at a bus stop over in Atlanta somebody called 911 thinking I'd had a stroke."

She thought, If I'd worn cut-off blue jeans and a red-checked blouse knotted midriff, all these men would be out of the competition by now.

Disc jockeys from WCRS judged the contest. The station was doing a remote broadcast from State Line RV World, raising a giant antenna with a satellite dish in the middle of the parking lot. People had come from a four-county area to see their favorite deejays: Morning Woody, Crazy Ned-Ned the Pumpkinhead, One-Stroke, Cyclin' Mike, and Hellbent Heidi. On air, Hellbent Heidi came off as a vixen and claimed to have a skin condition that caused her to work naked, but here in the sun, she wore a traditional Eileen Fisher dress over her size 18 frame.

Marguerite said, "I feel like we've met before."

"I'm an archivist over at the Steepleburg Public Library," Staff said. "If you've ever been on the third floor where we keep historical documents, maybe you've seen me."

Marguerite said, "Say that word again? Ach-what?"

"You the one insisted on taking the Stars and Bars out of the History Room?" Cy asked. "I wrote a letter to the editor about that. I don't want my tax money helping out no library won't honor my ancestors."

Marguerite said, "Arch-ive-ist?" stressing the middle syllable.

"Archivist," Staff said, pronouncing it correctly. "Archivist." Her face didn't change. She didn't smile or frown. But she turned to Cy and stared so hard that he held his hands up in surrender.

Ned-Ned the Pumpkinhead roared, "We're down to eighteen!"

Morning Woody cut short "Satisfaction" and segued into "19th Nervous Breakdown."

Marguerite said, "I can't say your job."

Cy looked at his hand like it had betrayed him.

Staff said, "Way to go, Cybernetics. Nice concentration. Maybe you come from a long line of ancestors who didn't concentrate when bullets came their way."

Hellbent Heidi stormed over, took Cy by the arm, and led him toward a tent set up with free bottled water for contestants. "I'm calling my lawyer!" Cy yelled. "That woman's evil!"

Marguerite fanned herself with her left hand. She said, "It's hot." She said, "I ain't asking for no sympathy, but I just got out of a relationship with a man who trafficked cocaine and heroin from Mexico. He said he worked for the Humane Society and that he rescued poor dogs and cats and goats from across the border down there in Juarez, but in reality he was shoving drug-filled rubbers down their throats, bringing them over, and then, you know, waiting for them to poop. I'm glad I got out of that! My mother warned me! But who wouldn't be attracted to a do-gooder Humane Society man? Anyway, he got caught, and I got questioned. The whole reason I want this RV is so I can do the Lord's work and travel around really helping animals in need."

Yeah, yeah, yeah, Staff thought. She'd braced herself for stories such as this. She'd done her research after hours in the library, reading up on scams, tricks, hoaxes, pity-me tales. A man up in Detroit lost his chance at winning a Cadillac because he believed another contestant's story about six kids and food stamps. A woman in Oregon didn't win a foreclosed house after being fooled by a man who claimed to have been on death row, falsely accused, for seventeen years.

Now Staff looked at Marguerite and considered what phobias her fellow contestant might possess. Dogs? Snakes? Tight spaces? Heights? But she needed something closer at hand. "It's supposed to get up to ninety this afternoon," Staff said, "and then the bees are coming out." As an archivist, she understood that 5 percent of the population suffered from bee-sting allergies, including, perhaps, one of her remaining competitors.

Marguerite said, "What?" and walked away from the Winnebago.

"And we're down to seventeen!" yelled out Morning Woody. He switched from the Allman Brothers Band into "19th Nervous Breakdown" again, blaring the song across the lot.

"I didn't want no RV anyway," Marguerite said as Hellbent Heidi escorted her to the contestants' tent. "Hey, can I get a four-pack of them WCRS koozies as part of my consolation prize?"

• • •

Staff had entered the contest soon after her fiancé, Leon—a math instructor turned semi-professional Texas Hold 'Em player—left her. He'd proposed after two months and then changed his mind, convinced that she made fun of him both at meals and in bed, because she kept a poker face at all times, something he could never do at the tables in Tunica, Shreveport, Vicksburg, Cherokee. After he was gone, she took the engagement ring to a jeweler in town called Spar-kleworks, only to be told that the diamond was a zircon. The man at the counter, who sported a bow tie, would offer only fifty dollars for it, which Staff took.

Now, in an attempt to escape the relentless this-is-not-worth-it thoughts that accompanied boredom and fatigue, Staff cataloged Leon's annoying mantras: *flush beats a straight; straight flush beats a full house; tapping fingers probably means a bluff; pair of kings beats a pair of queens; guy clears his throat twice when he's got a flush; pu-pils dilate when things look futile.* Next she occupied her mind by recalling, chronologically, the displays, shows, and collections she'd conceived and produced at the library: The History and Importance of Pine in the County; The History and Importance of Peaches in the County; Confederate Money; Nineteenth-Century Garments; The History and Importance of Dairy Cattle in the County; The Sib-ling Outsider Artists Hilty and Duck Dodgen of Rock House Springs; Hairstyles of Our Congressmen; The History and Importance of Blackberries in the County; Cherokee Weapons and Implements. She went through it all. Staff recalled a one-month show about modern-day treasure hunters who had searched for the lost gold and silver of the Confederacy, which sparked townspeople to buy metal detectors and shovels to excavate the farmland and backyards of unsuspecting fellow citizens. Though the library's director scolded Staff for caus-ing minor chaos, hardware stores on both sides of the river offered her discounts on any purchases.

Staff stared at the back end of the Winnebago, with its spare tire cover depicting the presidents' faces. She was still bored but undaunted. She thought about traveling to Mount Rushmore. She bet that, had she been born in a different time, and in South Dakota, she could have been a model for the sculptor, Gutzon Borglum. Staff daydreamed of sitting on a stool while Gutzon lovingly carved her in stone.

Next she daydreamed about Leon, seated for three-hour stretches, maybe in Biloxi, wondering if he could bluff a pair of ducks he held with a king-queen-jack showing on the river, knowing his opponents probably held face cards.

She ran down the list of famous archivists she'd learned about in graduate school. She wondered how her classmates—most of them plain, sincere librarians employed at colleges—felt about their career paths, if they'd grown as restless as she had. Staff thought about the periodic table, what she might plant in her summer garden, actors who might be attracted to her inscrutable stare.

By nightfall Staff had outlasted a woman on a Jazzy who'd tried to readjust her grip by scooting her machine to the front of the RV but braked too late, smashing into the grille and injuring herself. Staff then overtook a man with no arms—the crowd favorite—who had kept his forehead pressed against the end of the bumper until he fell asleep and slid right down to the pavement, disqualified. Within the hour she wished she'd brought along a sweater to go over her dress, but she stayed focused by thinking of warmer locales. She caught herself picturing El Paso. Another place she'd never visited.

One woman started crying uncontrollably when the radio station blasted "That Smell" by Lynyrd Skynyrd. She yelled, "That was our song!" ran to her 1988 Camaro, and peeled out of the lot, almost running over the woman on the Jazzy as she exited the first-aid tent.

"We're down to six contestants, folks!" Morning Woody said into the microphone. "And now it's almost time for our fifth break. Three . . . two . . . one . . . hands off! Let's see if Ms. Staffordshire Puckett might have to use the bathroom yet. We got bets going on whether or not she's wearing Depends."

Staff thought, Have I been so focused that I haven't eaten? Have I not used my breaks to devour protein shakes and granola bars, like I promised myself? She said aloud to no one, "Have I dehydrated myself unknowingly?" and then released her hand from the back of the Winnebago.

In the contestants' tent, Staff picked up a Gatorade, a bottle of water, and a blueberry muffin. She realized she'd stood there holding onto the RV in such a trance that she'd not comprehended the sun going down eight hours earlier, hadn't noticed the bats and night-hawks swirling around the giant antenna, attracted to State Line RV World's bright lights. She'd blocked the music WCRS blasted and replaced it with Shostakovich.

"You okay?" said one of the EMS workers, a stocky woman wearing cotton pants hitched past her navel. "We were worried about you. Thought you might've gone into a self-induced coma or something."

Staff nodded. She didn't smile.

"Your facial muscles don't seem to be working," said the EMS worker, shining a penlight into Staff's eyes.

Staff forced a tight smile. "Please don't do that."

The EMS worker backed off, and one of the remaining contestants sidled up. "I get drug-tested all the time," he said, "what with my being a professional athlete."

Staff turned to see the man with advertising logos all over his shirt. He wore polyester pants and had one of those unfortunate bald patterns with a small island of hair at the top of his forehead, surrounded by scalp. When viewed from above, Staff thought, this guy's head might look like a period surrounded by parentheses. Staff said, "What?"

"I'm Landry Harmon. I know that not a lot of people watch the pro bowlers' tour, but I'm in the PBA. I have two wins so far. I mean, I'm no Parker Bohn III, or Norm Duke, or Walter Ray Williams Jr., but I've done okay. I'm no Dick Ritger or Dick Weber, but my name ain't Dick. I'm no Earl Anthony or Pete Weber. But I've won. I've bowled a 300 more than I can count. Well, about seventeen times, in tournaments."

Staff noted that her ex, Leon, looked exactly the opposite of Landry Harmon. How could a semipro poker player have a BMI of 20 while spending so much time on his rear end, staring at cards in a smoky arena? And how could a man like Landry Harmon—who probably lifted weights between matches—end up so soft, frumpy, and glisten-headed? Did he eat nothing but French fries while his opponents took their turns? Staff said, "Hello."

"Have you ever bowled?" Landry asked. "Your face reminds me of a bowling ball, and I mean that as a compliment."

Staff shook her head. No one ever complimented her face, and what Landry had said sounded more like an insult, but he pored over her features with what appeared to be genuine admiration.

"Daggum, woman," he continued, "you have the most beautiful skin of all time. And I admire how you stood up during breaks like Muhammad Ali used to do between rounds, to get inside his opponent's head."

Staff said only, "Huh," and turned away so Landry wouldn't see her cheeks flush.

• • •

After the break, Landry Harmon followed Staff to the back end of the RV. He put his hand on the ladder. He said, "I should be holding onto the tow ball, make myself feel right at home, but it's so low I'm afraid my back will give out. I already got a questionable back. From bowling. On the Professional Bowlers Association tour."

Staff thought, The whole time I was mentally cataloging displays from the Special Collections Room, Landry Harmon probably recited whatever statistics people who played bowling kept in their heads.

She said, "You mentioned that."

"It's probably not a good idea for me to touch the spare tire, like you're doing. Get it? *Spare.* In my world, a spare's not a great thing, compared to a strike."

Later, she would wonder what kept her from attempting to irritate him. There was something about Landry Harmon's face—not blank and hard like hers, but soft and gentle. If his face were an animal, it would be a koala, Staff thought. If bedding, a down-filled pillow. She knew nothing of bowling and said, "What's your handicap?"

Landry Harmon's short-sleeve shirt was emblazoned with his sponsors: Brunswick, Vise, Dexter bowling shoes, Rogaine, Tanner's Natural Chamois, Newman's Own Dog Treats. He said, "Why you want to win this Winnebago? Please don't tell me you ain't got no-where to live and get me feeling all sorry for you."

Staff shook her head. "Just want to travel, see some places out West, nothing more than that." Of course, there was a lot more. Leon breaking up with her had been a splash of cold water. If she won the Winnebago, she could sell her sad little house in this sad backwards town, quit her sad sleepy job, and start living her life for real, every day an adventure.

Landry turned and stared at the sun coming up. The deejay started playing a George Harrison song. Landry said, "I don't have no sob story neither. Being a pro bowler, I pretty much live on the road. Right now I drive a Ford Focus. Sure, it gets great mileage, but it doesn't have a bathroom, a dinette, or a private master bedroom with a flat-panel HDTV and solar-blackout roller shades."

Staff couldn't explain the attraction she felt.

She thought, God put me here to meet this man Landry Harmon.

She said, "I read up about a man who tried to win a boat in one of these radio-station promos. It came down to him and a woman. The woman said she wanted the boat so she could give it to her father, who liked to fish. The man said he needed it because his wife had drowned somewhere off the Gulf coast, and they'd quit looking for her after a week, and he wanted to go down there and keep searching for her body. The woman put her hands up to her face and lost."

Landry and Staff kept eye contact even when two more contestants quit.

"My mother died," Landry said. "It wasn't sad, really. She died the way she wanted to. She had cancer and chose not to undergo chemo or radiation. She lasted almost three years."

"I'm not falling for it," Staff said. She didn't break into a smile, or laugh, or shake her head. She said, "Hg, mercury, 80. Tl, thallium, 81. Pb, lead, 82."

Landry placed his left hand over his right, one rung higher on the ladder. "Anyway, she got to see me win on TV. She saw me win

Southeast Amateur when I was in college. She had no regrets. Died peacefully at hospice."

There were only three contestants left: Staff, Landry, and a man covered in tattoos holding onto one of the windshield wipers. Staff peeked around the corner of the Winnebago as best she could, to see if the tattooed man had fallen asleep, but instead she saw Hellbent Heidi passed out in her canvas folding chair. Crazy Ned-Ned squirted Reddi-wip onto her hand. One-Stroke started to tickle beneath Hellbent Heidi's nose, and Staff yelled out, "Stop that right now!" as she might at visiting schoolchildren wanting to touch a fragile document in the Special Collections Room. Hellbent Heidi raised her head, and everyone else involved went, "Awwwww."

"There's nothing sad about my mother's death," Landry said.

Staff said, "Rn, radon, 86."

"Well, maybe one thing," Landry said. "She had a lot of jewelry, and I didn't know if it was worth anything. I ended up taking it to this place Sparkleworks, in downtown Steepleburg. It supposedly wasn't so much a pawn shop as a place that specialized in estate jewelry."

Staff stopped talking. She stared at Landry.

He said, "This man named Lou said two diamond rings and a locket and a bracelet weren't worth but three hundred dollars. I didn't know. It ain't like I've had time on the Professional Bowlers Association tour to take up night courses in gemology. So I sold it all for that amount. Maybe a month later, I looked on their website and saw one of my mother's rings going for $2,700 and the other for $4,260. The locket? Four hundred. That bracelet? Sixteen hundred bucks."

Staff said, "Stop." She said, "Who are you? Is this some kind of joke?" She thought of the ring she'd sold Sparkleworks for fifty dollars. She thought, Leon, Landry, Lou. She tried to remember if there existed an element with plain L for its symbol. She said, "Li, lithium, 3."

Landry looked through his armpit at Staff. "I have a feeling that estate-jeweler dude thought I was dumb as okra. Standing there so smug wearing his seersucker suit and a bow tie. Seersucker for a c-sucker, if you ask me. Excuse my language."

"It's a small world," Staff said. "I wouldn't want to caulk it. But that same pawn shop? I think that guy ripped me off, too."

Landry didn't waver from his eye contact. He said, "Know what I'd like to do? If I won this RV, I'd like to smash it right through the plate-glass window of that place. The front of the Winnebago's the same height and width as Sparkleworks' display window. That's one thing all pro bowlers are good at, being able to measure things out by sight. If I got caught, I could say I lost control of the wheel. If I didn't, I'd grab my mother's jewelry, and nothing else. After hours, of course."

Staff held up her free hand. She said, "Don't you think when they took inventory for the insurance claim, they might notice how everything stolen happened to be yours?"

"Huh," said Landry. "It might be fortuitous that I met a woman like you. Did I say that right? You're the smart one, I can tell."

"You said it right. Woman. That's the way to pronounce it."

Landry opened his mouth, then smiled. Staff noticed that one canine overlapped the next tooth, much like a bowling pin edging over to knock down its lane-partner.

"Can't use my own car to do it," he said. "It's one of those ad-wrapped cars you sometimes see around town. Somebody might go to the cops and say, 'Hey, I saw a little Ford Focus with Brunswick, Vise, Dexter, Rogaine, Tanner's Natural Chamois, Newman's Own Dog Treats, and PBA written all over the hood and sides.'"

Staff almost caught herself saying, "How come you and I never met about ten years ago?" Instead she said, "You're putting a lot of thought into a crazy idea. Are you getting delirious? Am I about to win this RV?"

The man with the tattoos evidently collapsed.

Ned-Ned the Pumpkinhead blurted out, "And we're down to two finalists!"

What Staff didn't say to Landry Harmon was, "I want to go with you."

• • •

In the history of hands-on competitions, Staff had learned while researching at the library, most winners suffered through at least forty hours. One man in Beijing withstood a challenger over four days and three nights just to win a rickshaw. A woman won a thoroughbred in Kentucky; a man won a champion bull in Texas; an eighteen-year-old college student with a fake ID put up five hundred dollars to participate in, and then win, a "Touch the Foreclosed Drive-Thru Liquor Store" contest in Shreveport, Louisiana, sponsored by a forward-thinking local bank, whose president later got charged for contributing to the delinquency of a minor.

Compared to those the Winnebago seemed easy.

The sun stood high in the State Line RV World parking lot. It had been forty-one hours.

"Just you and me now, I guess," Staff said to Landry.

He reached into his left back pocket, pulled out a handkerchief, and wiped his upper lip. Staff drew her fingers across her forehead. She couldn't tell if sweat trickled down her temple, or if a persistent fly kept landing on her. She untangled her toes back and forth, feeling nothing but moisture.

WCRS went into a long commercial after playing Steve Miller's "Going to Mexico," and then Hellbent Heidi showed up with her microphone. To Landry she said, "So. You thinking about going to Mexico if you win this nice Winnebago?"

Landry said, "No, I don't think so."

To Staff she said, "What about you?"

Staff shook her head. She said, "Matters who gets elected president next. Probably not Mexico, but maybe Canada."

One-Stroke, the sound effects specialist, went *"Boi-yoi-yoi-yoi-yoi-yoing!"* and then said—in the deep, sinister, stereotypical Hispanic accent he employed during a politically incorrect daily feature called What Would Hey-Zeus Do?—"It's time to spill the beans." Normally, callers in this segment had to admit some kind of immoral activity that involved spousal cheating or workplace theft in order to win two free tickets to a concert, or two free entrées at Wild Wings, or two free suet stations from State Line Bird Supply.

"Christ went forty days and forty nights," Hellbent Heidi said. "Y'all willing to go that far to win this fine Winnebago here at State Line RV?"

Both Landry and Staff said, "Yes," and then "Go away," at the same time.

Heidi said, "Well, it seems like we've gone completely into Stage Irritable, folks." She said, "What we got up next, Ned-Ned?" Then she turned off her mic and said to Landry and Staff, "Don't y'all turn hateful. If so we'll find a way to disqualify you."

Landry apologized. Staff avoided eye contact, knowing her face might be taken as a challenge. She said, "What if we take our hands off at the very same time? Would we split the prize? Would one of us have to buy out the other? I mean, would we split the prize, and maybe have to promise to accompany one another to, say, professional bowling games all over the country? Plus Mount Rushmore?"

Heidi said, "That's a good question. Let me go ask our manager."

Staff turned to Landry. She said, "Just in case, you know."

Landry said, "It's called a tournament. Professional bowling *tournaments,* not games."

Hellbent Heidi returned and said, "They decided that if y'all happen to take your hands off at the very same time—and they used the word 'indiscernible'—if y'all take off your hands in such a way that no one can say something like, 'He pulled his hand off one-hundredth of a second before she did,' or vice-versa, then it would be up to y'all to decide how you'd share the RV. Hell, Bobby said he'd buy it back from you for thirty grand, and y'all could split the profit. There's property taxes and insurance to think about, too."

Staff and Landry shared a look, and Staff knew they were both thinking about the estate jeweler, and how they weren't about to let themselves get ripped off again.

Staff said, "This Winnebago's brand-new."

Landry said, "Blue Book has it going for right under a hundred grand."

Staff said, "Anyway, who's Bobby?"

"Bobby owns State Line RV," Hellbent Heidi said. "It's up to y'all. Easiest solution, if you ask me, is for one of y'all to quit before the other one so's we ain't got no quandary."

Morning Woody leaned into his microphone and said, "You might add that we'd appreciate one of them making a decision soon, Heidi. They saying a summertime thunderstorm's headed our way. I ain't too keen on getting electrocuted." And then, perhaps using the same techniques employed by the FBI during long-term standoffs, he began a loop of four excruciating songs by the heavy metal band Jackyl, one of which included a chain-saw solo.

Staff and Landry plugged onward. They held onto the RV through the night. During breaks, they used porta-potties. They opened Nutri-Grain granola bars for each other, and Landry laughed when Staff said she'd poured prune juice for him instead of Gatorade. Landry mentioned how he didn't have groupies like some of his pro bowling competitors. He said, "I used to be completely bald on top before using Rogaine."

Staff said, "I'm thinking about retiring early from the library. Somebody needs to do a study about the effects of breathing musty books eight hours a day for sixteen years. I bet it's on par with asbestos." Rain began to spatter. Lightning spasmed in the distance. Later on, Staff would tell Landry that this was the moment when she first imagined them driving the RV through the front glass at Sparkleworks.

On and on they talked. Landry pulled his shirttail out, and the deejays made a pact to stand up to their bosses should they ever want to hold another hands-on contest. At the forty-eight-hour mark, Landry said, "You ever seen that movie *48 Hours*? That's a good movie. It's on about all the time, one channel or another, on cable." He looked up at the clouds. At only 8:00 a.m., the sky had turned dark.

Staff said, "I've never seen it."

"When this is over," Landry said, "maybe we can rent it on the Netflix. That movie should've won some Oscars. You ever seen *Another 48 Hours*? It's not as good, but it still should've won some Oscars. I met Nick Nolte one time. He likes to bowl in between making movies. At least that's what he told me."

A long rumble of thunder rolled in from the west. Staff said, "I'm not playing around, but I don't know how much longer I can do this."

"No, no, no, no, no," Landry said. Later he would tell Staff, "What I was really thinking was, 'This is the best date I've ever been on.'"

The rain beat down, soaking their clothes and shoes. Landry tightened his grip on the ladder. He said, "No matter who wins, let's promise to see each other again."

Before Staff could say, "That would make me happy," a bolt of lightning zapped the WCRS radio antenna, sending an explosion of sparks across the parking lot, followed by a clap of thunder that roared harder than anything Jackyl could've captured on vinyl. Staff and Landry let go simultaneously—they agreed that they did so, and Hellbent Heidi later lied and said she'd seen it too, them releasing in such a way that even an Olympic stopwatch couldn't have detected an outright winner.

Staff and Landry ran to the tent, where they found the deejays huddled with Bobby. There was supposed to be an official ceremony for the winner of the RV, complete with a photographer, in Bobby's office, but the lightning had knocked WCRS off the air. Bobby said something about how rules change every day, and then asked which one of them would sign the title papers. When Landry and Staff shrugged, he pulled a quarter from his pocket. "If this don't work out," he said, "we'll do rock-paper-scissors-dynamite."

Landry won the coin toss and asked what Staff wanted to do. He said he had a feeling, and that he trusted her.

Staff stared at him. "We could both sign," she said.

Bobby said, "I don't give a good goddamn what y'all do. I already got my free advertising."

And so Staff and Landry signed their names to the RV's title as the storm continued to pelt the tent. Bobby handed over the registration and an owner's manual. The radio people scrambled to their cars, leaving the tent and the busted antenna behind. The wind still blew, and Staff and Landry stepped out into the rain. The cars they'd come in, a Jeep and an ad-wrapped Ford Focus, sat with two spaces between them, like a 7–10 split.

"Your cars will be safe," Bobby said. "You can pick them up later. We got an automatic fence around the place. And let me tell you, if someone wants to steal something, I don't think it's going to be one of y'all's junkers. Listen, it's been two and a half days. I'm out of here. Congratulations." Bobby headed straight for his car, got in, and drove off.

• • •

Staff didn't have second thoughts until she and Landry were inside, alone, drying themselves off at the kitchenette with hand towels bearing the logo of State Line RV World. Maybe she shouldn't have had them both sign the title, she thought, or maybe it was the most prescient thing she'd ever done. All she knew for sure was that she wasn't ready to part ways with Landry Harmon.

"Well?" he said, rapping his knuckles on the faux-marble countertop. "Shall we take this baby for a spin?"

Staff nodded. Landry thought to take off the temporary tag. Staff rode shotgun. Landry guided the big RV onto I-85. He didn't seem to have a destination in mind, and Staff didn't care. Soon they were crossing the state line into South Carolina. Just beyond the first rest area, they listened to the mechanical voice of the emergency weather channel: People living in low-lying areas should seek higher ground in case of flooding. Yet, people should seek low-lying areas if tornadoes develop. They passed a highway patrol car attending to a fender-bender, then a white pickup truck angled sideways in a ditch, then two tractor-trailers that had pulled over to wait out the rain, their hazards flashing. The interstate was no place to be. Landry took the next exit, which happened to be Steepleburg. Staff hoped he wasn't planning to drop her off at home, but Landry just talked about taking the RV to Milwaukee, the site of his next tournament.

Staff thought: If you talk about something too much, you might make it real. She pointed out the library where she worked, saying, "That's where I've spent way too many hours." They passed an all-night pharmacy and a mall so vacant of anchor stores that older people called it "the track," because that's where they walked early mornings. Landry straddled the white lines as they passed a hamburger joint once featured on a cable show about out-of-the-way dives. A prop plane flew across their line of vision, wobbling its way toward the county airport. Two dogs briefly splashed along beside the RV, barking at the tires.

Staff thought about everything she had to lose, and it wasn't much. More lightning flashed, its prongs reaching the ground like an upturned vase of a half-dozen dead roses, and then the rain went horizontal.

"If there are power failures downtown," she said, "there'll be no security cameras working, no burglar alarms. We'll know for certain if the traffic signals are out. If they are, we could drive right through that jeweler's window and no one would know."

Landry gave a low whistle. He looked at her. He said, "How serious are you?"

Staff gave her best impression of a concrete slab. She said, "How serious are you?"

By now they were coming into downtown Steepleburg.

Landry shook his head and then nodded. "If we were to do such a thing—and mind you, I'm not saying we should—we'd want to get in and out real quick-like. I'd only take my momma's stuff. But you could take whatever you wanted."

Staff didn't care about the ring from Leon. But wouldn't it be funny, she thought, if they sold china at Sparkleworks? Wouldn't it be funny if the headlights of the Winnebago shone on a nice set of Staffordshire?

"Maybe I'd get a little something so I could look fancy rooting you on at that tournament in Milwaukee," she said. "Earrings, or a bracelet. Something nice but not ostentatious."

Neither of them said a word as they passed under a darkened traffic light.

Then Staff put out her left hand, and Landry took it. Staff felt her face begin to soften and relax, and then she broke into a bright smile, showing perfect, straight, white teeth.

"Wow," Landry said. "What's wrong?"

Staff said, "Ha ha." She gripped his hand tighter. Her heart pounded faster than the windshield wipers. Up ahead, through the crashing rain, a plate-glass window reflected their headlights like a beacon.

COLUMBUS DAY

Every night at bedtime, my wife turns to cable stations that show back-to-back-to-back-to-back episodes of murdered spouses and the forensic technology that prevents questionable and error-prone outcomes. This one particular channel airs these programs' reruns exclusively. It's like the Killer Channel. Sometimes I wake up at three o'clock after hearing the narrator go, "They exhumed the body a second time," and open my eyes to find Lisette sitting straight up, staring at the screen. I should mention that she leaves the house six mornings a week before four o'clock, to travel down our clay, rutted half-mile driveway, get dough in the oven at her ex-gas-station-turned-bakery Pure Tarts, and await both locals and travelers in need of diet-regardless nourishment. It didn't use to be this way, back when we held regular jobs—Lisette a pharmaceutical sales rep, me the VP of marketing research firm Piedmont Consumer Pulse. Before our early-midlife resolutions to move out of a city, to do something that wasn't slightly immoral, we punched the channel changer thirty or sixty minutes and fell asleep before the local news's sports segment. In the old days, in our late twenties and early thirties there at the kitchen table in the mornings, Lisette might say something like, "That's sad about the Humane Society burning to the ground" or, "It's not supposed to rain until late this afternoon." She might've said, "Someone needs to teach that anchorwoman how to pronounce al-Qaeda, Illinois, Guantanamo, Cairo, Putin, and Angelina Jolie."

But now it's all How Did That Person Almost Get Away with Murder? It's all patricide, fratricide, matricide, filicide, sororicide, and—what scares me most—mariticide, the killing of one's spouse. When it comes to that last one, on the TV show, inevitably the graven-voiced narrator, five minutes from the episode's conclusion, goes, "Was it coincidence that Walter bought a $600,000 life insurance policy on Doris only three weeks before her supposed bludgeoning while he was out of town? Hmmmmmmmmm? Hmmmmmmmmm? Curious, don't you think?" And then the cops go into Walter's computer and find that he researched living in Borneo or Tongatapu or southern Alabama to find out that people could live in those places elegantly for a hundred years with a mistress, so long as they had exactly $600,000, plus airfare. Then the truth comes out about how Walter worked two jobs—one as a sous-chef, the other in a chemistry lab—and he folded a tasteless poison into Doris's omelet one breakfast, she died, the coroner chose "heart attack" or "natural causes," Walter moved to an island, and then he got drunk in a tiki bar and blurted out a confession to an FBI agent there with his wife celebrating a second honeymoon.

Lisette watches those shows. She runs a bakery. Almost every night she wants me to sample her latest tart. I don't want to sound paranoid, but some mornings I'm a little surprised to wake up without blood surging from my eye ducts.

"Did you remember to bring your Fitbit?" Lisette asks as I drive us some thirty miles from the outpost where we live to the mall. The fucking mall! Lisette's never been there, but I have during cold, rainy days when I needed to get some steps in. Usually I say, "I need to drive around and think up some ideas for a client," but really I head straight to the mall and merge into the stream of men and women trying to lower blood pressure, raise libido, or limber up those mechanical hips and knees. There's a Williams-Sonoma going out of business or moving to a place where people actually use stovetops instead of fire pits. Lisette wants to check out their whisks, their nonstick muffin pans, their fluted tart pans—all on sale.

I say, "Yes." I think, I don't know why I joined a Wellness Plan. The insurance company said if I did so along with a number of other self-employed insurees, it wouldn't add an extra hundred bucks a month. Me, I thought, rightly, I can buy a lot of cigarettes and booze with an extra twelve hundred dollars a year.

We take two-lane roads on our way to I-26, which will eventually get us to an exit for the Southgate Mall in Steepleburg, an ex–textile town that dwindles both spiritually and population-wise daily, though the locals—pure southern gothic descendants of the once-respected rich and powerful—insist the town's going through a rebirth. Steepleburg called itself "Church City" a hundred years ago because there were more congregations per capita than anywhere in the Southeast. Then it went by "Biscuit City" because a 1950s band called the Flaky Biscuits had a hit. I got hired one time to help remoniker the place, and the only thing I could come up with went "We Don't Blow" because city employees worked rakes instead of the leaf blowers used in every nearby southern town that had, indeed, reinvented itself: Asheville, Greenville, Columbia, Augusta, Charlotte, et cetera. Hell, Atlanta'd gone past leaf blowers into the realm of giant detritus-gathering vacuums, which made me think how Atlanta might consider "We Suck" instead of "Empire City" or "Hotlanta."

The mall looks a lot like Main Street, only covered, which is to say Vacant Storefront, Vacant Storefront, Vacant Storefront, Place That Sells Ball Caps, Vacant Storefront, Place That Sells Leggings, Place That Sells Tennis Shoes, Vacant Storefront, Vacant Storefront, et cetera. Kay Jewelers, New York Watches, Diamond Couture, East Coast Jewelers, We Buy Gold, Vacant Storefront, Vacant Storefront, Zales Jewelers, Vacant Storefront with the Piercing Pagoda across the way. A place to rent tuxedos and that place Spencer's to buy rubber chickens and whoopee cushions. Lisette says, "You got your phone? I'll go in the store. Take your time walking. I might want to check out the Sears and see if they have a good cordless hedge trimmer. Our boxwoods have gotten out of control, in case you haven't noticed."

We enter at the food court. I check my Fitbit—somehow I've put in nearly four thousand steps already, probably pacing the floor thinking about a tiny twinge I feel down toward my appendix—between Vacant Storefront and Yankee Candle. The mall holds few shoppers, which is weird because it's Monday, and Columbus Day. Don't kids still hang out in malls when they're not in school? Are they all at home staring at their Facebook pages, tweeting, doing the Instagram, bullying others?

I look at my wristwatch and say, "If we somehow get separated, I'll meet you at the car at, what, three?"

"Goddamn, Renfro, how far do you plan to walk?" Lisette looks at her watch. "You want to walk in circles for four hours?" She reaches down and practically places her elbows on the floor, stretching.

I do not say, If this place stayed open until midnight I'd walk until then, to keep you from watching those TV shows. I say, "I'm joking. Don't kill me." I try not to think of ways a person could die from a cordless hedge trimmer.

• • •

I take a lap at what I consider a four-mile-an-hour pace. With hardly anyone else here it's easy. I see other mall-walkers—people forty years older than I—shuffling along like zombies. Most carry bags of jellybeans they bought over at Candy World, or hotdogs wrapped in pretzels from Auntie Anne's. One man wears a portable oxygen tank. More than a few have canes or walkers. Except for the vacant stores, it doesn't look that much different from the orthopedic floor of a hospital specializing in hip replacements. I'm the youngster here. If I lived in the same neighborhood as these comrades of mine, I'd be out at night with a baseball bat knocking down mailboxes.

One lap's 2,200 steps. They say it's a mile, but according to my Fitbit it's more. I do the lap, and see my wife, wearing her out-of-the-house/out-of-the-bakery attire, namely blue jeans so tight I worry about her getting a yeast infection, and an Akris long-sleeved notch-collared blouse. I know the particulars because I said, "What the fuck?" when the American Express bill showed up.

I do the lap, passing others easily, wondering what they listen to on their iPods, wondering how in the world such old people could ever succumb to iPods, suspecting that they probably keep Billy Graham podcast sermons somehow available on iTunes lined up one after another.

On the second lap I notice a man sitting on a bench across from a place called Brows 'n' More—a joint where people sit *in public* to have their eyebrows waxed. Who does that? There's another place called the Relaxation Station where people get chair massages and sea-salt foot baths *right in front of everyone* walking by. Listen, I don't consider myself a prude. I had a cocaine problem. I've drunk at least fifty liters of every bourbon ever bottled. Sitting in my home office I crank Hüsker Dü, the Ramones, even Joy Division. But Jesus Christ, there are some things that mall-walkers shouldn't have to encounter daily.

The man wasn't crying on my first lap, but he's obviously pained when I'm right around Step 7,000. I veer over and say, "You okay, buddy?" He's older than I am, but about halfway between me and the zombies. Mid- to late fifties.

"I'm okay," he says. He wears wingtips, which means he's not a walker. "I've been better, but I'm okay. Better than my dad, I guess."

I should say, "All right." I should say, "Glad to hear it," and get on my way as if I'm in need of Squirrel Nut Zippers and Mary Janes at the candy store. But I care about my fellow human beings—which should keep me from getting poisoned, right?—and say, "Because your father never had to sit outside a waxing place while your mother got her unibrow eradicated?" It's what came out.

He shakes his head. "It's stupid," he says. He crosses one leg over another—polyester pants—in a way that makes me think he might have gas.

I get passed by the second-fastest mall-walker, Pete, an eighty-year-old wearing those red-and-black golf pants and going about 1.5 miles an hour. That bugs me a little. Pete brought his son with him a couple times and said his name was "Re-Pete," like some kind of Bazooka Joe joke. I say to Crying Man, "The economy will rebound.

As a matter of fact, I hear that it's rebounded just about everywhere except here. And Alabama." What else can I say?

"My parents used to bring me here when I was a kid. My father had two broken hips because he fell off a three-story roof. He was a roofer. Anyway, we came here, Mom shopped, and my father would make it this far and sit on this very same bench." The man bends his head toward the waxer and waxee. "Right in there used to be an organ store, organs like the instruments. Keyboards and organs. Maybe pianos, though I remember only organs. This old guy working inside would always be playing, and my father would sit here and sing loudly if he knew the song. Big fat man named Joey, though everyone called him Blowey. Great man. Everyone loved him. Worked as the organist at First Baptist, and no one ever asked why he never got married."

I think, I need to get out of here. I think, I need to walk around the parking lot of the mall instead of the inside. I say, "Yeah," like an idiot.

"Wiley Rose Jr.," says the man, sticking out his hand to shake. Now he's blubbering. I say "Renfro Truluck" and hope he's never worked for a company that makes products I've intentionally hammered wrongly in order to get my clients' merchandise advertising-worthy. I'm not proud. Anyone who's ever seen one of those "Nine of Ten Pepsi Drinkers Like RC Cola Better" has me to blame. Easy to do: Bring in taste-testers, make sure the Pepsis are flat, et cetera. America. "Nine Out of Ten Pizza Hut Lovers Choose Deno's Greek-Style." Close down Deno's for the day. Have their best chef make perfect pizzas. Order twenty Pizza Hut Meat Lover's pizzas hourly, during lunch, when their workers are frenzied anyway. Offer two slices to stooges. Deno's wins. Marketing research.

"I'm waiting on my wife," I say. "She's buying a baking sheet, or something." I start cataloging in my head everything Lisette could purchase on sale if she held a secret wish to murder me: Knives. A high-speed hand-held mixer. Ice picks.

Wiley Rose Jr. says, "I am the exact age as my father when he died. Exactly. He used to sit here and sing along with Blowey and make me sit with him while my mother shopped. I was so embarrassed, you know. I wanted to hang out with my friends, maybe get an Icee, or at least pretend to be smart and hang out at Waldenbooks."

I think, That's what's missing: There's no bookstore in this mall. I think, Is there a bookstore in any mall? I say, "What was the story with Coke-flavored Icees? I mean, there was Cherry, and then Coke? Who got *Coke*?"

"*Exactly* his age. I figured it out. Fifty-two years, ten months, eleven days. If I live until tomorrow I'll live a day longer than my father." Wiley Rose Jr. turns toward me, then back to the waxing station. He says, "It's not right. It's not right, this sacred spot being used for whatever they're doing in there."

I nod. I nod and nod and nod. I think about where there might be a place in the mall that sells Kleenex or handkerchiefs, but know there's not one unless Belk's got a sale. Maybe in the old days when they sold musical instruments where a gay Baptist organist moonlighted, but not now.

• • •

I stand up to leave. I want to pass Old Pete—and get enough laps in to clear 10,000 for the day. I visualize the mall's tentacles and try to figure out how to avoid walking past Wiley Rose Jr. another three times. Lisette saunters up, though, lugging two paper bags with raffia handles. She sees Wiley Rose Jr. crying. "Are you okay?" she asks. To me she says, "Are you having heart palpitations a twentieth time? Did your back go out again?" To Wiley Rose Jr. she says, "I get allergy attacks in here, too. All that perfume clouding out of the entrances like evil specters."

He says, "Yeah. Just allergies."

I say, "You ready?" and try to widen my eyes so she'll know I want out of there. I figure I can go home and walk the yard, the driveway, the adjacent pasture where my neighbor Sutton Glane keeps two pet heifers, Helen and Totie, both with withered legs, their manure somehow a veritable magnet for psilocybin mushrooms. I say, "My heart and back are fine."

Lisette says to Wiley Rose Jr., "I watched this show one time about a woman who was deathly allergic to perfume. So her husband took out a gigantic life insurance policy on her, then at night when she slept he not only wafted, but dabbed Chanel on her upper lip."

I say, "Nice to meet you," to Wiley Rose Jr. and take Lisette's bags.

"The coroner said she died of natural causes, you know, but her parents always questioned the report, and sure enough, they eventually exhumed the body and found that swath of good perfume under her nose. The parents said, 'She would *never* wear perfume—she was deathly *allergic* to it.' Next thing you know, the husband's got a life sentence. Big dickhead. He had out a million-dollar life insurance policy on her. They had two kids, so for a while everyone thought a million dollars was about right. It wasn't! It wasn't!"

I say, "Is it 'swath' or 'swarth'? I've never been able to remember that word."

Wiley Rose Jr. stands up and says, "I'm fifty-two years, ten months, and eleven days old," then says his name and sticks out his hand to shake my wife's. Me, I take the time to sneak a look in the bags, but Lisette has bought up only a bunch of spatulas and nonstick pans, plus two magic egg-separators.

"There used to be an organ store in here. Wiley and his folks used to come here back in the '70s or whenever, and his father sat right here on this bench and enjoyed the organ stylings of a man they called Blowey." I find myself walking in place, like some kind of marching band member. Like I play the fucking clarinet.

Lisette says, "Are you sure you're okay, Renfro?"

"I wouldn't mind taking a lap or two with y'all," Wiley Rose Jr. says. "That would do me some good. Make sure I live to see tomorrow. Hey, if I have a heart attack, I ain't got one of those Do Not Resuscitate provisos. And I'd rather you perform the duties," he says to Lisette, though he slaps my back.

"You got it, Wiley," my wife says. She's not nonplussed, a word I know but notice how everyone uses wrongly.

I look at my wife and say, "I'm only doing another half-lap," which wouldn't have been true had I not been an A-one marketing researcher, able to foresee both complications and dilemmas.

She says, "I heard a good one in Williams-Sonoma. Hell, if I'd known that the employees there knew such great jokes I guess maybe I'd've shopped here more often, and then they wouldn't be out of business."

Wiley Rose Jr. waves goodbye at the wax technician, but I can tell that in his mind he's waving at Blowey playing for immobile listeners. I say, "What?"

"Are you a really religious man, Mr. Rose?" Lisette says.

We bend around a sign that reads YEP: YOUTH ESCORT POLICY and details, in small print, how everyone under eighteen needs an adult with them on Friday and Saturday nights after six. I say, apropos of nothing, "Lisette here owns Pure Tarts, Wiley. You probably haven't ever been out to this area they call Pure only because there used to be a Pure gas station at the crossroads. This is out past Pauline. Kind of between Pauline and Cross Anchor. East of Forty-Five. West of Calloustown."

We pass three or four vacant storefronts, then a place where kids can get their photo taken with Santa from the day after Halloween until Christmas Eve. We pass The Finish Line, Foot Locker, Lady Footlocker, Journeys, Payless Shoes, Rack Room Shoes, and the Army/Navy/Air Force/Marines recruiting station. We walk toward the food court. Wiley Rose Jr. says, "I used to be religious, up until today. My daddy died way too young."

I nod. Lisette says, "You know why lesbians always buy their weightlifting needs and hiking boots at Sports Authority or Cabela's or Academy Sports?" She doesn't wait for us to offer an answer. "Because they don't like Dick's."

I laugh, certainly. I think it's one of the funniest things I've heard since moving to Pure. Wiley Rose Jr. walks a little quicker than us, which makes me think that maybe he's offended, but he slows back down and looks at both of us. "I got one. Hope y'all ain't all political correct. Listen, a lot of people remember that Yogi Bear had Boo-Boo for a pal, but then they forget about his little black friend. Know what his name was?"

I can't imagine. I get ready to say "I don't know" right away. Lisette does say it.

Wiley Rose Jr. says, "Shit, y'all, you ain't thinking. Little black friend. Ends with 'boo.' Think hard, now. This one ain't hard. Where y'all from? Goddamn." He says, "Jigga-boo-boo," and holds his mouth open and head sideways to let us know that if we don't know the answer, then we might be outright do-gooders from north of the Mason-Dixon Line.

• • •

I say to Lisette in the car, "Goddamn. I was feeling sorry for the guy until he told that racist joke. Jesus Christ. I wonder if he kept on walking around the mall in search of a place to buy a white robe and hood." After Wiley told the punch line, my wife and I veered right to the first exit. Then we wandered around trying to figure out where we'd parked and ended up going about seven-eighths around the exterior of the mall in the wrong direction. In the end, I got over 10,000 steps.

Lisette clears her throat twice. "Tell me again why you were hanging out with him?"

I shake my head and take a wrong turn out of the lot. There's a series of backroads we can follow to get home, which will take twice as long, but through some beautifully dilapidated countryside. I say, "I can't believe we still celebrate Columbus Day, can you? I mean, he didn't land on North American shores. There seems to be enough evidence that Vikings did, right? And maybe some Scottish people?" I don't want to talk about what made me stop and check on Wiley Rose Jr. I'm thinking about how I'm past the age of my father at his extremely early and unsolved death. I'm guilty for not having considered, back on my thirty-seventh birthday, that this was as far as my father made it in life. I say to Lisette, "He was getting nostalgic. And then he got racist, I guess. Those two things go together often in the South, if you ask me."

I don't know if Lisette can read my thoughts, but she stares at me for a good five seconds, then turns her attention to the road. We go through Steepleburg, pass city workers who didn't get a holiday—all of them raking leaves on the Square—and turn right onto Union Avenue, which becomes Cedar Springs, which becomes Highway 56, which, eventually, reaches near Pure.

We get to a section of the road where houses and trailers stand a good hundred yards apart, small pastures in between. It's bleak. Lisette points to the mouth of a gravel driveway and says, "Those people haven't been home for more than a week." Then a half-mile down she says it again, pointing to the other side.

I ease up on the accelerator and notice a yellow, rain-damaged bag she's pointing toward. "How do you know?"

Lisette reaches into the backseat and retrieves a spatula. She inspects it, looks out the windshield through the holes. "We got our telephone directory flopped out at the end of the driveway a week ago. You went and picked it up, remember?"

I remember. Because of my paranoia, I thought the plastic bag next to the mailbox might contain a pipe bomb, a dead cat, a bag of excrement unworthy of use as nightsoil. At the time—I poked the bagged directory with an available length of bur oak branch—I thought about how I hadn't used a telephone directory in some time, that they might be going the same route as the Sears catalog of my parents' generation. "That's good thinking. Thieves could roam around here, notice how people didn't pick up what's at the end of the driveway, then go right inside and rob the place."

"At least steal their heat pumps for the copper," Lisette says. "I read an article the other day that the average heat pump costs way more than a thousand dollars, but there's only about sixty bucks' worth of copper inside. And all these sad-ass crackheads and meth addicts are going around, probably spending more than sixty dollars' worth of gas in their trucks. You see a *For Sale* sign in somebody's yard? There's a meth addict that's eyed the heat pump out back, that's what I read."

About three miles from our house, I say, "If Columbus hadn't gone back home and said he found our continent, those Pilgrims might not have taken off for here. If they hadn't shown up, England wouldn't have gotten all pissed off. Then there wouldn't have been the Revolutionary War. There wouldn't have been the Declaration of Independence, followed by the Constitution. Slavery. Jokes like the one Wiley Rose Jr. told us. There wouldn't have been the Second Amendment—which probably made some sense 250 years ago, but I doubt those old boys had automatic weapons and hollow-point bullets in mind back then." I slow to about twenty miles an hour seeing as we're closing in on Pure. For some reason I want to finish this conversation before we hit our property.

Lisette says, "The speed limit's fifty here."

I say, "If Columbus hadn't said he found us, we wouldn't have had genocide in regards to the Indians. No Great Depression. The Civil War. Vietnam. Insurance, pharmaceutical, and the medical industry holding so much power that they can keep me from trying to live my own day the way I want because I have to go get 10,000 goddamn steps in a day for some fucking Wellness Plan."

I keep my eye on driveways to see if our closest neighbors' telephone directories lie out in the open, like invitations. My wife says, "Yeah." She says, "Outside the fact that you're all over the place in terms of a historical continuum, yeah." She says, "War of 1812. Mexican-American War. Hollywood. McDonald's, Walmart, disco."

I step on the gas and get up to about thirty. I laugh. "Iraq and Afghanistan. PTSD. Slavery—did we mention slavery already? The poor Chicago Cubs."

We turn left into the red clay driveway. To the right is Pure Tarts. She says, "The Ford Pinto. That obnoxious guy who does infomercials. Reality TV."

Our dog Myrtle, a quadra-breed, comes running toward us wagging her tail, smiling, nothing but the best greeter in the world. I stop, open my door, and let her jump in. She sits between us and licks Lisette's face. Myrtle's tongue flips in and out like a piece of flypaper hanging in front of a window unit.

"I may never go to a mall again," I say. "If Columbus hadn't gone back to tell Queen Isabella and whatever her husband's name was that he found a New World, we wouldn't have malls. If we didn't have malls, we'd have a better economic situation on Main Street. If we had a better economic situation on Main Street, everyone would talk to one another in a civil fashion, and no one would even think to find a need to own pistols."

I open my door, and Myrtle jumps across my lap and onto the ground. Lisette says, "All right. That was fun. Maybe we can do this again on the next Monday holiday. When's Arbor Day?"

I look up and see two clouds verging toward one another from opposite directions. I think, Beginning of a tornado? I think, Is it still hurricane season? How many times did Columbus look up in the sky from either the *Nina, Pinta,* or *Santa Maria* and see such clouds? Did he understand what irreversible problems he set forth?

My wife says, "Race you!" but she's talking to the dog. They hit the back door simultaneously and go inside. I stand there like a fool staring upward, wondering if when the two clouds hit there'll be lightning. It's bright and sunny with the exception of these two cumulonimbus clouds on a collision course. Down below the house I hear Helen and Totie mooing, both on the ground just like the old-timers say bovine and equine are wont to do with approaching storms. I reach behind the backseat and pull out Lisette's two bags, then shuffle inside, still thinking of Wiley Rose Jr., still thinking of my own father. I want my mind to wander elsewhere, but I can't stop from wondering if—had Lisette and I had children—my sons or daughters would one day sit somewhere pondering their lives when they reached the age of my death.

Lisette's got channel 44 on, watching *Forensic Files*. She sits on the couch, beautiful, with a bag of pretzels. That narrator says, "Hmmmmmmmm? Hmmmmmmmmm?" as if on cue.

I say, "We're not too old to have a baby. It's not like you've gone through menopause or anything. You're not even close."

Lisette says, "I'll tell you something cool: We could leave a telephone directory at the end of the driveway so people thought we weren't home. But we'd *be* home. And then, when they came up to break into the house or steal our heating unit, we could kill them. We have enough land to bury a bunch of meth-heads. Maybe we could throw them down that old well, and then put a big cement pad over it, and then a raised-bed garden over that, just like that one dude did in Ohio or wherever. Or maybe not kill them, but hit them with one of those stun guns. At least spray them with bear repellent and call the sheriff's department."

I set her bags on the kitchen table. I walk over, kiss the top of her head, and tell her I love her. She points the open pretzel bag my way as a commercial airs concerning some kind of electronic cigarette, which is something else that wouldn't have happened had Columbus's fleet got caught in a relentless storm and drifted down toward, say, southern Argentina. I shake my head No. My Wellness Program sends me e-mails about salt intake and blood pressure two or three times a day, pointing out how too much sodium might kill me—and now that I think about it, maybe that's how Columbus got gout, or reactive arthritis, or however he died.

Lisette says, "What? What did you say?" and curls the top of the pretzel bag.

The show's back on, and I sit down, mesmerized again. Later I'll remember why we probably shouldn't procreate, as shouldn't most people I've seen or met in the recent past.

HEX KEYS

The fourth woman stood outside her trailer, wearing a smudged-orange pants suit, holding a dead three-foot-long rat snake by the tail, near the roadside ditch. The look on her face said something like, This is nothing, comparatively speaking. She looked like she might bellow out, "This ain't as bad as dealing with smoke damage inside the bedroom." Later on, I couldn't imagine my father planning a better scenario. What did he expect when we pulled down that clay-rut road? I would've bet that he plainly wanted to drive by the single-wide, maybe see the woman out there sweeping her dirt driveway with a cheap rake missing prongs, if anything, then his getting back onto some valid blacktop as soon as possible. He would've said, "See?" or "There you go," or "What do you think you'd be doing inside that place, if she'd been your mother?"

"I almost took that woman to the prom," my father said. "We were dating, I asked her, and then her daddy said he didn't like me. Said I wasn't what his daughter deserved, or something like that. Anyway, she could've been your mother."

This occurred in June, Father's Day, 1972. I was twelve. My father had friends in Vietnam. I had a couple older cousins over there, too, plus neighbors with sons and relatives unlucky enough to serve. I'd bought my father a new set of Allen wrenches and had them wrapped up nicely on the kitchen table for when he got up and ate his everyday breakfast of Cream of Wheat with blackstrap molasses.

We didn't eat breakfast on Father's Day, 1972, as it ended up. He woke me, had my pants and shirt laid out on a chair, and said, "Come on. Hurry up. We got some places to go today I want you to see."

Our first stop was a breakfast joint one town over called Mama's Nook. Somebody had spray-painted an "ie" after the name on the side of the cement-block building. This wasn't any kind of raised-letter sign, or neon. It wasn't a nice porcelain sign or even a cut-out piece of plywood attached to the cinderblock. It looked as if the owner hired out someone with a proper stencil set to flat-out paint right onto the exterior. I didn't know the term "nookie" yet. I knew "poontang" only because, right after my mother took a temporary hiatus from the family in order to "tend to more important tasks in the long run," my father took grease pencils and wrote P-O-O-N on the labels of Tang that he drank each morning with his Cream of Wheat.

I said, "I got you a Father's Day present."

My father turned into the narrow lot. He stared straight ahead and, without moving his lips much, said, "Mama's Nookie's the place to be."

At this point I didn't know that my father had an established plan for the day, and that he'd been saving it up. I'll give him this: He didn't seem to blame my mom for checking herself into some kind of clinic that treated chronic depression and pain. Me, I'd said some bad things about her to friends. When my buddy Clay called up to tell me how his mom made him wear ironed blue jeans, or told him to quit eating Milk Duds, I'd said, "At least your mother doesn't mind seeing you in the morning" and "At least you have a mother who doesn't want you to ruin your teeth." To be honest, I didn't quite understand my mother's alleged predicament. She'd been gone two months, and I doubted that she would return ever.

We walked in and sat down at a booth. This was a Sunday, so everyone else inside, it seemed, wore church clothes. The men—all fathers—sported boutonnieres, and I felt a certain shame for not thinking to clip a rose from one of our bushes out front.

The waitress who came to our table wore a name tag. My father said, "Hello, Arlene."

"Well, well, well. I heard you might be back to alone. Wondered when you might come crawling over here." She wore a yellow dress with a stain along the right side. Her hair probably wasn't formed into tight pin curls naturally, nor platinum. Arlene's head reminded me of a vegetable scrubber we had under the sink.

She tossed down two laminated one-sheet menus, front only. She said, "We out of liver mush, so don't ask. We had a run on liver mush, and Mama ain't had time to go to the store."

My father said, "This is my son, Preston," and nodded his head once across the table, my way.

I said, "Hello."

Arlene smiled. She had all of her teeth, which kind of surprised me. She said, "Hey, Varlene, get on over here," without taking her eyes off me.

Varlene wasn't a twin, but the two women looked alike. They wore the same uniform and went to the same hairdresser, at least. Varlene showed up from behind the cash register and said, "Buck Hewitt. Hey, Buck. Is this Buck Jr.?"

She didn't look at me. My father said no and introduced me again. For some reason I thought it the perfect opportunity to set these two women straight. I said, "A lot of people call me Presto, like if you took the 'n' off my name. I do a lot of magic tricks." "A lot" was an exaggeration. I knew about four card tricks, and could make a quarter disappear about half the time.

Varlene said, "Magic. Like father, like son." Then she returned to the register without saying goodbye.

My father said, "I'll just have an egg sandwich." To me he said, "Hey, Preston, Arlene and Varlene have a sister. Guess what's her name."

On my second try I figured out "Darlene," and then I ordered a waffle.

"Waffle," Arlene said. "I could've guessed that one from a Hewitt." I figured out her allusion years later.

My father didn't move his lips much and spoke quietly. He said,

"When I get the sandwich, I'm not going to eat it. You eat up your waffle just fine, but I'm going to plain sit here."

I leaned across the table. "Say that again?"

My father looked to his left, at all the people bowed in prayer before their breakfasts showed up. For the first time ever I noticed how his face resembled a half-melted back-porch citronella candle. He said, "Never eat food served to you by someone you've hurt, Preston. If I can teach you anything, that's it. Well, it's one of the things." Then he went on, quietly, to tell me how he'd dated Arlene and broken up with her, dated Varlene and broken up with her—even took Darlene out to a movie once, but halfway through she stood up and made a scene. My father said that her two sisters paid her five dollars, which was huge money back in the early 1950s, to break up with him. "It's not like we were going together, you know. But it was kind of embarrassing in front of all those people watching Marlon Brando."

Our food came. Varlene brought it out. She set my waffle down lightly, and pretty much slung my father's plate down. It rattled and wobbled like a dropped dime on a cookie sheet. My father placed a five-dollar bill on the table. I said, "I got you a Father's Day present."

My father said, "You ain't got to give me nothing, Presto. Just coming out to meet women who could've been your mother is enough gift for me."

I'd decided on Allen wrenches—they'd been used, sure, but I'd gotten some three-in-one oil and sanded off the rust—because my father'd broken a couple of little ones while unsuccessfully trying to unstick gravel from the treads of his tires. My father called them "hex keys," and he needed them for the Fortuna automatic skivers and United Shoe Machinery splitters he worked on at the behest of independent textile supply companies and cotton mills that demanded his presence when their machines ran afoul. My grandfather started the business, and when he died my father dropped out of college— where he met my mom—and took over.

I said, "What I got you is better than this, I bet."

My father shook his head. He said, "We got a couple more places to go."

• • •

We left Mama's Nook and took Highway 54 toward the town of Glen Springs, where—according to my father—a special curative mineral water got bottled and shipped to high-ranking members of the Confederacy, and the entire operation dwindled once General Lee or someone accused an interloper of bottling a tainted tonic that induced dysentery in the troops before the First Battle of Kernstown or the Battle of Appomattox Station. Maybe it was Stonewall Jackson who blamed Glen Springs water, or the white supremacist Lieutenant General Jubal Early. One of them. Glen Springs still featured a number of wooden two-story antebellum houses owned by the descendants of bottlers and shallow-water-spa attendants, but each house fell more and more into disrepair.

I didn't speak during this twenty-minute trip. Maybe I got all obsessed with how either Arlene or Varlene might've sprinkled rat poison in my waffle batter. I thought about how it wouldn't be all that hard to stir some kind of liquid poison in a syrup container. My father took a left turn and said, "It's around here somewhere." He hit his brakes, accelerated, hit his brakes, accelerated, and I rolled down the window of his truck in case I needed to get sick.

About ten o'clock we turned down a pea-gravel and pine-straw entrance to what ended up being one of those Sears Craftsman bungalows. My father pulled up to the house and opened his door. I slid out his side, for he parked way too close to a rock wall on the right. "I'm back here. Hey! I'm back here," a woman called out as my father approached the front door.

My father took me by the right shoulder and directed me around the house. He walked with a sudden and pronounced limp, it seemed, and leaned on me as we curved around.

"It's Buck and Preston," my father said when we reached an open chain-link fence. He and I both looked around eye level, swooping our heads this way and that like half-lighthouses, like indecisive street-crossers, like adamant naysayers. My father said to me, in a louder-than-normal conversational voice, "We're here to see Rayelle Purvis."

"I'm up here," Ms. Purvis said, and we looked up into the limbs of the kind of oak tree usually seen in movies that involve hangings. She stood on an eight-by-eight-foot platform of two-by-twelves, at least twenty feet in the air. No ladder stood nearby, and no low limbs protruded from the trunk. She said, "Buck Hewitt? What the hell are you doing here? I thought you were smart enough to know better."

My father said, "What're you doing up there?" He didn't introduce me. I craned my neck. I tried to figure out if this woman scrambled up the tree like some kind of squirrel, or trick pit bull.

Rayelle Purvis looked up at the sky, then back down to us. She said, whispering, "I hope you didn't go to the front door and wake up Floyd."

My father shook his head no. He whispered back, "I just wanted to see how you're doing."

"Floyd would kill you if you came to the door. If you woke him up or not. You know that." To me she said, "Hey, little fellow."

I waved but said nothing. My father said, "We're just out on a tour today seeing who's alive and who's not. Maybe I'm feeling middle-aged, you know."

A live brown field rat fell off Rayelle Purvis's platform, landed closer to me than my father, then skittered off slowly. I won't say that I didn't jump. I won't say that I didn't maybe let out a little squeal. She said, "Damn it to hell." Rayelle squatted down out of sight, then stood back up holding a silver industrial stapler. I guess she'd had her toe on the rat's tail up until this point.

"Do you want me to try and catch that thing?" my father said. He said, "I wanted Preston to hear about how you and Ginny used to be roommates. I wanted for you to tell him how his momma's smart and normal, I guess."

"Smart and normal" seemed an odd thing to push a stranger into admitting, I thought, even then. I looked off to where the rat ran—under a pile of what ended up being the past winter's butterfly bush clippings—then back up to Rayelle Purvis. She stared at me and said, "Your momma and I used to be roommates in college. We were KD sorority sisters. I introduced her to your daddy, and my lot in life got decided because of *Ginny's* drive."

My father said, "Well. That's not exactly how I remember things, but okay. Come on down from there, Rayelle."

For some reason I felt empowered enough, maybe because this woman said my mother's name in a way that almost sounded like a curse, to say, "Are you more comfortable with rats than with people?" I'd read some kind of *National Enquirer* thing my mother left behind about people who cared more for vermin than humans. There were human beings out there who held Cheerios in their mouths and let rats climb up their shirts.

Rayelle said, "It's a good thing you didn't go to the front door and wake up Floyd. He was up all night trying to catch an owl. I'm trying to catch a hawk. We got us a dream to travel around showing the schoolchildren injured birds of prey."

My father said, "So you'll catch a normal bird, then injure it?"

"Hey, you shouldn't be so unaccustomed to such a thing, Buck," Rayelle Purvis said. "Am I right or am I right?" She pointed off in the distance and said, "We got another platform over there with roadkill possums and coons stacked up for turkey vultures. I got to keep an eye out for them, too."

I said, "Mom was in a sorority?"

My father said to Rayelle Purvis, "I wish you nothing but the best of luck. You should be proud. You and Floyd both should be proud."

I said, "Was she a cheerleader or something?"

My father waved upward, and took my right shoulder again, and led me to the truck. We got in. He said, "That woman's insane, you understand. I knew it would be bad, but I didn't know she would be that crazy."

He started the truck and turned his head to back out of the long driveway. He put his arm around the back of the bench seat, and I could smell Ivory on his skin. I said, "Is her husband mean or something?"

My father said, "Yes, he's mean and out of control. He's a loose cannon. I went to high school with him. Floyd got kicked off the football team for beating up a trumpet player in the pep band he thought blew off-tune. He could headbutt a Coke machine into spitting out bottles."

"What if he'd answered the door?" I asked. My father swung the steering wheel hard. He put the truck in first gear and peeled out on the asphalt.

"I was going to say we had the wrong house. That's what you do. I was going to say, 'I'm sorry. We're looking for the Snopeses.' Listen, Preston, in these kinds of situations, always say you're looking for the Snopeses. It's kind of a joke. It's a long-winded joke I'll tell you about sometime. I learned it in college. Floyd wouldn't remember me, for one, and he never read about the Snopeses, for two."

I said, "Let's go home. I want you to open up what I got you."

He didn't say, "Two more," didn't say, "Having you spend the day with me is Father's Day enough." I think I heard him mumble, "Still better than checking in voluntarily." He drove back toward town a couple miles, then took a left. He said, "Old Canaan Road. Old Grist Mill. Old Stone Station," to himself, like a mantra.

Between us he had a folded map of the entire county, which he didn't need, for he'd memorized his routes.

● ● ●

We got home right before noon. My father pulled into the driveway. We lived in a normal middle-class subdivision, one of those places that emerged in the early 1960s filled with brick ranch-style houses, all 1,600 square feet, some with half-basements that always flooded. I wanted to hurry inside and see the look on my father's face when he unwrapped the hex keys. I foresaw his pulling those things out one by one and twirling them between his thumb and forefinger, maybe saying, "This little L-shaped wrench will work perfectly on a skiving machine." Maybe he'd say something like, "It's three inches long," and I could say, "That's 76.2 millimeters!" seeing as we'd been going over the metric system in math class right before summer started.

My father closed his door and said, "Let's take a little walk."

He held out his hand for me to grab. I did. I said, "Come on. Come inside so you can open up your Father's Day present." Maybe I stomped my foot like a big baby.

"Two more," my father said. He looked at his wristwatch. He said, "Your mother would want it."

When I say "normal middle-class subdivision," I should mention that it was only half a subdivision. It was a sub-subdivision, a circle divided by two streets. We lived on Great Smoky Circle. The two streets that intersected Great Smoky were Yosemite and Yellowstone. Everyone who lived on Yosemite pronounced it "Yozemite," two syllables. We walked down Great Smoky for a while, then continued on a path surrounded by kudzu on both sides. My father took me through a place where—years later—two children would be found dead. We walked down a path that, when the subdivision developers continued their project, would turn out a slave cemetery on either side.

We walked what must've been a half-mile, until we reached what I learned later was an old unpainted heart-pine sharecropper house between two creeks, set in a four-acre expanse of bottomland. My father hunched low and whispered, "I should've brought the binoculars for this one. Be quiet."

A woman came out in denim overalls. She didn't wear a shirt beneath them. She had her head wrapped in a red bandanna. This might all have taken place about fifty yards away, not far. Two mixed-breed dogs trotted behind her, wagging their tails, their heads lifted in search of any scent, I imagined. Twenty chickens stood high on the gutters of the house. The woman held a silver two-gallon metal bucket that she swung by her side. A hawk went *scree-scree-scree* overhead. I don't know if she hummed a tune, or if music merely followed in her path. If we'd gone to this woman's house first I might've said to my father, "Witch!"

Except I'd never seen a more beautiful woman in my life. My mother was pretty, but this woman held an exotic appeal that could've been recognized by Ray Charles and Helen Keller alike. I said, "This woman could've been my mother?" I felt ashamed for saying it. Betraying my depressed mother wasn't something I planned to do on Father's Day.

"Shhh," my father said. "No. No, never."

The woman stopped and turned our way. She looked perplexed for a second, then started laughing and said, "Is that you, Buck?"

My father eased up to his full height. I didn't. If anything, I crouched down farther. My father lifted his right hand and said, "Hey, Bess. I'll be damned. Is that you? Me and my boy here are looking for his dog. His dog ran off. And we're looking for it." My father ambled slowly toward this Bess woman. "You haven't seen a dog out this way, have you?" To me he said, "Come on, boy, don't be shy."

Understand that I'd never been shy in my life, but this woman's beauty apparently stunned my synapses to the point where no muscle knew how to function. My father walked back toward me, grabbed my collar, and stood me up. Bess said, "I ain't seen no strange dog out here since these showed up to live here. What kind?"

When we entered what might be considered her yard, my father said, "I don't know. What kind of dog would you say you got?"

If it weren't Father's Day I could've called him on all of this. But I said, "Oh, it's a mixed breed. Maybe part collie and part something else." I couldn't think of one breed besides collie. I'd seen *Lassie,* but never *Rin Tin Tin* or *Old Yeller.* To my father I said, "Maybe if he shows up here it would be good for her to know its name."

My father said, "Richard. The dog's name is Richard."

Richard? I thought. My father must've been thinking of the president or something.

Bess lifted her arm to wipe sweat from her brow. A rooster ran off under the house. I noticed about two inches of blond hair emerging from Bess's armpit. Off to the right a mule brayed, then kicked at nothing with both back legs. He stood in a corral of sorts, surrounded by a large garden of tomatoes, corn, and sweet peas. I said, "My name's Preston. The dog's name's Richard." Again, I cannot explain this woman's outright sublime nature. *Two inches of armpit hair,* I thought, *equals 50.8 millimeters.*

My father said, "Yeah, looking for the dog. You still growing your 'organic' vegetables?"

She nodded. She said, "You need to change your ways, Buck. The government's into killing off people with chemicals they spraying on. Oh, the government's telling people they depend on to not eat store vegetables, but everyone else don't know. They got secret ways of letting their rich backers know to buy from me, but they ain't telling no one else. You know why? Because of integration. Ever since the integration, the government's been happy to kill off every black and white-trash linthead who can't afford private schooling so's to start up a new race of people, just like Hitler wanted. You know who buys from me? I'll tell you. Both our senators, for one. Funny thing is, they send they slaves down here to pile up the backs of they Cadillacs full of peas, corn, tomatoes, beans, and sweet potatoes. I might look like I live in poverty, but I got a bank account you wouldn't believe." She said all this fast, like she had it memorized and wanted to get it out of her throat.

There on the outskirts of Bess's garden I said, "Dad."

He said, "Well, okay, Bess. I guess we better go look for Richard elsewhere."

She walked up and squatted down to me. She said, I think, "Go to a private school, if you can talk your daddy into it. You need to be around people only like you, always. They's going to be a race war in time. You and your dog need to know about it."

I thought, *How can my father have ever been interested in a racist woman?* What would have happened to me had this Bess ended up my mother? Would I have been driving around in a convertible, wearing a hood like all the Ku Klux Klan members I'd seen driving through our sub-subdivision? Would I forever make fun of people not like me?

We got back home, and my father turned on the TV. I kind of forgot about the hex keys, which still sat atop the kitchen table, next to an empty bowl.

Finally my father got out of his chair with a grunt and walked into the kitchen. I heard him tearing apart the wrapping paper. Then, I couldn't tell if he laughed or cried. He made noises. I never asked.

The next time we visited my mother, he brought the hex keys along to show her. He said, "They make me remember how adjustments need to take place daily." When my father knew his death loomed, three decades later, he gave those tools back to me. Over the years I've kept them in my pocket, and roll them between my thumb and index finger often, instead of saying to my own son, "She could've been, she could've been."

FOUR-WAY STOP

G. R. prided himself on both historical and traditional figures. He felt as if he knew quite a bit about pop culture, too, at least movies and music. This was Halloween at his and Tina's front door, far from normal suburban neighborhoods. He'd already pointed at masks and said Batman, Iron Man, Superman, Spiderman, Incredible Hulk, and common zombie. Clown, ghost, Pocahontas, ninja, Iraqi War Special Forces Seal. He'd correctly identified Reagan, Bush, Napoleon, and Rush Limbaugh. Ballerina, pro wrestlers (André the Giant, Lex Luger, Ric Flair, The Undertaker, Macho Man Randy Savage, Hulk Hogan, Dusty Rhodes, Rey Mysterio Jr.). Football players (Cam Newton and Peyton Manning). G. R. waved at parents waiting on the roadside in cars, gave a thumbs-up, said how he liked the way their little Lady Gagas looked, their Mileys, their MacBook Airs and cans of Red Bull. "Goddamn, how many miniature Snickers we got left? We got any of those Reese's Cups?" G. R. said to his wife. "I don't remember Halloween being like this the last few years. The churches must've quit having parties. I thought parents got scared off by razor blades and white powder."

Tina sat in the den, with the door open to the living room where her husband stood at the front door. "I told you to wear a bloody bandage on your head like some kind of Civil War amputee. That might scare some children away," she said. "We already spent almost fifty damn dollars. Please don't tell me I got to go back out. They aren't even from around here. Some of them aren't even kids." She picked up the channel changer and moved from one food network program to another. She went from a tips-on-vinegar-barbecue show to one on noodle-making in Southeast Asia. Tina wore flannel pajama bottoms with giraffes printed on them, and a T-shirt advertising WSPA because she called first to the station one morning when she knew the trivia answer, which happened to be "avocado-green shag carpet."

"We might," G. R. said, and then looked out the door and said, "Jesus! Jesus! Two Jesuses! Are y'all with each other?" Two young men limped up the walkway, both burdened with crosses fashioned from four-by-four lengths of pressure-treated pine normally used for flowerbed edging.

G. R. yelled out, "Jesus and Jesus! Y'all are the first biblical characters we've had tonight. Good job, boys!" He focused on the teenagers, but handed over a couple small Butterfingers and Milky Ways to a young hobo and Snow White who elbowed in. They didn't say "Trick or Treat" or "Thank you," but he didn't mind. To the two Jesuses he said, "Man, this has to be tough," for they had to hold their arms out to the side, with plastic orange pumpkins strapped to their wrists, which were strapped to the wood.

"We're not Jesus," the kid on the left said. "I'm Impenitent Thief."

"Penitent Thief. Sorry," said the other kid.

G. R. looked at them and thought, Did a Mormon family move nearby? Are these boys Jehovah's Witnesses? He said, "Say all that again, what y'all just said?" He didn't say, "Aren't y'all a little old to be trick-or-treating?" but thought it. He also thought, "It's almost ten o'clock," and remembered seeing a news item one time about how the last visitors on Halloween often case a house.

The thieves' father slid out of the shadow of the tea olive bush and said, "It's what they wanted. They wanted to go out one last time. What can you do as a father?"

G. R. said, "Jesus. Jesus Christ." He said, "I doubt I have anything y'all might want," and he stared. "I mean, I got candy, that's it." The father had long brown hair and a beard, and when he stood between his boys it looked like a painting G. R. saw one time in a book in the emergency room's waiting area. "We ain't got no manna, or silver."

"I'm allergic to peanuts," said Impenitent Thief.

G. R. dumped what he had left in both boys' candy receptacles and turned off his porch light once they trudged back to the road. He didn't think, at first, about how he didn't see a car out there for them, and the next house stood a quarter mile away. He tried not to think about how his own son kind of looked like Penitent Thief.

• • •

At ten o'clock Tina went to bed without saying goodnight, leaving G. R. in the den. He turned to the early local news on the right-wing channel he watched to stay in tune with the enemy's movements. The anchorwoman came on saying, "Some people are calling it a Halloween miracle," then went on to say she'd get to that story right after the weather forecast.

The weatherman said, "It's forty-five degrees outside now, and I got your miracle right here, Amy—it's going to be in the mid-seventies tomorrow, but rain will be moving in over the weekend, with lows near freezing. Near freezing! So much for global warming!"

"Thanks, Pete. That sounds wonderful. As you know, I was brought up in Portland, so a little rain doesn't bother me at all."

G. R. wished he hadn't poured out all the candy. He got up, went to the refrigerator, and thought about eating whatever Tina cooked earlier in the day that involved diced kidneys. He took out two cans of beer and heard Amy say, "And now for the Halloween miracle."

Back in the den, he looked at the TV screen and saw Jesus and the two thieves. He yelled to Tina, "Hey, those guys were here," but she didn't respond.

"They was here, and then they wasn't," a woman being interviewed said to a reporter. "I seen them, and then they vanished. Like, I don't know, I thought maybe I blunk my eyes, but Vanessa here seen them, too, and she says she didn't blink none either."

The camera swung to the woman's daughter, still in her costume. G. R. said out loud, "Vampire."

"I come back from my boyfriend's momma's boyfriend's party, and they was standing right dare," said Vanessa, pointing to the stoop. "I said, 'Y'all ain't right,' and took me a picture using my cell phone." She held the phone up close to the camera.

Her mother said, "I normally don't do Halloween, you know. Something tode me this year, though, to go out to Big Lots and get me bunch of them little Skittles packs. We had a bunch of kids show up, and then right at the end come Jesus and them two robbers, you know. I gave them one Skittles pack each—well, two for Jesus—and then they disappeared. We all lit up out here! Ain't no way to just take off without no one noticing."

The camera turned to the reporter. He looked, to G. R., like the kid on *The Addams Family*. G. R. couldn't tell if the guy wore a costume or not. "Amy, I'm on Old Roebuck Road—and three other people say they had the same experience, but they didn't want to be on camera. If anyone out there witnessed Jesus and the two thieves, we'd like to hear about it. Back to you."

G. R. said, "I witnessed it," to himself, then louder to Tina in the bedroom. "I witnessed it. Hey, I might've witnessed a Halloween *miracle*, honey."

He drank his beer and accidentally hit LAST on the channel changer. A man wearing a toque looked straight at G. R. and said, "Never, *ever*, underestimate the remarkable flavors of sweetbreads."

G. R. called the station to say he'd seen them, too, but the line was busy for five minutes straight. He finished his second beer, went back to the refrigerator, extracted the rest of the six-pack, and went out to his truck. He looked at his watch and tried to remember when his last trick-or-treaters came by—9:45, he figured. Now it was 10:20. He knew that people walked about three miles an hour because Tina's doctor had put her on a regimen. G. R. thought that anyone sporting a cross couldn't make more than a mile-and-a-half an hour at most, and if they stopped at houses working a late-shift Halloween, it wouldn't even be that far.

He thought, If I can find these guys and deliver them to the station, maybe I'll get on the news. What would Tina think about that? What would she think about turning on the television in the morning to see G. R. standing there next to Jesus and the two thieves?

He thought, Maybe I can tell our story.

• • •

Near the end of Old Roebuck Road, a quarter-mile before it teed into 215, stood a useless four-way stop. On three corners stood pastures, and then there was a cement-block convenience store where sheriff's deputies hung out waiting for people to ease through without holding their brakes properly. G. R. had his window down. He'd called out "Jesus! Jesus!" about every fifty yards, driving twenty miles per hour, his high beams on.

At first he thought he heard the pop-pop-pop of a pistol from behind the store, but then realized the sound to be planks of lumber dropped upon one another. He sat at the four-way a good half-minute longer than needed, an open can of beer between his legs, before releasing his clutch and rolling into the store's shallow parking lot and then around back, where, sure enough, Jesus and the two thieves stood around a fifty-five-gallon drum, the crosses standing upright in it, Jesus holding a lit Zippo in one hand and some wadded newspaper in the other.

G. R. pulled up beside them and turned off his headlights. The three men stood motionless. "Y'all was on the news just now," G. R. said. "They said anyone could find y'all, call up the station and let them know."

"We haven't done anything wrong," the father said. "We were hungry. Candy isn't the best for a body, but it's better than nothing." The boy who introduced himself as Penitent Thief apologized again, but his brother said, "And then we'll eat this crap, get cavities, get diabetes, and die."

G. R. got out of his truck. He said, "Is the store closed? What time does this store close? I don't come down this way very often any-more." He thought, Certainly they'll have cans of sardines or something inside better than candy. He thought, I don't have enough beer to share.

"Name's Darmon. You can have your candy back if you feel like we duped you," the father said. He lit the newspaper and dropped it into the drum. His two sons stepped closer and held out their palms.

G. R. put his beer can on the roof of his truck. "Okay, listen. You men were at my house. I don't know if I looked away, or what, but you disappeared. And then this woman came on TV and said y'all disappeared from her. People out there think you're really Jesus and the two thieves."

"People see what they wish to see," Darmon said.

G. R. said, "Yeah, I know what you mean." Without the crosses on their backs, and without the porch light providing a shadow, these three looked like normal unemployed construction workers. They looked like hobos, grifters, Irish Travelers. If they had shown up without the *accouterments*, G. R. thought, he would've pointed at all three and yelled out, "Welder," or "Landscaper," or "Shriner."

"It's a long story," said the father. "Last year we had a roof over our heads. Now we don't."

"Mom does," Penitent Thief said. "She's at the shelter, but there wasn't enough room for all of us."

Impenitent Thief reached into one of the plastic jack-o'-lanterns and culled out the packs of M&Ms. "We got to remember she likes these best, tomorrow."

G. R. reached into his truck bed and wrestled out two logs he'd picked up where Duke Power workers had trimmed trees that neared electric lines. He had prided himself on not buying half-cords of de-livered wood for three years. He said, "Wait a minute. I could give y'all this, and you'd have heat for the night. Or I guess I could drive you around and show you how to find wood, so you can have heat for a lifetime. Ha-ha-ha. You know what I mean?"

Then he dropped the tailgate and held out his right hand to help both Penitent and Impenitent into the back. Darmon got in the passenger side, after sliding the beer over.

For a couple seconds G. R. thought about taking them straight to the TV station. He thought about saying, "Don't worry. I was never a soldier."

At the four-way stop he lingered, again, too long. Darmon said, "You got it both ways."

G. R. said, "This is right where our son got killed three years ago."

• • •

After he pulled out the push mower, riding mower, edger, leaf blower, and then the stacked rakes/shovels/post-hole diggers/limb cutters/ rolled-up extension cords/rolled-up extra garden hose/boxes of Christmas decorations, there was enough room inside his storage shed to house three stray men temporarily. G. R. manhandled a roll of hurricane fence he didn't need, and a roll of barbed wire he thought he might need some day, then humped out a number of clay flower-pots Tina said she'd one day use to plant lemon trees and ficuses. He moved bags of potting soil, pine-bark mulch, playground sand, and lime. "I'm embarrassed that we have all this shit," he said.

"You have a nice house," said Darmon. "What you got here, two acres?"

G. R. said, "One and three-quarters acres. Y'all can sleep here to-night. But you'll need to leave before my wife gets up. She just won't understand, you know. It's one of those things. Hey, who wants to eat some kidney pie?"

G. R. went tiptoeing back inside the house, picked the casse-role dish out of the refrigerator, opened a drawer for three forks. He placed the dish on the dining-room table, got a roll of paper towels out of the closet, and listened for Tina's snoring. He said "Tina" in a normal speaking voice. She didn't answer. The bedroom television aired nothing, which meant the remote's timer had shut it off. As he stepped out on the back porch he heard one of the boys say, "That wouldn't be right," which made G. R. wonder if his father or brother had just said, "We can break in later."

"I heard all that," G. R. said when he approached the shed, a hundred steps away, in hopes of calling a bluff. "Don't get any ideas about breaking in later. I have no money hidden."

Penitent Thief said, "What? We were talking about what to do if we needed to use the bathroom. Peeing won't be a problem, but in case one of us has to go number two. I was saying it wouldn't be right to use the wheelbarrow."

"We can use one of the jack-o'-lanterns," Darmon said.

"And these paper towels," said G. R., handing over the kidney pie. "Here, my wife said for y'all to eat this," he lied. "Well, anyway, stay warm. Put some charcoal in that hibachi and light it up, but keep the thing outside the shed. I wouldn't want y'all to asphyxiate."

Darmon said, "We appreciate everything. Listen, I'm sorry about your son. I appreciate what you're doing for mine. For me and mine."

G. R. said, "There's a pull cord for a light in here. Let me go back inside and see if I can find some blankets." He started, then turned and said, "There's a smashed-up car over on that side of the property. Don't sleep in it."

"This kidney stuff ain't bad," said the Impenitent son. He said, "Is there a hose out here? Would you mind if we drank some water?"

"Right over there. Help yourself."

• • •

G. R. had not stood in his son's bedroom more than a half-dozen times since the accident. Tina sat at the desk daily. G. R. couldn't. He sat outside—no matter the season—from dawn until dusk most days. Although he didn't have to return to work after the settlement, G. R. wouldn't have gone back anyway. He ran through images of his boy turning a double play in high school, throwing a stick to the dog, sitting down at the desk to work out algebra problems. G. R. knew that he would've ended up just like Jesus and the two thieves had the insurance company not agreed to pay seven million dollars for their client's negligence. Seven million didn't seem like all that much money, G. R. and Tina thought, but they agreed with their lawyer that they didn't want to fight longer. If Sam had lived to be eighty, that would mean a hundred grand per year and some change. Good money for something like a minister or teacher. Not much for what Sam could've done in life had he indeed made the pros.

G. R. went into his son's bedroom and stripped the mattress. Then he opened the closet and pulled out an extra folded-up blanket.

• • •

"The water's running," Tina said at 5:00 a.m. She nudged G. R. "Did you turn on the washing machine or dishwasher?" G. R. didn't answer. She said, "Someone's outside running our hose." She sat up and elbowed him hard in his upper ribs.

G. R. opened his eyes and stared at the pebbled ceiling he had wanted to scrape smooth since buying the house. He felt Tina looking at him. G. R. thought, Work, and then remembered he didn't have to show up at Kohler. He didn't need to check the kiln's temperature. He didn't need to tell anyone not to mess up.

And then he remembered. I got Jesus and his two thieves out back! G. R. thought. From Halloween. I should've called the TV station about this. I could've gotten on there and said some things about Sam.

The running water turned off. G. R. said, "It was the refrigerator. It was the freezer, making ice."

"No it wasn't," Tina said, throwing off the covers and getting up. "I know that noise. I know every noise this house can make. I remember the ones it used to make, too." She grabbed her bathrobe.

G. R. turned on the bedroom television to drown out what sounds a thirsty thief or son of God might likely emit from the business end of a tangled hose. That same chef came on talking about the organs and glands of farm animals. By the time G. R. got out of bed, his wife had turned on the porch lights already and grabbed a flashlight she kept in the china cabinet. "Wait a minute, wait a minute," G. R. said. "Let me go out first," but she'd opened the back door and stepped out, shining a beam.

"It's just a homeless man and his boys," G. R. yelled out too loud. "They're just staying for the night, honey. I felt sorry for them."

Tina held the light on the three men. She said nothing, and they stood motionless, twenty feet away, all three with their hands above their heads—though the two boys held theirs out to the side. Darmon said, "We couldn't sleep, and we thought we'd water your plants. If you water things at dusk they tend to get mold. What time is it, anyway?"

Tina turned and looked at her husband. She kept the flashlight pointed toward Darmon and his sons. "What the hell are you doing to us? Why can't you do anything right? First Sam, and now this. And everything that's happened in between."

"That was a fine casserole you baked," one of the sons said. "We appreciate the food you cooked, ma'am."

Tina stared at her husband. She said, "What?"

"I gave them your kidney pie," G. R. said. "They were hungry. I couldn't let them live off of Skittles and Snickers, you know. Didn't you hear me yell out to you to turn on the news and see the Halloween Miracle? It was these fellows here I was talking about."

Tina asked G. R. how much he'd had to drink and went back inside. She turned off the back-porch floodlights. Darmon said, "We didn't mean to get you in trouble." His Penitent Thief son said the same.

"Y'all have to forgive her. She doesn't know how she comes off sounding. I keep waiting for her to turn a corner, but it doesn't seem to be happening."

Darmon said there was no need to explain. He asked if G. R. needed help putting the mowers back in the shed, and thanked him for his kindness, and said they should be walking toward the shelter, anyway, in order to give some candy to his wife. The Penitent Thief handed over folded blankets and linens and apologized for any scuff marks. G. R. said he'd be looking out for them as the evenings got colder, and reminded Darmon to look for already-cut firewood beneath power lines.

G. R. returned inside and went straight to his son's room. He unfurled the sheet and blankets, then lay atop the bed. G. R. fell asleep praying for his wife to revert back to being the gamesome woman she'd been before the accident. He pushed his head deep into his dead son's pillow and wondered what kind of willpower it would take to suffocate himself.

Four hours later he heard the doorbell. Tina answered. Before he could get up he knew already that a merciless and committed person stood there—if not the Impenitent Thief, then another. He thought about how he would finally be able to tell his family's story to anyone watching the early local news.

TROMBONES, NOT MAGIC

Again, I don't want to tell my son the full story. What I should say concerns everyday advice offered by afternoon-talk-show hosts, high school counselors, and incarcerated men paid off to be part of the Scared Straight traveling show. I should go all "Attend the best college, get your degree, find a job, keep your nose to the inner seam of your boss's pants." Unless his boss is a woman, and then my advice is, "Never allow your eyes to drop below about five feet two inches or she'll think you're staring at her cleavage." If my son has a woman boss, I hope it's in the area of weather forecasting, so he's always looking at the sky. Maybe he can get a job as an air traffic controller, or ornithologist, or astronomer. If he goes into one of the bluer-collar jobs, maybe he can specialize in the installation of ceiling fans.

We're alone at the Amtrak station so he can get on a 5:00 a.m. train to New Orleans to see his mother, Wendy—a woman I still love—who released herself from our marriage ten years ago when she understood that she was a lesbian, when she realized that she loved a coworker named Janette, when she and her partner decided to give up middle-school teaching for new careers in home renovation. This occurred a couple years after Hurricane Katrina, if it matters. Wendy needs to see our son Odom for one last visit before she succumbs to a cancer that has metastasized into her lymph system, liver, everywhere. She and Janette played trombones, too, and I think they wished to join up with some kind of Dixieland band when they weren't tearing out walls.

I should tell Odom Jr. something like, "The process of death begins at the moment one escapes the birth canal." I should say, "Tell your mother I still think she's the best-looking woman on her old softball team."

I say, "When you get down there, it's okay to cry. But try not to fall apart in front of your mother or Janette. I imagine they're already pretty fragile emotionally."

Odom Jr. says, "I'm going down to the French Quarter and get some Mardi Gras beads."

I say, "Do you have enough money? Did you get that extra hundred dollars I left on the kitchen table?"

Odom Jr. says, "I promise not to walk into one of those bars and drink. I know about our family's history."

An old white man walks by with a cane, making motorboat noises with his mouth. He wears a houndstooth hat and a sweater with GAMECOCKS stitched across the front. It's not store-bought, and part of the lettering ends up beneath his armpit. He says to us, "If we lived somewhere in civilization, we could get on a train not in the middle of the night," without turning his head our way.

I smile. Odom Jr. looks down at his tennis shoes. I say, "If your mother offers you money, don't take it. Janette needs it more than we do. But if she offers you a Sawzall, bring it home. I've been wanting one of those things. I've been thinking about cutting some wood."

Odom Jr. says, "I hope I don't have to sit next to a smelly person on the train. Then I'd have to move to the bar car. And because of our family's history, I shouldn't be in the bar car."

I say, "I kind of need a regular circular saw, too. Listen, if she gives up any of her tools, take them. Money, no, but hammers and shit, yes."

My son sweeps hair out of his eyes. He has one of those-type haircuts. He says, "Next week I have a dentist appointment."

It's February 14. I'm with my seventeen-year-old son in a train station in South Carolina. He'll be sitting with his mother, bedside, in sixteen hours, before the day ends. Odom'll have four hours of Valentine's Day with her, then another full day and a half before getting on the same train back. I say, "You don't want to hand over melted candy to your mother. See if the conductor will let you keep your chocolates cold. Probably not the conductor. An usher, or whatever they're called." I've never been on a train, and don't know the proper occupational names.

Odom Jr. says, "I looked on the Internet and saw where people are hanging around the station in New Orleans trying to trick people into believing they're taxi drivers." He says, "That didn't come out right. It's a misplaced modifier."

I say, "You are never going to be a taxi driver. Nothing against taxi drivers, Odom Jr., but you won't be one." I'm happy that he knows about misplaced modifiers. Unlike most kids his age in America, he has an English teacher who cares.

We both look down the track. There's no single light coming our way. Cane Guy takes his stick and starts rummaging around the garbage can. My son says, "Did you ever play the trombone? Did you ever play a musical instrument?"

• • •

I should've told Odom Jr. this story earlier: I had this one trick, see, that mostly involved getting the stooge to forget anything that happened five seconds earlier. I don't want to say that attention deficit disorder emerged from my hometown, but it seems to be the case. Maybe everyone got distracted by my smoking cigarettes at age twelve, I don't know. It's a trick that's easy, seeing as everyone's thinking about anything else besides what's happening to their hands, right in front of them. Nowadays they're thinking about Facebook, Twitter, Yik Yak, Instagram, and all those other technological advances that sap the brain's ability in regard to concentration. I tried to learn some card tricks, too, and just couldn't get them right, plus I underwent puberty. I went back to my old standby. My father suggested it all. He said I might be able to pay for my own college if I did it right.

Here you go: Find a way to stick your right index finger in an ashtray when no one's looking. Get a good gray/black ash on the tip. Then come up to anyone, man or woman, child or adult, and say, "You like magic?" Most everyone says, "Yeah." If they don't, then they're maybe blind, or they go to science fiction movies and walk out saying, "They don't make spaceships like that." Most everyone likes magic, that's a common fact. I don't know how many times I executed this trick from ages twelve to sixteen, then seventeen until my ex-wife left, and had people say, "How'd you do that?" or "You're Satan."

It's important to say right up front, "I will not hurt you. You must do what I say, but I won't hurt you." Smile and nod. Make everyone in the room feel comfortable, whether they're plain watching or part of the performance.

People believe that shit about "I won't hurt you." You can point a gun at someone's head and say, "I won't hurt you," and they'll quit peeing in their pants. I got a story about that, too.

They can be seated, or standing, it doesn't matter. Say, "Stick your hands out flat, palms down." They will. Say, "Higher," and take their hands—making sure to touch the ash on your right index finger onto the bottom of their left hand—then raise both hands a little and say, "Close them into fists as tight as you can."

They'll do this. Keep eye contact. Don't go waving your right hand in front of their faces or anything, because they might say, "What's that slightly gray/black spot on your index finger?" If you have a propensity to talk with your hands, maybe find a way to slyly wipe your hands on your pant legs. Unless you're wearing white pants. Or a white skirt. This is a magic trick that can be performed by both men and women equally.

So then say something like, "Bang your fists together three times like this," and give a visual example. Tell the person to waggle those fists up and down a couple times. Right about now the person has forgotten all about your ever having touched his or her hands. Say, "Repeat after me: 'What roots clutch / what branches grow / out of this stony rubble.'"

They say it. Then say, "That's from *The Waste Land,* by T. S. Eliot." If it appears that this person might be intelligent—like if his or her mouth isn't wide open breathing—you might provide additional information about T. S. Eliot: that he worked in a bank, that he was from St. Louis, Missouri, that he also wrote a poem about a guy named J. Alfred Prufrock, that he was known as a modernist. If this person cocks the edges of his or her lips, go into a long explanation about modernism vis-à-vis postmodernism. Maybe talk about Yeats. Keep the focus on poetry, because that'll get 99 percent of people thinking in their inner voices things like, "I hated my English teacher in high school" or "I need to remember to take my dog to the vet for its shots soon" or "They're making great strides in the vegetarian meat industry, and fake sausage almost tastes real." They'll start daydreaming about ex-boyfriends and -girlfriends, cars they've owned in the past, good martinis they've concocted or drunk, the sound of slapping screened doors, people with mucus hanging from their nostrils, the exciting nights when clouds fly quickly in front of a full moon, an unbelievably offensive soccer match that ended up 3–2. They'll think of anything. They'll go into making pacts with God that if this stops they'll tithe *20 percent* from now on. Oh, these people will run through the presidents in a row, maybe the periodic table. They'll think things like, "I would rather my favorite pet be dead than be doing his magic trick."

In the early years I didn't say all this shit about T. S. Eliot. I didn't know it at the time, to be truthful. Back then I said something like, "Say this: John Wayne, James Kirk, Ronald Reagan, and the rest. Coca-Cola's pretty good, but Pepsi is the best." That's what I said. My father taught it to me. He sat around watching old-school movies and TV shows most of the day.

Okay, so after the person with an unknown ashen smudge on his or her left palm is completely mesmerized and forgetful—it might take another few "Bang your fists together three times'es" —say, "I am not going to hurt you."

Take an unlit cigarette and rub it on the top of both of his or her hands. Say, "I want you to think of this as being lit, and burning hard, like a kiln." If there are other people in the room, say, "I want *all y'all* to think of this as being lit, and burning hard, like a kiln." Make a sizzling noise with your tongue and palate.

Make a big point of saying, "Is there an ashtray around here? Is anyone smoking a cigarette?" and someone will hand you the ashtray you dipped your index finger in ten minutes earlier. Put a thin veil of ashes on the backs of the stooge's hands, and say some more poetry. Say something about burning. Say something about pet cremation. Maybe say, "Good fences make good neighbors," and explain how it's Frost, and then go into an explanation about how he was being all ironic. Have the person bang his fists together three times, then have him or her blow the ashes off his own hands.

Say, "Pick a hand."

I don't know how many people say, "Left," but it's a lot. People say, "Left hand!" I bet 86 percent of the time. It doesn't matter. You know that the smudge is on their left palm. If they say, "Left," then tell them to put their left hand behind their back. If they say, "Right!" tell them to put their left hand behind their back.

This is hard to explain, in terms of pronouns. Believe me when I say that I know it should be "their left hands behind their *backs*," but to me it sounds like a single person has more than one left hand and more than one back when I say it correctly.

Say, "I bet you two dollars I made your hand burn straight through." Say, "I bet you two dollars I magically caused your hand to become sullied." Say, "The power of fire can be either cold or hot at times. It can be 98.6 degrees and unnoticeable. You want to bet me two dollars I seared your palm without your knowing?"

Again—86 percent of the time they'll say, "I'll take that bet."

Then say something like, "You wish for your right hand to be kept unsullied, because you eat with your right hand more often than not," and have them open it up. It'll be clean. Have them pull that left hand out from behind their back(s). Dirty Smudged Palm, marked with old cigarette ash.

They'll say, "How did you do that?" or "You're Satan." Then someone—if there's a group—will say, "Do it to me."

It's a once-a-day kind of trick. You can't go, "Okay, hand me the ashtray and let me dip my right index finger in it."

Oh, wait: If you're twelve, go for two dollars. Sixteen? Four dollars. Drinking age in a bar? Ten dollars.

My name's Odom Tobe. I've done this particular magic trick one too many times.

• • •

My father missed his left ring finger. Well, he hit his left ring finger with the blade of an ax, I mean. He didn't have a finger between pinkie and middle. It happened when he was in high school. Whereas I went around pulling ash magic tricks on people so I could pay for college, my father lived on a farm cutting the heads off chickens for extra cash. He hesitated and swerved on the very first one, and the blade came down in a way that left only skin dangling. After that, well, after that he took to chopping heads off with a vengeance. It's not hard to imagine. That first rooster it took two chops to kill? His name was Odom.

My father denied it over and over, but in the end I understand that I got named for a dead rooster, one that splattered my young father's shirt, face, and arms with blood. Evidently he took and cradled me straight after birth and pretty much the same thing happened: He underwent a flashback, and there, holding his son in the delivery room with nine fingers—holding his son with nine fingers in the delivery room—goddamn it: there, my nine-fingered father held his son in the delivery room and thought, "Odom."

Misplaced modifier, like son like father.

During the *Star Trek* craze, he could never play Spock. He could never wear a wedding band correctly. My father said that's what took him so long to marry, that most women he met held traditional notions concerning all the vows and impedimenta of betrothal, and the rest of them plain got freaked out by a nine-fingered chicken-killer.

I'll just go ahead and say that my mother had a couple webbed toes, so they kind of evened out in regard to imperfections. My father couldn't do that Live Long and Prosper gesture, and my mother focused on Kermit the Frog whenever *Sesame Street* aired.

"You need to go to college in order to prove my theory," my father told me often, starting at age twelve. "Do you know the word 'vicarious,' Odom? I want to live vicariously through your scientific proofs."

My father believed that life once existed on Pluto, because the sun was something like a thousand times hotter. Then over time the sun cooled, and life moved to Neptune, Uranus, Saturn, Jupiter, and so on. It moved to Mars, then Earth. In time the sun would dwindle into nearly nothing, and life would evolve on Venus, then Mercury. Then the sun would die out and everyone on Mercury would freeze to death.

"I know the word," I said, though I didn't. I thought "vicarious" meant "victorious." That made sense, too—"I want to live victoriously through your scientific proofs."

My father held only a high school education, but he read a lot of science fiction novels and borrowed my mother's issues of *World Weekly News*. He believed that germs lived everywhere in the solar system, that they traveled around in a systematic fashion not unlike comets and asteroids, and that once the temperature dropped because of the sun's fizzling, those germs would crash into the soil and multiply in evolutionary fashion, et cetera.

I bet my mother said, "You're scaring the boy, Jobe," four thousand times during my childhood.

That's right: My father's name was Jobe Tobe, two syllables. I'm glad he had that lurchy chicken named Odom, for I would not want to be named Jobe Tobe Jr. As an aside, every resident of minuscule Testate, South Carolina, inherently understood that our family name rhymed with "lobe" or "robe," except for this one poor squirrelly man named Mr. Ludd who got fired at six different school districts starting in Delaware and working on down the East Coast, who showed up tenth grade and lasted one year teaching English. He insisted on calling the roll and saying, "Odom To-be-or-not-to-be." He taught drama classes, too.

I never raised my hand.

As another aside, no one in my hometown growing up thought it hilarious when we said something like "I live in Testate." They didn't have the will to laugh about how it sounded, evidently.

One would think I couldn't pull the magic trick off very often growing up, seeing as there weren't but forty people in my graduating class. I did those forty, their parents, some people who showed up for Fourth of July reunions at Lake Testate, the forty people in the class below me, some of their parents, maybe half of the original people in my class another time because their memories faded quickly, their parents again, maybe some lost people down at the Testate Feed and Fuel who couldn't find I-26, and all those one-year-and-out teachers who came through Testate. If I'd've lived in a normal-sized town of 10,000 I could have made enough money to forget about college altogether and sit around the rest of my life reading science fiction novels and grocery-store tabloids.

I went to college, paid for it myself, got in a physics class, and mentioned to the professor my father's beliefs. I went into detail, that very first day. It's not like I sat at the edge of my desk barely able to contain myself. The professor said, "Do any of you have a background in physics?"

I raised my hand. Like an idiot, right there with a bunch of football players behind me all grouped up sweating, one of them being the long snapper who would later ask the professor if there was physics in a perfect low spiral, I said all that stuff my father asked me to figure out involving dwarf stars, black holes, traveling molecules, and so on. I didn't hold back. I said it's exactly how things started on Earth: single-cell organisms divide and multiply, there's water, there's aquatic life, fish become amphibians, amphibians move onto dry land, there's a monkey all of a sudden. I watched as the professor's mouth dropped slightly, watched as he opened up a notebook and wrote something down. I deflated somewhat when—after my diatribe—the professor said, "That's nonsense. Are you crazy? It's impossible. What're you doing here?"

I should mention that this college wasn't the best in the nation. It wasn't even on one of those Best Regional Top 100 lists. Hell, it wasn't even a real college, as far as I could figure—a satellite school where half the students commuted from their parents' house(s), or maybe lived in a trailer park on the west side of the campus until the state allocated enough funds to build a real dormitory.

I never knew for sure, but I think that professor ran off to his office and started writing research immediately. Me, I walked over to the registrar, dropped out officially, went to the Business Office and got a refund, then returned to my off-campus trailer, realizing that I would not be attending another class ever. I understood that I could only hide from my father for the next few months, feigning higher education, maybe learn more bar tricks until my roommate caught on that I wasn't supposed to be there anymore.

I thought, There are some things my father should never have asked me to do.

I thought, No woman is ever going to want to be in a relationship with me.

Four years later I met Wendy in a bar called Duck and Cover, which was bordered on one side by a hunting compound and the other by the Savannah River Nuclear Site. Wendy'd just graduated from the same college and worked on a master's degree from an even less prestigious institution of higher learning that allowed for distance learning.

I got work at Milling Plastics, spent my extra money on books and computer-technology courses, rose in the company, invested well, rejoiced in Odom Jr.'s birth, and then Wendy left me for a trombone-playing woman.

I spent way too much time researching microbes that may or may not have circled the solar system, looking for places to seed themselves. I drank, trying not to think about how my father drank. I drank, trying not to think about my grandfathers on both sides.

• • •

I say, "I take it back. If you want to cry, cry. I don't know what's the right thing to do. Hell, your mother might think that if you don't cry, then you don't care. You care, don't you?"

I look down at the ring finger on my left hand. I took the wedding band off a month after Wendy left. There's still, I think, a white circle there, even after all these years.

The blind man leans out in such a way that I fear he might fall off the platform. I sit up a little, thinking I might need to take off running toward him. He eases back and taps his cane a few times on the concrete. My son says, "I'm not gay. Do you think Mom might be upset with me?" He says, "I mean, what if she's about to die and asks if I'm gay? I don't want to disappoint her."

I shake my head no. "Your mother loves you if you're straight or gay. As do I. What the fuck are you talking about?"

Cane Man starts walking toward us and says, "My father took me to Grand Central Station once. I was brought up here in South Carolina. We took a train to Grand Central Station, got off, then stood there to take a train right back home. He said, 'Now you can say you've been to New York City.' That was it. Only time I went. Now I'm here, going the other way."

Odom Jr. says, "Are you going all the way to New Orleans now? The train stops in New Orleans."

I say, "I thought you were going to fall off the platform earlier. Don't lean so much." But here's what I'm thinking: *My own father used to tell a story of his father taking him from South Carolina to New York, then turning right around.* Same scenario.

"It's Valentine's Day," the man says.

I say, "My son Odom here is traveling to New Orleans all by himself," even though Wendy would be pissed off that I said his real name and offered his destination, what with pedophiles and scam artists. "He's a big boy now," I say, then punch my son lightly on the arm.

The man says, "I took a plane one time to Memphis, but I got out and had some fun there." He walks down the platform and sits at the far end of the next bench. He says, "I know," but I'm not sure if he's responding to Odom's name, or destination, or if he's merely spouting off random words.

We hear the Amtrak train's whistle, but it's hard to tell how fast it's going, or how far away. I start thinking about that Hank Williams song and know that it'll be stuck in my head a good rest of the day. I say, "I know it's bad luck to make such a prediction, Odom, but I think you've gotten enough of your mother's DNA to break the curse."

He turns toward me, and I can see that he's tearing up. "Your grandfather lost a finger and got a divorce. I kept my finger and got a divorce. I think you're sensible and smart and sensitive enough to remain in a relationship for a long, long time. And moral. You don't like to trick people."

My son says, "You want to tell me something else. I can feel it."

That's how smart he is. And peculiarly intuitive. "Well," I say. "I don't know. I have some things I'll tell you when I'm on my deathbed, I imagine. I don't know all the ins and outs of sexuality or whatever it's called, but maybe your mother discovered her love of Janette because of me. It wasn't all trombones, is what I'm saying."

He curls up one side of his lips. Is it a smile? Does he smirk at his old man? He says, "You and Mom and Janette had a three-way and Mom found out that Janette's better."

I shake my head. I say, "Now you're talking like an old-time Tobe. I might have to reconsider the DNA."

The train comes closer. Its light shines on some pine trees, maybe a half mile away. Odom Jr. says, "You hit her in some kind of drunken brawl, and then you felt really bad about it and quit drinking altogether."

I scrunch my eyebrows down and shake my head. "I hit a boy in about tenth grade after he hit me. I did my ash trick, and he kind of flipped out. He called me Satan, he hit me, I hit him back, and then his parents made him pay me money owed."

Cane Man gets up from his seat and holds his stick out at a ninety-degree angle, pointing at the train's engine. He yells out, "Heeeeeaaaar that loooooonesome whiiiiiistle . . ." but the engineer hits the whistle so loudly that Cane Man gets drowned out. I don't know if Cane Man overheard any of my son's and my conversation, but he holds his cane—tip first—to his lips as if he's playing a trombone.

My son says, "You tried to poison her after she said she wanted to leave."

"Odom," I say. "No."

The train's brakes make a noise that hurts my molars. My son grabs his bag. He says, "Gambling! Mom got upset because you needed to join Gamblers Anonymous."

I should shrug. I should say, There you go, you got me.

"Not close," I say.

Wendy never considered it date rape until she read an article that involved college students signing pacts and waivers, asking questions that involved permission. Neither did I. Back then, men and women—boys and girls, really—met at bars, connected, somehow ended up at one another's apartments or trailers. They drank and/or smoked dope. They said, "Hey, *Saturday Night Live*'s coming on," or "I hope something's good on MTV." They put vinyl albums on the turntable, or cassettes in a stereo, or CDs—if they were rich—into a deck. They ate large bags of Cheetos, Doritos, Lay's Barbecue, and Fritos. They either said things about the Middle East and the government, or they pretended the world would never see another major conflict. Wendy and I came back to my trailer from Duck and Cover, and she said that she admired my sink for not being filled with dirty dishes. I tried not to stare at her bralessness. I did my best. The brown faux-Naugahyde couch sat across from the boxlike Zenith I'd bought at Goodwill.

I thought it necessary to do my smudged palm trick, which caused Wendy to open her mouth wider than I've ever seen a person do. She didn't call me Satan, or ask how it was done.

I put my arm around her.

She smelled of cigarettes, Charlie perfume, light perspiration. Wendy's hair winged out on both sides, as was the fashion fifteen years earlier. Maybe I nudged her sideways until she lay prone. I cannot remember exactly. Maybe I said, "I like zippers better than buttons." Maybe I pulled her long-sleeved T-shirt up before she had the chance to say no. I would like to say that she nodded in approval, that she helped me get my blue jeans down around my ankles. I would like to say that Odom Jr. was not conceived while someone made a joke on television, or a rock band played a song about the skin of celebrities.

My son was born nine months later. Wendy and I got our lives together, got married right after Odom Jr.'s arrival, and did our best. For some reason—perhaps we hailed from too-conservative backgrounds—we thought it unnecessary to tell our son about all this. "Bastard" is such a rough and misused term.

Wendy read the article, made her accusations, then took off with Janette.

I turn to say, "It's all my fault" and "I love you" and "I have done the best I can do raising you alone" to my son, but somehow—as if he performed the greatest levitation/vanishing act of all time—I look up to see him standing on the first step of the train, ready to embark. I glance over to Cane Man, but he's gone.

"I'll be here to pick you up," I say. My son smiles and nods. We both know there's a good chance that I'll sit here for a few days, waiting. I look down between my feet and see a black smudge, where someone's stubbed out a cigarette. I press my index finger down hard, and hold it there. I want to push it until it disappears.

GLORYLAND

If I'd not punched out my previous three bosses, I wouldn't have fallen prey to graveyard shifts trying to block that losing Confederate anthem from my head nonstop, which I knew wouldn't disappear entirely until my "security guard" partner Dickie Land quit or died. Dickie Land! Were his parents not thinking ahead? Dickie Land, the simplest of the Land brothers, worked with me at Land Concrete Recycling. During daylight hours dump trucks came in, paid fifty bucks a load, and dropped enormous broken chunks of parking lots, sidewalks, and buildings. The daylight workers broke it up and *sold smaller* chunks to contractors in need of sturdy and uncomplicated fill. To be honest, I could only surmise what went on inside Land Concrete Recycling. Even the company's name confused me. Somehow the owner, whom I never met—Dickie Land's father—got people to pay him for using his acreage, and got people to pay him for taking useless shards off-site. What kind of perfect scam is that?

"You've not had a job in the last ten years?" Dickie Land's brother asked when I handed him the half-filled-out application.

I was forty-four years old, single again, living in an apartment complex that didn't have a pool or laundry facility. Before everything fell apart, when I still had money, I checked into a fancy rehab with a psychologist who told me I needed to love and admire myself. He wore a toupee. I got out, didn't drink, found another job, punched out another boss.

To Rudy Land I said, "Nothing worth wasting ink on. Day trader," I said, which wasn't true.

"Man, that bubble sure burst, didn't it? Listen, this job's for insurance purposes more than anything else. It's better for us to pay eighty bucks a night under the table than have kids come in here and crush their legs fooling around. Plus, there are some less-than-moral construction people out there who want to dump after hours." Rudy Land wore two gold pinkie rings. I recognized him from various Happy Hours a decade earlier. He talked and talked, but he never mentioned his little brother. "You walk the perimeter once an hour with a flashlight, turn a key at a handful of posts. It takes seven minutes, tops. If someone gives you trouble, you call the police. Number's in the hut. Don't play with the front-end loader or jackhammers."

I said, "When can I start?" and in my head figured out the money.

Rudy looked at the Rolex on his left wrist, then jabbed his right arm out and looked at another one. Two pinkie rings and two watches! I tried not to think, Now this is the kind of boss I'd love to beat up. "Tonight if you want. Did I mention that it's six days a week? Sundays off, but that's it. Stay with us a year and we'll talk vacation."

Four hundred eighty dollars a week, I thought. Nothing taken out. If I could keep my temper in check and stay away from liquor stores, I figured—if I could empty my mind like one of those guest-lecturer yogis instructed at the rehab center—I might could revisit that mysterious notion of self-esteem.

"I'll do you proud," I said, just like I said on my last series of jobs—one teaching Pop Culture in the American Studies division of the History department at a college whose administrators should suffer egregiously in the afterlife; one as a despised state employee working the extension service, charged with telling people what they couldn't do on or to their own property; and one trying to talk people into buying electric scooters.

"You'll be working with . . ." Rudy Land said, but his phone rang, he answered, and then he started yelling, "Do we call ourselves Land Concrete *and Rebar* Recycling? Did someone fuck up in the Yellow Pages? Y'either get the rebar out before bringing it in, or go dump it somewhere and risk fines from the EPA and ten dozen other environment watchdogs."

I said, "I'll just come on in at eleven," and left his office. I didn't ask if there would be a timeclock to punch, or if anyone would be around for me to relieve. Rudy Land nodded hard once, flipped the back of his hand toward the door, and continued to berate a rebar-impaired contractor.

As I drove away in my thirty-year-old Toyota, I thought about calling my ex-wife to tell her the good news, that I hadn't slugged anyone in months and might be buying a used RV within a year to live in wherever I wished so long as a dump station stood nearby. I heard myself saying to her, "You still like to travel, don't you?"

I heard her saying, "What kind of gas mileage does a Winnebago get? I thought you were all about the environment. You're still a fraud, Jackie."

• • •

I parked and walked into the only building with a light on. The guard hut, one of those prefab Dutch-style barns sold in the parking lots of Home Depot and Lowe's, stood near the entrance. A heavy-duty extension cord ran from the main building, where I'd met Rudy Land twelve hours earlier, to the post where—if I did my math correctly—I would spend fifty-three minutes of each hour.

I opened the door to find an overweight man with black, wavy, heavily greased hair standing against one wall and looking at the other. I said, "Hey there, buddy." One of those therapists earlier in my life said I should use "buddy," "pal," or "friend" at the end of every other sentence when talking to men, and avoid Honey, Darling, Baby, Dear, Dearheart, Sugarbritches, or Slick when conversing with females.

"I'm Dickie Land," Dickie Land said.

Immediately my head filled with "Look away, look away, look away—Dickie Land," and that verse would remain during my stint at Land Concrete Recycling.

I said, "Hey, pal," and introduced myself as I stepped inside. "So I take it you're one of the owners."

Dickie Land didn't turn his head. Against the wall stood a four-by-eight-foot piece of once-white pegboard. The top half appeared smudged. "What I'm doing here, see, is I'm writing the entire Bible—Old and New Testaments—on this here piece of wood. And then another. When it's done, I'm going to wear it across my front and backside, you know, like one of those things. And I'm going to walk around."

I said, "They didn't tell me if I was supposed to wear a uniform. Those things are called sandwich boards that you're referring to. Did Rudy leave some kind of uniform for me to put on, friend?"

Dickie Land revealed the most cocked eyes in the history of ophthalmology. He said, "Don't mind me. My daddy says I can use this space any time I want. I can't during the day because I work at Gloryland. It's the biggest church in the tri-county area. Do you go there? We're not related to the church. My last name's Land, but I'm not related to Gloryland. There's so many people at Gloryland I wouldn't know if you were there. I sit up front. They let me sit up front. Preacher says when I get done with printing out the Bible, he's gone let me walk from one end of the stage to the other."

I thought how I'd almost asked Rudy Land why the last guard quit or got fired. Is Dickie Land simpleminded? I wondered. Obviously he can write, or at least transcribe. I said, "I've seen Gloryland out there on the highway. First time I saw it I thought they'd built one of those mega Walmarts." I walked up to the placard. Dickie Land used a special one-hair paintbrush—and the hair must've been from a chinchilla, otter, or field rat, it was so thin—in order to print out, say, "She may not eat of any thing that cometh of the vine, neither let her drink wine or strong drink, nor eat any unclean thing: all that I commanded her let her observe," across one inch of the board, maybe a half millimeter high.

"You should go to Gloryland. It's the biggest church in the tri-county area. I cut the grass there. You should go to Gloryland. I cut the grass at the biggest church in the tri-county area." I looked for my promised flashlight. I thought how maybe Dickie Land got stuck and needed one tiny pop upside the head to get untracked. "Daddy told me to use these pegboards so I'll have air come through. So it won't make me die of heatstroke."

I said, "That's a good idea. Ventilation." I said, "How're you going to walk around, though? That board's eight feet tall. See what I mean? You'd have to be nine feet at the shoulders to walk around wearing such a pair of signs."

Dickie Land walked up to his project. He looked at me—maybe, I couldn't tell what with those eyes—and said, "Hey. Hey. What can I do? Daddy didn't tell me anything about this."

I said "Stilts," right away, which shouldn't've come out of my mouth so quickly. I would regret the idea later. That therapist who told me not to call women Honey used to put his finger on my lips when he thought I blurted things out before thinking. He did it a lot. And called me Sweetheart one too many times.

● ● ●

I walked the perimeter. I tried to figure out why an insurance company thought a concrete recycling company would be better off paying someone like me twenty-five grand a year so that a drunk or teenager might not wander in and succumb to silicosis. Why wouldn't the Land family flat-out build an eight-foot-high hurricane fence with concertina wire looped across the top? And seeing as they paid me under the table, how would an insurance company really know that they had a nightly guard? Something wasn't right, but I didn't bring it up.

I shuffled along at a less-than-seven-minute pace while Dickie Land plodded through his odd project. Sometimes, unfortunately, I beat myself up for my previous mistakes. I bet no one thinks more on the job than a night-shift security guard. Why did I think it necessary to clobber a dean, or a chemist, or a scooter dealer? I thought about my ex-wife—whom I never even raised my voice to, she'll admit it—and wondered if she ever found a mate with no vices, a man not obsessed with American movies post-1950 wherein northern actors couldn't grasp southern dialect, not obsessed with how all American music post-1950 owed a nod to Sonny Boy Williamson II, a man not obsessed with how American cardiologists secretly worship videogame designers, and contemporary chefs who find a need to use fatback in their recipes.

"I'm starting on Proverbs!" Dickie Land yelled out one night, magnifying glass in hand. "I'm done with Daniel!" he said another.

"That's real good, Dickie Land," I always said between laps, and then I'd think, "Oh, I wish I was in the land of cotton," or "In Dixie's Land, where I was born in," or even fragments of the song that no one knew, because I hung out in the public library sometimes and found myself looking up just *about everything*. I said, "You know, people collect this kind of folk art, Dickie Land. After you get done walking around on stilts showing your tiny-lettered Bible off, you should see about selling it."

Dickie Land didn't seem to comprehend art collectors or the future. He painted, humming what I assumed were hymns he memorized at Gloryland. Sometimes—this was mean, I know—I'd bring along a book to work, say *Raise Your Jelly Jars High, Boys: The Reemergence of White Lightning in the Upper-Middle-Class South So That Lawyers and Bankers Can Feel Dangerous,* and say to Dickie Land, "Hey, man, read this paragraph right here." I'd shove the book his way.

"If it's not the Good Book, then I don't want nothing to do with it," he would say.

Each Thursday Dickie pointed to the desk, where a brown business-sized envelope with my pay, usually in twenties, lay. Rudy wrote "Good job," or "Dickie prays for you every day" on a torn-off sheet of Land Concrete Recycling stationery. I asked Dickie where he went after work, and he said "Gloryland."

"Where do you live, Dickie? Do you live in your parents' house?" I asked about forty days in a row.

"Gloryland," he'd say.

I'd done some research on his particular megachurch and learned that Pastor Leon Speth slayed congregants in the spirit and worked as a faith healer. "Have you ever asked your preacher to stick his palms on your eyeballs and fix them?" I asked Dickie more than a few times.

He would turn my way and said, "Fix them from what?" He always stood in front of his pegboard, special paintbrush in one hand and magnifying glass in the other. I wanted to buy him a jeweler's loupe just to see if he shoved it in his eye socket sideways, but those things cost a lot of money, even used, and in an effort to move out of that apartment, I'd been good about not wasting wages on booze, electricity, water, scratch cards, and fast food, much less buying extra gear for superstitious, slow, primitive artists.

I walked my perimeter. I sat in the guard shack, poring over *Entertainment Weekly*, *People*, *Southern Living*, *Cosmo*, *Prevention*, and *Appalachia Now!*, just in case I got another job teaching Pop Culture in a Southern Cultures Studies program inside an American Studies program inside a History or Sociology department. I needed to keep up. I wanted to remain fluent in all things current.

One night in April, with Easter nearing, Dickie Land set his brush down and looked over at me. We had been ignoring each other as best as possible for three months. I still wasn't sure what my responsibilities were, to be honest. Dickie said—in a voice that came out somewhere between Tom Waits and Sir Richard Burton—"Do you really think you'll gain insights to our problems there between the covers of that monthly? What are you perusing tonight, anyway, *Pen and Ink*?"

I could've dropped my jaw, or reconsidered some of the more pessimistic contemporary philosophers who argued that our lives were a reality TV show orchestrated by intelligent life forms from another galaxy. But I smiled. "You can read and write and think," I said.

Dickie Land's eyes turned normal. I had read about a strain of people in south Georgia who could go double-cockeyed as easily as everyday folks can cross their eyes or roll their tongues, but I figured it to be another rural myth. "I did some mathematical calculations early on," Dickie said, jerking his head for me to come look at his two-board Bible, "and realized that if I lowered myself to text-talk I'd have enough space. Do you know how many times somebody said 'O my God' in the Bible? Psalm 25, 3, 4, 83, 59, 22. Answer: A lot. Just in Psalms and just off the top of my head. So I've decided to go 'OMG.' It'll seem more cool, you know, and it'll click with the teenagers."

Now someone might rightly say, "Jackie, how come you didn't piss your pants, or punch Dickie Land seeing as that was your usual response to things?" I don't have an answer. And I don't know why my first response went, "'MOS' means 'Mom Over Shoulder.' I bet Jesus says that somewhere in John, Mark, Luke, or Matthew."

• • •

To say that our graveyard shifts together took an unforeseen direction would be an understatement. I found a way, usually before one in the morning, to ask Dickie Land, "How long have you been acting like you had the IQ of one of the lesser-used Monopoly pieces?" or "Are you planning out a long, drawn-out trick on Gloryland?" or "Does this have something to do with your father's estate?" or "Are you trying to get in the *Guinness Book of World Records* for writing out a tiny Bible and feigning being a mentally challenged adult?" or "Is this some kind of experiment you're conducting à la *Black Like Me* or *Fat Like Me* or *Facially Deformed Like Me*? Are you in the Psychology department at the college?"

For what it's worth, I'd twice been cleared of public intoxication charges by convincing the arresting officers that I worked on a soon-to-be published nonfiction narrative titled *Drunk Like Me*, with footnotes and everything else scholarly.

Dickie Land never answered my questions. He transformed from a single-focused, cock-eyed, slow-witted evangelical into a man conversant on topics that ranged from intricate combat maneuvers starting in the Peloponnesian War, to classical music and its influence on prisoners, to current products on the market that he'd feel comfortable promoting. Dickie Land spoke highly of Buck knives, and axes manufactured by a company in Finland called Fiskars.

"Did you hit your head? Do you remember hitting your head?" I asked after every circuit around Land Concrete Recycling.

Nothing. One time Dickie Land said, "I tell you one thing. You might lose your job here if construction comes to a halt. If construction comes to a halt, we'll go out of business. If I were you, I'd go around in the daylight—or, hell, in between walking the perimeter—carrying a sledgehammer. Nobody's looking?—smash up some good concrete. People have to find a way to fix their parking lots and sidewalks, you know what I mean? They'll call their insurance agents, get their money, haul off their bad cement to here, and so on."

I took to pretending that I heard someone walking across the gravel, or car tires slowing outside in a suspicious manner. Understand, I started this job uncomfortable with Dickie Land's supposed deficiencies, and without a logical progression I became uncomfortable with Dickie Land's nonstop rational behavior and thought processes. I guess when Dickie felt I stayed away too long, he'd come outside the guard shack and yell, "Cancer no longer exists, you know. They're making it all up so's the money keeps coming in. People go in with a common cough. Doctor orders an X-ray. They'll say they see a spot on the X-ray, and then order a computerized axial tomography scan or magnetic resonance image. Then they'll open you up, pretend to take out the spot, close you up, order more X-rays and scans and MRIs—I get those confused—say that you need radiation and physical therapy, and six months later, when you're feeling better, they talk you into participating in some kind of cancer-survivors walkathon to raise money *for them*. It's a regular Circle of Greed."

I would stare off at the road hoping that someone would show up trying to dump concrete without paying. I would stare off thinking, Dickie Land's making some sense, and fantasize about getting another Pop Culture teaching job so I could bring him in as a guest lecturer.

One morning I called up Rudy Land and said, "Hey, bossman, has Dickie been acting any different around y'all? I mean, have you noticed a bizarre turnaround in his behavior?"

Here's what I expected from Rudy Land: "Yes, it's a miracle!" or "No" or "Have you started drinking again? I don't have a brother." I didn't expect, "Man, that's cruel."

I said, "What? Wait. I didn't say anything mean."

Rudy turned his head from the phone and yelled, "Not there! Dump it over there, you idiot," and in my mind I envisioned a new gigantic mound of ex-foundation marring my usual hourly round. Back to me Rudy said, "I'm sorry. Who is this?"

I said, "It's Jackie. Your security guard."

He laughed. He said, "I don't know what kind of scam you're running, friend, but it won't work here. I don't have a security guard."

"Jackie!" I said, but then realized that Rudy Land feared the IRS, or Social Security, trying to catch him on paying me under the table. I hung up.

• • •

"You shouldn't be calling my brother, comrade," Dickie Land said. "Ever." He pointed to the corner of our office at two things, a sledge-hammer and a pair of stilts.

I said, "I'm not going to go around breaking up good cement, Dickie Land."

I thought, "Old Missus marry Will de Weaver/William was a gay deceiver"—one of the verses—and wondered what the Confederate flag–waving reenactors thought about their anthem having "gay" in it. Or about the song being written by a man up in Ohio.

"Help me get on my Bible, and let's see if I can maneuver around on the stilts," Dickie Land said. "I've been practicing on the stilts by themselves no problem."

I said, "I'll help you if and only if you ever answer my question."

Dickie shook his head no. He said, "I'm going to need a trumpet, and seven golden candlesticks. You need to come to Gloryland this coming Sunday, Jackie. This Sunday's the day. They're wanting me to show off my handiwork, like I said."

I said, "Hey, it's Thursday. I need my pay," for I knew that I wouldn't be coming back. I foresaw my getting talked into breaking the law, then the Lands killing me so I wouldn't blackmail them, then my body showing up amid crushed concrete used as a foundation for a megachurch built atop an old landfill or a sacred burial ground or a swamp. I foresaw my ex-wife, years later, trying to find out whatever happened to me. As much as I held a grudge for her not keeping, cherishing, and following our wedding vows, I wouldn't want her to spend time worrying that, perhaps, I'd disappeared in order to make her think I might lurk around her new life.

"Oh," said Dickie Land. "Damn if it ain't. So. What say you about coming to the service on Sunday?" He patted his back pocket to let me know that my $480 rested inside his wallet.

"I look forward to it," I said, which, oddly enough, I meant. One time I saw a Fourth of July fireworks extravaganza go terribly wrong, and I figured Dickie Land's showcase might offer a similar disaster worth experiencing.

We strapped the pegboard Bible to his shoulders. There, on a clear night, Dickie Land strode around the parking lot, unstable. I began humming "Dixie" like an idiot, which I probably did unconsciously most nights on the job. Dickie Land found his stride, went straight out onto the road, and never returned. In the distance, though, I swear I heard him yell out, "Just as no one can be forced into belief, so no one can be forced into unbelief," which—if I remembered correctly—was said by Sigmund Freud. Freud! Who comes across Sigmund Freud while guarding used concrete?

• • •

I'll go ahead and say that I didn't get saved at my first and only Gloryland Sunday performance, at least not in an outward and official manner. This isn't one of those stories that ends up in *Reader's Digest* or the *Ernest Angley Newsletter*. I wasn't overcome by a searing laser-light, only to find my body transported onstage to have goatee-sporting Leon Speth slam his palm on my forehead in a way to make the chloroform on his coatsleeve hem knock me backwards stunned. No, I just sat there halfway back in the pews—I should say that I've been to Division I basketball games with fewer spectators—moving my mouth to contemporary hymns that everyone else seemed to know. A six-piece rock band led the way, with two drummers.

Pastor Leon said some things about Jesus dying for our sins, about the devil being bad, about Jesus being betrayed, about Satan being strong but not strong enough, about how knowledge puffeth up, but charity edifieth.

Then they passed around plates, which were really KFC buckets.

I'd like to say that I took the bucket from Karla—she made a point of introducing herself when I sat down—and handed it over to what appeared to be another slow-minded congregant who kept saying "Jimmy Bishop, Jimmy Bishop" while a long string of mucus dangled from his nose, but I reached in my pocket, pulled out a two-dollar bill I'd been keeping for luck, and tossed it in.

"Now, y'all know that we have a special good member of our flock here named Dickie Land," Leon Speth said. He wore a headset and held his arms out like Jesus on the cross. Some people yelled out "Amen!" and others "Go Dickie!" and others "Praise the Lord!"

I had to hold back the urge to scream, "Oh, I wish I was in the land of cotton!"

"Dickie Land has been doing the Lord's work for some time now."

The preacher looked offstage. "How long you been working on your project, Dickie?"

Dickie wore a headset, too. His voice came out to the audience—the original, half-witted Dickie Land voice that I had known—"I don't know. Maybe thirty year." Then there was the sound of his stilts pegging up and down, clump-clump-clump-clump. "Six month."

"Ladies and gentlemen, our Dickie Land has painted the entire *Holy Bible* on two pieces of plywood . . ."

"Pegboards," Dickie Land blurted out from backstage. I might've said it out loud myself.

Reverend Leon Speth nodded and laughed. He said, "I stand corrected."

Karla nudged me and said, "I know Dickie. I used to date Dickie in hi-skoo."

I don't know why I thought it appropriate to say, "My wife left me because she thought I was irresponsible. I'm not drinking anymore, and I pay my bills on time."

Karla put her left hand on my belt buckle. She said, "You're a good person, I can tell. Jesus hasn't steered me wrong yet."

I was about to say "Lower," about her hand, but Dickie had high-stepped his way across the stage toward Pastor Speth. The congregation stood up and clapped.

I did, too. And I couldn't wait for Dickie Land to hold his hands over his head, quiet the crowd, and say something about cancer, or Freud, or economics, maybe a couple new views he had pertaining to all the smoking bans in hotels and restaurants in town.

But he said nothing. He clomped to the lectern, reached beneath the front pegboard, and pulled out that trumpet he'd talked about earlier. When he blew into it, not much happened outside of a long, slightly whistling noise, just like anyone who's never played a brass instrument might make.

I, of course, felt disappointed. I wanted to be a part of Gloryland history. I wanted to live vicariously through a supposedly witless man addressing a thousand people and telling them how they hadn't taken the Golden Rule seriously, or something. As Dickie Land exited I looked over at Jimmy Bishop, who had his hands down his pants. Karla looked at me in the same way my ex-wife looked at me on our wedding day.

"I chickened out," came across the speakers. "Goddamn it, I wanted to say some things about superstition and people who've given up on everything else." I couldn't tell if he berated himself or talked to a stagehand. Pastor Leon looked offstage, then took off walking at a pace best known to cancer survivors at a fundraiser.

Someone said, "Shut up, brother," and then I heard the sharp rap of stilts hitting a hardwood floor.

I don't remember shoving my way down the pews, nor climbing the steps to the stage. My first punch connected with the preacher's chin. Subsequent punches hit the second drummer, then a man I didn't know who wore a plaid jacket, and then, almost, Dickie Land. I don't know if his headset still worked when he yelled, "You don't know me, you don't know me, you don't know me!" right before he picked up one stilt and swung it hard at my knees.

I don't know if the congregation out front caught me yelling, "Dickie Land, Dickie Land," in a singsong voice. From the apse— if megachurches indeed own apses—I heard the first couple lines of "Amazing Grace." Dickie took off running down passageways he must've memorized, followed by Speth, Drummer #2, and the guy in the plaid jacket.

I turned to find Rudy Land—I didn't even see him emerge from the pews—standing on top of the pegboard Bible. He said, "How can one man cause so much trouble?" I didn't stop to wonder if he talked about his brother or me, and I punched the guy hard, one of those punches with enough upward force to cause the nose to explode in a grand splatter of blood. I hit him with my left hand, too, right on target but not with as much force. He retreated, crying, into the bowels of the building.

I thought about how I used to spend class periods covering how Americans paid a lot of money in order to create an identity—Botox,

Nikes, hair extensions, diet pills, and the like. I thought about how—with the surge of reality TV—everyone considered it his right to gain fame and fortune even without appropriate skills or intelligence. That particular lecture lasted an entire M-W-F.

The congregation sang. Pastor Leon Speth didn't return. I had no choice but to go front and center with my blood-spattered hands to say some things I'd noticed about what drove people to do what they did. I would be bringing up both Charles Darwin and John Maynard Keynes. I drug Dickie Land's work behind me, careful not to scuff the edges.

LINGUISTIC FALLACIES AND FACIAL TICS, SEX ED AND DEATH

A month after my parents rightly underwent unlawful and inferable retribution—maybe twenty-seven days after Uncle Cush arrived, insisting that we move to his abode on the other side of the Savannah River nuclear facility, for he foresaw arson, which, indeed, occurred—I attended my first and only Optimists International meeting. This was July 1990. I'd turned fourteen the previous March. Already my uncle explained to me how do-gooders, philanthropists, volunteer literacy coaches, and foreigners forever tempt arsonists and lynch mobs in a town like Poke, wedged between a nuclear dumping ground and a covey of bankrupt and abandoned ex–cotton mills. Cush told me that until my parents felt it safe to return, he would be managing *in loco parentis*.

"Why didn't they take me with them?" I asked more than once, usually when Cush served up MREs for supper that he'd acquired and stockpiled before, during, and after the Fall of Saigon. "How come you and I can't go where they are?"

"Thing about freeze-dried mashed potatoes, they go good with everything. Hell, I like freeze-dried mashed potatoes with mayonnaise on Sunbeam bread." He always pulled on his extraordinarily repulsive Fu Manchu and draped it above both ears during mealtimes. If I looked across the table I felt as if I dined with a man sporting hirsute oxygen-supply nostril tubes. My uncle stood six-five, also, and probably wore about a size nine hat. He wasn't someone most people would pick as a dinner guest nightly.

The Optimists met bimonthly, second and fourth Tuesdays, always at Poke Pancake, off Denim Street in the nearly vacant mill village. I hoped that no one sat at our table, for I didn't want to hear a stranger gag over my uncle's facial hair. Also, I didn't feel like fielding all the questions I'd seen my parents undergo from locals: Where you from? Who you with? What's your church?

In the past, I'd heard my father say, "The United States," and "My son. Are you visually impaired?" and "Ha ha ha ha ha" when the answers—if you didn't want to feel obligated to disappear unannounced and have your house torched—should've gone something like "Other side of Barnwood County" and "Poke Plant No. 6" and "First Baptist." There were a couple of acceptable substitutions: Graywood County. The nuclear facility. Bolt Baptist. But not much else, and never ending with laughter.

My uncle and I arrived on time, though all the Optimists had, evidently, arrived at daybreak. A waitress cleared their tables, and another showed up out of swinging doors, plastic Corning cafeteria plates fanned up both arms like rigid playing cards.

Everyone turned and stared, of course. Years later I wondered if these men—could women not join the club?—thought to themselves, "How dare these strangers consider themselves Optimists? *No one*'s more optimistic than me."

By everyone, I mean six men who totaled at least 420 years in age, two boys just older than I, both wearing ties, and a professor from the local college.

Uncle Cush put his right hand on my shoulder and held his left out in greeting. "Good morning, fellow soldiers!" he said too loudly. "Taking the boy around to rub elbows with some of the finer civic-minded folks of the region. We already been to a Lions Club meeting. Going to meet up with some Shriners and Jaycees later in the week." If I had held three drops of blood below my Adam's apple at this moment I'd've been surprised, that's how much I could feel my face blush. "Cush Truluck," my uncle said. "There's here's my nephew Drum."

The president of Poke Optimists stood up. He wore a paper napkin tucked into his waistband and another in his collar. "Music contest's in December!" he yelled at about the same volume as my uncle.
"Today here's the finals for oratory contest. Bring them drums in
December and you can enter, long's you less than nineteen year old
and in less than college."

My uncle pulled out a chair at the table closest to the door. He
turned forty-five degrees, I understood, to keep a panoramic view of
his environs. I said, "Let's go." He wrapped his extraordinarily large
hand around my neck. "Go on," my uncle said to the man in charge.

"Well, y'all all know me. I'm Marty Cromartie, and I guess the
rest of us is here." He counted off the members with his index finger
pointed. I squinted to make sure I witnessed correctly: His remaining fingers weren't balled up in a semi-fist. This particular Optimist
only *had* one finger on his right hand. I wished that we'd shown up
earlier to espy his eating pancakes. "Mr. Lesley, you ready to give our
invocation?"

A man with a comb-over on par with a wheat field during gale
season stood and started right with, "Lord, we want to thank you for
giving us such wonderful and glorious organizations, molded by your
hand, such as Optimists International and Junior Optimists Octagon
International. And we want to thank you for inventing the pancake-
and-bacon breakfast." Mr. Lesley continued. I looked at my uncle
to see if he bowed his head and closed his eyes. He didn't. For some
reason he thought it necessary to stand, walk to the kitchen entrance,
and peek through the door-window. He returned and got seated just
as Mr. Lesley quoted something from Psalms about cultivating faith-
fulness, then said "Amen," to which the five other members shouted
in response. During the entire prayer, one of the oratory entrants
licked his palm and slicked his hair. The other held his own dick,
probably nervous and needing to purge himself of limitless coffee,
orange juice, and water.

Mr. Cromartie said, "Let's all now repeat the Optimist's Creed."

What followed was a chaotic din that made me wonder if I'd lost my cognitive skills. It sounded like every man got every word eventually, but not in the right order. The recitation came off sounding like one of those stupid rounds the music teacher at New Poke Elementary thought so brilliant, exotic, and experimental: "Hey, Ho! Nobody Home"; "Frère Jacques"; "Row, Row, Row Your Boat"; "Three Blind Mice." More often than not—when I wasn't telling the teacher long-winded stories without an apparent plot (she sent a note home once) or beating up classmates for saying things about black, Native American, and Hispanic people that weren't true (the principal sent notes home about that, weekly)—I spent music class conjuring up and then failing to shake a sad narrative of rodents chasing a French kid out of his home and he tried to escape via canoe.

My uncle and I stood during the creed, and continued upright during the Pledge of Allegiance, the National Anthem, a harrowing interpretation of "America the Beautiful," the Lord's Prayer, South Carolina's official state song, and—I'd be willing to bet this wasn't an official requisite of all Optimists International Clubs—"Dixie."

Uncle Cush cleared his throat. He stared forward. Later, after my parents felt no qualms in traveling back to reunite with me, Cush purported to envision the entire arson event while those old men sang, gaping at a Confederate flag they'd brought into Poke Pancake, hands over pacemakers, at the same height as the American flag and above the state one. Even I knew that wasn't right. Cush told my parents some years later, "It was as if the back of those six fat heads blended together into a screen, and my mind projected correctly the whole scenario, movielike. I'll admit that I might've undergone some flashbacks from when I did some good acid over in Dong Bong Phong," or something like that.

I'll admit that Cush figured things out, but it wasn't on the backs of Optimists' heads.

"If it looks like I might rush forward, step hard on my foot," he said as we stood there not singing "Dixie" with everyone else.

I said, "My parents don't allow me to sing this song," which was true, and indirectly has to do with our house getting burned to the ground.

"Your father believes in the union," Uncle Cush said, right about when the Optimists squeaked through "to Dixie Land I'm bound to trabble." "I ain't talking about the North. Not the Union North. The *unions*. It all makes sense, now that I think about it."

Uncle Cush kind of swayed forward, I mistook the movement as belonging to the "furtive" camp, and I gouged my left heel hard onto the bridge of his right foot.

"Okay," Mr. Cromartie said. "I believe we should all be sung and recited out by now. So let's get started with our oratory contest. We got us two finalists, Mr. Frank Liner Jr. and Mr. Leonard Self IV. They had to come up with five-minute speeches"—Mr. Cromartie shuffled some pages at the lectern—"on the topic 'If Only.'"

"If only," Uncle Cush said, loud enough for everyone besides the ancient Optimists to hear.

"Our judge this year is Mr. Alan Chalmers, from the English department over at Barnwood Community College, where he's been a professor since 1979. Mr. Chalmers has a master's degree from the University of Tennessee, and has had his poetry published in . . ." Mr. Cromartie eased his face down toward the page about an inch from the text he'd written. "In *Toppled Pig Review, Little Glandular Scares, Angry Checkbooks,* and *Too Many Harpsichordists in One Room.*"

Judge Chalmers raised his hand, turned to the Optimists, and said, "I just found out yesterday that two of my recent sonnets have been accepted at *Bean Tooth*. It's a highly regarded journal, maybe the best in the Southeast in regards to poetry." He sounded like he might've been half-Irish, or at least visited Belfast in the last twelve months.

"Well there you go," Mr. Cromartie said. "*That's* optimistic, ain't it?" He prompted his comrades to applaud. "Today's winner will go on to compete in the district oratory competition, and that winner will get a big old check for twenty-five hundred dollars. Two thousand five hundred dollars!"

Leonard Self IV stood up and said to Frank Liner Jr., "You win. I got twenty-five hundred dollars scattered beneath my Beemer's seat, man." He walked out, doing that get-the-hair-off-my-forehead swish, his neck jerking, a sneer on his lips.

Uncle Cush said, not too quietly, "Please understand that you need to hate people like him, Drum. Tell me that."

I have to say that, at age fourteen, I thought the guy was cool. I kind of wanted to perfect such a twitch, learn how to keep my mouth open, et cetera. It took maybe another, oh, day with my uncle to reconsider. I know that I swished my nonexistent bangs ten or twenty times before saying "Let's go" again. It's not like there was a bridge across the Savannah River site. We had to drive thirty miles north to Augusta, then backtrack to Edgefield—where the great potter Dave the Slave once worked—then drive back thirty miles to Cush's odd estate of added-on rooms. I said, "We're not Optimists."

The Optimists didn't respond to young Self's exit. Mr. Cromartie looked at happy Frank Liner Jr., then toward me. I'm talking he zeroed in on my face and said, "I forgot the order. Hey, everyone makes mistakes!"

"Who died?" one Optimist said. "You forgot to tell who died. That's the order. That's what's supposed to be next."

I had to pee. And no one offered us pancakes, so I felt some hunger. Uncle Cush—I don't want to say that my father's older brother possessed soothsayer qualities, though he did—said, "Biscuits Bojangles later" in his minimalistic language. He said, "Soon."

Mr. Cromartie held up his palms toward his Optimists. "My fault. Daggum. Yeah, we want to remember Lloyd Snoddy, who died last week. Lloyd was a good Optimist with us from 1963 until the Carter administration. Billy D. Bobo passed ten days ago. He was always first in line at our annual barbecue, remember?"

Mr. Cromartie went on through ten dead people, I bet. Me, I

watched the Optimist International Club oratorical winner, and the judge. Both looked as if they'd been granted reprieve from the most dastardly of henchmen. I can't know for certain, but I think Judge Mr. Alan Chalmers, M.A., wrote a new poem on his Poke Pancake napkin during the obituarial list.

"We need to send our prayers and positive thoughts," Marty Cromartie said, "to Mack Mackey, who dodged a deer and crashed into a tree over on Old Elberton Road. Mickey McNutt's wife's got the brown lung. Pat Patterson still recovers from accidental carbon monoxide poisoning in his garage. We need to remember Steve Stevens for when his shotgun engaged while he cleaned it. Last week Pete Peterson slipped up there at Table Rock and fell some ninety feet, but only broke his back, both knees, both hips, his pelvis, his neck, one elbow, five fingers, and a wrist. Y'all remember that Pete lost his arm in a thresher machine two-three year ago. In a way, I'm thinking having only one arm might've saved his life. One more broken bone might have tipped the scale when it comes to pain tolerance, you know."

I caught myself thinking, How come these people feel the need to call themselves optimists? Uncle Cush leaned down and said, "It ain't right, right?"

Mr. Cromartie said, "Well. I guess this'll make the agenda go quicker. Are you ready?" to the one contestant.

Frank Liner Jr. nodded once. He walked up to the lectern—I would like to say there was a microphone there, but I doubt it—and said, "'If Only.' By Frank Liner Jr. Copyright 1990."

"Pay attention," Cush said. "You might have to go back to public school one day. Don't want you falling behind." But he didn't pay attention. I caught him staring at a man up front that I later learned was the so-called Human Resources Director at Poke Plants One through Six, a job that couldn't've been that difficult, seeing as plants two through six stood vacant and the flagship cotton mill had gone from three shifts to one.

"If only I could change the world. And tell them all how socialism's wrong. We live in the best country on Earth. Our bands play the best songs. If only I could change the world. And tell them how Jesus is the only way. How can Chinese people think they're right? During Armageddon they'll have to pay," Frank Liner Jr. said. Then he bowed and, spine erect, performed that bang-swish his once-formidable oratory competitor had demonstrated upon his frivolous departure. He said "Copyright, 1990" again.

I didn't clap, but everyone else did, as if Frank Liner Jr. was some kind of poet laureate/Chamber of Commerce representative/seminary graduate. They acted as if they had a future Country Music Hall of Fame inductee in their midst, or a CIA informant. Uncle Cush yelled out "Whooooo-hooooo! That's what I'm talking about," and laughed maniacally.

Mr. Cromartie got up from his cheap vinyl chair and said, "That's fitting. Wait—I should've mentioned this with all our deaths and prayer needs. Y'all know Ronnie Virgil McKinney? He used to be a member up until 1970, when . . ." He trailed off.

"When integration got set in here, I'm betting," Uncle Cush whispered. "Many a white man around here dropped out of their supposed philanthropic or service-geared organizations when the court said blacks had the right to join in and pay their dues."

Mr. Cromartie said, "Y'all know R. V. Well, I should've mentioned it last meeting, but I just found out: Twenty-three days ago he got transported to Augusta for some terrible third-degree burns he got on his arms and legs. They say he might got *fifth*-degree burns on his face, and that he'll need some that reconstrictive plastic surgery if he wants to ever go out in public."

Uncle Cush made a couple throat noises. He kind of growled, then rattled. He raised his hand, and I could feel my face redden again. "How'd R. V. get such a burn, if you don't mind my asking?"

Actually he said "asting," to fit in.

"They say he had a lawnmower gas can that blowed up on him," Cromartie said. "That's what they say. They say it blowed up right as he passed a propane tank for his grill, and it blowed up, too."

"Who is 'they'?" my uncle asked. No one turned round. Frank

Liner Jr. looked up at the ceiling, and I followed his gaze. Poke Pancake had a mold problem, if it matters.

"Who are *you*?" Mr. Cromartie said to my uncle. "You know, we was being nice letting you sit in on Oratory Competition Day. Now I'm of the belief we might've made a mistake. Optimists, as a rule, don't cotton to agitators, brother."

Then the Optimists turned in unison, each having to shift hard in his seat, grunt, and hold his mouth in that half-open way known mainly to men and women distraught by a workman's outlandish estimate.

"I believe you know me," Cush said. "You know me, and you know my brother. Why don't we all just drop the pretense and go on from there?" I thought I heard the click of a pistol, but it ended up being Frank Liner Jr.'s temporomandibular joint popping, which he continued to do over and over. Sometimes I pretended to suffer relentless TMJ problems during the MRE fiascos.

On a side note: my uncle liked to say, "You know how they always tell two kids with braces not to kiss, seeing as they might get locked up? That actually happened to me one time. I was dating this girl with braces *on her legs*. Her daddy wasn't happy to walk into the living room and see my head down there."

Uncle Cush stretched his right arm out slowly and pointed to each Optimist, down the line, accusingly. He said, "We got what we came for. I thank all of you."

Marty Cromartie fell right over, I guess fainting. Mr. Lesley got up and started a second invocation that began, "Lord, you do work in mysterious ways."

My uncle pulled me up by my collar and led me out of Poke Pancake, a diner I could never enter again over the next twenty-five-plus years.

• • •

In my uncle's Chevy pickup, driving parallel with the Savannah River, then taking about a 179-degree turn back south to his house on the other side of the nuclear site, Cush said, "All little boys hate broccoli. The president hates broccoli. What can you derive from that, Drum?"

I looked out the window and counted off all the different kinds of litter I spotted: beer cans, hamburger wrappers, plastic bags, liquor bottles, dead does, cigarette packs, Styrofoam cups, and an aluminum baseball bat at the base of someone's bashed-in mailbox. I said, "Can't we at least *call* my parents?"

"All pens have ink. A squid has ink. What can you deduce from that?" Uncle Cush said. He drove with his wrist draped over the steering wheel. He said, "I'm hungry. You? I feared those pancakes might be tainted, so I'm glad we didn't partake."

Dead possums, newspapers, a rectangular can of what I knew to be Klean-Strip paint remover seeing as my father kept some in his shed, a pair of panties, Hardee's sacks, filled Hefty bags that must've fallen off someone's truck bed on the way to the dumpster, sunglasses: I ticked it all off, and thought how I might want to be, later in life, an archaeologist. Or a cop who specialized in arresting idiots who threw stuff out their windows.

I rolled my window down farther. "Did the air conditioner ever work in here?" I asked. My uncle had his window down fully, and that ridiculous Fu Manchu blew all the way to the back window.

"Can't take AC," Cush said. "Back in Nam, you think we had any kind of air-conditioning? Shit, boy, if it's less than a hundred ten degrees, I feel like I might need a sweater."

Understand that I had been under Cush's supervision for one month at most. At this point I didn't fully grasp his questionable service to our country. I said, "Just tell me where they moved. I promise not to run away."

"All ceiling fans have blades. A Schick razor has a blade. What's that tell you about throwaway razors?"

I said, "I think I just saw one of those blades in the ditch."

"Concentrate, boy. I know if you're truly my brother Newly's son, the one thing you can do is concentrate." Uncle Cush turned into a

Little Pigs BBQ, leaned forward until his face almost touched the windshield, looked in the plate-glass windows, then put the truck in reverse and eventually drove out of the lot. "We got food at home. I like to keep a supply of food close to where I live."

I said, "If you give me my parents' new phone number, I won't tell them about what you have me eating. Those MRE things. They suck."

"All MREs suck. A woman I met back in Nam named Fenfang sucked. What can you make out of that information?" Uncle Cush opened his door and stuck his left foot out, scraping his boot sole on the pavement. "I forgot to do that earlier. I stepped on some gum, I think. Made me feel off-balance."

I said, "I don't know what it all means, Uncle Cush. School doesn't start till August, if I just go into New Poke High like I'm supposed to do."

"Homeschool's the way to go," Cush said. "(A) You'll learn more; (B) You won't have anyone to beat up like you kept doing in elementary and junior high; (C) I don't care if you can't tell a story in chronological order—I think you and me might have the same DNA when it comes to that little problem; (D) Ain't no reason to buy new school clothes, wasting all that money; (F) Ain't nobody at the high school can teach you both logic and sex ed like you're going to get from me." He honked the horn for no reason. "A, B, C, D, F. Just like regular school."

"I can't drive, for one," I said. "And you don't know me well enough to know, but I'm too lazy to take off running to, say, Charlotte or Richmond to search out my mom and dad. Miami. Omaha, Kansas City, Milwaukee." I looked at my uncle closely to see if he'd reveal anything via "facial tics." I said, "Sacramento, Olympia, Bismarck, Pierre, Dover, Nashville, Atlanta, Montgomery, Jackson, Baton Rouge, Raleigh, Albany," but then I kind of ran out of capital cities I knew for sure. I kept wanting to say "St. Louis," though I knew it wasn't right. I wanted to say "Dallas," and "Louisville," and "New Orleans." Fine cities, sure, but I'd somehow wedged myself into listing off places where I thought do-gooders might hide out among legislators.

My uncle stomped on the accelerator, let off, stomped, let off. It felt like what I imagined a Disney World ride would feel like. He didn't raise his eyebrows. "I ain't telling," he said. "Look, Little Grasshopper—I don't expect you to know what 'Little Grasshopper' means, seeing as your parents didn't own a television set—you won't get anything out of me. That 'Grasshopper' thing is called an allusion, by the way. And from now on it's all right if you call me 'Master Po.' Shit, boy, *Kung Fu*'s what it's all about. I don't know how anyone can be alive today without knowing *Kung* fucking *Fu*."

Okay, so I hate to contradict my friends and family, but later— after my uncle's weird and complicated death—I looked up *Kung Fu* on Wikipedia and saw that it aired between 1972 and 1975. Those were years when Cush purported to serve the army, escape the army, and rove from village to village mesmerizing locals with his spoon-playing abilities in both North and South Vietnam, *much as Kwai Chang Caine traveled around.* But there in the truck, right after my first and only Optimist experience, I could only vaguely intuit what he meant.

I said, "I don't know the answers." I placed my hand on the dashboard so as not to bang my head into the glove compartment. "Give me a hint. Hey, is there something wrong with your gas pedal?" I noticed a tricycle on the roadside, followed by a plastic wading pool, followed by a Wiffle Bat, followed by a Hula Hoop.

"No hints. You'll go a long way in life being able to understand logic, Drum. Here: All lawnmowers run on gas. After I eat pinto beans, I get gas. What does that say about me?"

Then there was a Frisbee, a deflated football, a smashed Etch-a-Sketch, a naked GI Joe, and one of those sand-weighted six-foot-high plastic basketball goals. I said, "A father got frustrated with his spoiled child. He put all the kid's toys in the back of a truck, forgot to close the tailgate, and everything eventually flew out."

"Very, very good," Uncle Cush said. His right foot remained steady on the accelerator for the first time in miles. "I believe you're correct. I hope that spoiled kid didn't have a fancy dog, or any of those other pets rich kids require."

I laughed. I jerked my head around like a fool, to no effect, for I didn't possess bangs. "Were those men at that meeting mean or stupid or both?"

Uncle Cush shook his head. "Those two boys? The ones in the speech competition? Both they daddies grew up in Poke. Both they grand- and great-granddaddies grew up in Poke. Best-case scenario? Those two boys will go off to Georgia, Clemson, or the University of South Carolina. They'll be in fraternities made up of other boys from Poke, or at least Barnwood County. Then they'll come back. They'll marry they high school girlfriends, who went to Georgia, Clemson, or the University of South Carolina. Then they'll have children of they own. And the downhill genetic dilution continues. Over and over and over."

Of course I had to say, "Do you mean 'their' when you keep saying 'they'? That's not correct English, you know."

Uncle Cush stomped on the gas and looked over at me. He took his hand from the wheel. I felt the urge to urinate. "I got good front end alignment," he said. "Okay, listen. All slugs move slow and leave an unmistakable trail. R. V. McKinney has to move pretty goddamn slowly seeing as the bottoms of his feet burned off and he ain't got no more face."

I said, "He's the person who burned down our house."

"And?"

"He had something against my parents and wanted to kill them. That's why they took off and went into hiding."

My uncle smiled. He bobbed his head up and down like one of those trick pink drinking flamingoes dipping over a saucer of water. "R. V. McKinney's a Klansman. He worked for the mill in a middle-management capacity. Or in an advisory role. What don't mill owners want, Drum? Literate workers. What did your daddy do in his spare time for a number of years before the mills started fading?"

I said, "Worked in his shop turning finials?"

"Well, yeah, but he also ran the literacy association. I don't know if he ran it, really, but he put some effort into keeping Barnwood County residents able to read the fine print. So. Now we know. Now we got us some direction, boy." He kind of swerved. He pointed through the windshield. "They's a great meat-and-three up ahead. Let's go get us some real food and celebrate. Plus we need to chart out your upcoming curriculum."

My uncle pulled into the lot of a place called New Dam Meat and Three Diner. The magnetic sign out front read "Welcome Young Republicans." I said, "Why are you doing this to me?"

"Weird coincidence. But, hey, you got to know the enemy to beat the enemy. Come on. We'll see if they're having some kind of contest inside. We'll sit in the back again and act like we belong."

I got out of the truck. I couldn't tell him he would never be confused for a conservative man, what with the abnormal facial hair, the wild eyes, his propensity to blurt out koans. I tried to think of what meat and three I might order. Would it be pork chop, mashed potatoes, cole slaw, and lima beans? Would I choose Salisbury steak, macaroni and cheese, French fries, and applesauce? Meatloaf, stewed tomatoes, okra, and squash casserole? Flounder? Banana pudding?

Uncle Cush stopped. "I smell something wrong," he said. We both looked farther down the road. I think I had my hand on the door to the diner. There on the berm lay a dead standard poodle, followed by a Shetland pony.

Then we went inside, strutting like two idiots, proud, I guess, both of us. When my parents finally felt it safe to return, I would mention what we ate, only—liver and onions. I don't know why I've never mentioned this whole set of events to anyone—from optimism to reality, I guess—though I've thought about every detail, for the most part, daily.

FLAG DAY

My wife, Alicia, told me that she never knew she could swim until six years into her first marriage. We sat on a nice well-stained second-floor porch at a lake rental house, thirty miles from where we lived, overlooking a cove. Below us floated a dock, a pontoon boat, a metal canoe painted green, and across the water only one other house stood in view. I'd gotten the place free for the long weekend, so long as I set the place up for Wi-Fi and figured out how to get these people's entertainment system to work. My job was to type up and print out a step-by-step process so future vacationers could come to a lake house surrounded by Nature, then have no problem getting online, or watching endless movies on premium channels. Normally I'd've said something about how I needed payment, not a four-day weekend at the lake, that unfortunately I couldn't barter with Duke Power, Piedmont Gas, or whoever my mortgage lender happened to be this year. But Alicia needed some time away. She felt as though she might be on the verge of a nervous breakdown, and had walked off her last job two weeks earlier.

"Because we moved around so much, I never got the chance to learn how to swim," Alicia said. "It seemed like every summer my father got stationed in places without lakes or pools."

We'd arrived at noon and unpacked in the master bedroom. This place had four single cots downstairs, two queen-sized beds on the main floor, and then another two upstairs in a crow's nest. The owner, Carnell Henderson—he'd hired me to run some cable from his house to his wife's new greenhouse, and while I was there he asked if I knew computers, and so on. I kind of lied. I mean, I knew that I could figure things out, but it's not like I have a degree in computer science or electronics. Me, I had a bachelor's in psychology, plus a grandfather and father who worked as electricians and taught me the trade. I told Carnell no problem. He made a point to tell me this investment property of his normally pulled in fifteen hundred dollars. I didn't ask if that meant nightly, long-weekendly, weekly, or monthly. I didn't care. He sounded like a landlord more than anything else, and maybe I held bad memories of landlords back before my second marriage.

Psychology ended up being a perfect degree for my future job as an electrician. I had no fear of mice or rats living deep in crawlspaces.

I poured some wine into Alicia's glass—we'd brought two coolers filled with chicken wings, catfish, pork chops, hamburger meat, and veggie burgers should we finally decide to go healthy—and got up to get myself the bottle of Four Roses. We had kale, and early first-harvest cucumbers, tomatoes, squash, and jalapeños from our own garden. I'd gone by the Bi-Lo on the way out and bought corn, charcoal briquets, and lighter fluid, plus four different six-packs of fancy beer I'd never heard of. If we'd had this lake house for a month we'd've had enough food and booze, is what I'm saying. We brought along pumpernickel, rye, sourdough, and French bread. Edam, cheddar, and brie. Three bags of Doritos. French onion and bean dip. Salsa. Hummus. Alicia's eight bottles of merlot and rosé. Two fifths of bourbon.

My second wife pulled her legs up and set them across mine. She wore a green-and-white sundress adorned with monkeys all linked together hand by hand, swinging, like that Barrel of Monkeys kids' game. I'm not sure where she got it. This might sound mean, but I was glad we had all that food and didn't need to go out to a restaurant, if there were any nearby. Alicia looked like a regular woman worried about her appearance in many ways—she dyed her shortish hair and worked a treadmill most mornings before dawn—but sometimes she chose to clothe herself in getups she thought either chic, suave, or hipsterish that I didn't see other women our age wear when I showed up to keep their houses from sparking on fire. I picked up a pair of binoculars left on the table and looked out at someone doing figure eights with a Jet Ski in the lake's main channel.

"I didn't even care about swimming. I never thought about it! And then Tony and I were at his family's reunion down at Lake Poke. I must've been a little drunk. I told you all about his family history. Anyway, he talked me into this canoe, it flipped over when he went to stand up, and I found out that I could swim. All the way back to shore. We split up about a month later. You think it had something to do with my realizing I could swim and all?"

I shrugged. I wanted to say something about how her last boss was named Tony, too, and that maybe she subconsciously looked for trouble. Alicia complained for a year that he put too much pressure on her. She worked for an audiologist, pretending to be a nurse of sorts, as far as I could tell. Mostly she worked the front desk and tried to figure out Medicare. Sometimes she sat patients down and made them respond when they heard a beep from this audiology machine. "You were, like, twenty-eight? You didn't learn that you could swim until you were twenty-eight? Wow. I never thought about it. Have we never been swimming?"

Part of the "pressure" she perceived from this doctor might've concerned his wanting her to always speak just above a whisper to everyone who walked into Hub City Audiology, and then to talk everyone into buying the most expensive hearing aids.

"Yeah, I know. After I had to swim out of Lake Poke and leave Tony, swimming became my favorite exercise for a couple years." Alicia recrossed her legs over mine. She raised her glass, then pointed it across the cove. Just as she did, a dozen boys spilled out onto the porch, all wearing orange shirts. By "boys" I mean frat brothers, and by "orange" I mean they must've gone to Texas, Tennessee, Clemson, or Syracuse. I had a prime suspect: I doubted that a fraternity would come spend the second week of June a thousand miles from their colleges, and Tennessee has a number of fine lakes. I tried to think of other colleges with orange jerseys, but couldn't. I thought back to a number of gated-community houses where I'd been hired to do something as simple as changing a fuse, but couldn't remember an orange motif in the family rooms.

I picked up the binoculars and looked at the lake house situated maybe a football-field-and-a-half across the oblong-shaped cove. After adjusting the cylinder and scanning our new neighbors, I noticed one guy looking back at me with a pair of his own binoculars. He gave me the finger. I set the binoculars down and didn't say anything to Alicia. She didn't need more strife, what with her pressuring audiologist ex-boss and those horrific flashbacks that involved a capsized canoe.

Luckily Alicia and I didn't speak first, after those guys came out. One of them said, in what I would bet was a normal conversational tone, "Hey, let's make some bets about that pontoon boat." He didn't scream it out. What with Alicia's background in audiology, and this geography elective I took in college that let me understand the tricky echoes that can occur in valleys and over water, I put my index finger to my mouth and whispered, "We can eavesdrop. We need to speak quietly."

She said, "Oh, I got that down," and smiled.

From across the water one of the college boys said, "Hey, man, someone put on some tunes." Then for five minutes the air filled with a basic drone, background noise, like a group of a dozen people talking at once, mixed with bass-heavy music. I barely said to Alicia, "I hope they're not up all night."

She said, "I bet I didn't dogpaddle but ten feet, and then went straight into the standard Australian crawl. Maybe in the morning we can go out there—take out the pontoon, anchor it, and swim around."

I picked up the binoculars and looked to the side of the house across the cove. Sure enough: breaker box right there in plain view, eye level. I thought, Do not do anything that would make Alicia look for a third husband.

I poured easy-light charcoal into a standard black smoker on the far end of the porch. Alicia said she would wait until the coals burned down before she decided what she wanted on the first day of our vacation. I'd agreed to take the pontoon out in the morning, but then I wanted to fix Carnell Henderson's problems, then recheck everything on both Sunday and Monday before we went home, where, I assumed, Alicia would begin looking for a new job and I'd catch grief from my regular customers—I catered to a wealthier clientele who would not admit that they had mice chewing wires to the HVAC unit's fan-circuit board, or that they bought elaborate ceiling fans for their verandas before understanding that they didn't run on batteries. Or they forgot how to run their own dryers, blamed me, and then I had to come over and close the door to the Samsung before pushing the Start button. House call. Five minutes. Eighty bucks.

"I'm not even hungry now," Alicia said. "I feel like I'm not going to get hungry for some reason. Hey, did we bring any aspirin?"

The fraternity boys started playing old-school disco loudly, bands that I recognized even though they were before my time: Earth, Wind & Fire. The Commodores. Mother's Finest. The Ohio Players. I got out the binoculars again to make sure the partiers weren't in their fifties, or maybe their parents had shown up for the evening. The bass reverberated across the water and made the foundation of Carnell's house throb. I said, "Fuck."

"You didn't bring the aspirin? I put it out on the table before we packed," Alicia said.

I lit the grill and, in my mind, *thought* I foresaw what I'd be doing later in the middle of the night. I said, "I got it. It's on the kitchen counter inside."

"Come here, Ted," Alicia said. She tapped the chair beside her. "Let's just sit and do some drinking." She'd gotten up and relieved the freezer of its ice bin, poured it into a cooler Carnell kept on the deck. "You're the smart one here. Tell me what I should do."

Though Tony demanded too much of my wife, he didn't harass her in any way. Alicia and I weren't litigious people anyway. We met two years after both our divorces—mine had to do with an ex-wife who cheated—and we married two years later. In six months we'd celebrate our tenth year together, our eighth married. At parties people liked to hear how we met: She had moved to an upscale apartment complex, I was hired to install lights around the pool, and we flirted. The next day Alicia called her landlord and said that her dining room lights no longer worked, could he please call the electrician who had been there the day earlier. She had tripped the breaker on purpose. A day later, Alicia put on rubber gloves and tennis shoes, then shoved a paperclip in one of her outlets, which caused a gigantic scorch mark. She called the landlord. Alicia and I went out to a fondue restaurant the next night.

I said, "Baby doll, we don't really need the money. You do what you want to do." This wasn't all that true, but it seemed like the right thing to say after two tumblers of bourbon and Coke. I said, "You want to go back to school and take some classes? Do that. You want to come with me and help out every day? That's fine."

Alicia had a college degree, too. She had majored in early childhood education, spent three years teaching second grade at a public elementary school, said Screw this, and decided to never have children. She told me that at one point with Tony the first husband she took the pill, had an IUD, used a diaphragm, and shoved a sponge up there. By the time I came around she was down to the pill and a diaphragm.

"I need a job, Ted," she said. "Those three years I have in the state retirement system? It's not even getting interest, what with the account being inactive. If you died, I don't know what I'd do."

I didn't say, If we had a couple kids maybe they could take over All Out Electric. I said, "I got a life insurance policy. We have money saved. The house will be paid for in fifteen years. I ain't going to die."

The boys across the way dumped a bucket of golf balls onto the ground. When their CD was between tracks I made out one of them saying, "Whoever hits the pontoon, everyone else has to do a shot. Hit the canoe? Two shots." I got out the binoculars and looked over there. It appeared as if they dumped out nothing but brand-new Titleist Pro V1s. Those things cost four bucks apiece.

"These are really good binoculars," I said to Alicia. "They're going to play a drinking game that involves our pontoon and canoe. Or Carnell Henderson's."

She said, "I can tell you what got me depressed," as if we had been talking about it for a solid month. I'll admit that at times I get consumed with work, but I felt sure that Alicia had not admitted any form of depression until this point.

I said, "What?" but held the binoculars back up and watched the first guy swing a nice Ping pitching wedge. He fell short by a good forty yards. I pulled the binoculars down, then swung the strap around my neck and let it rest on my lap. I said, "Depression about the job?"

Alicia poured out the rest of the first bottle. She said, "This is a weird story. You have that degree in psychology. Tell me if this makes sense. It's the only thing I can think of, as far as a cause."

"I don't have any advanced degrees, honey, you know that. It wouldn't be right for me to offer up any kind of diagnosis. Or prognosis. Which is the right word? I never remember."

Another guy swung hard, topped the ball, and it dribbled into ankle-deep water. My wife said, "This woman came into the office about a month ago. Tiny woman, maybe four-eleven. You could tell she used to be taller, and regal. She had a pretty bad hunched back, you know. I know for a fact that she was eighty-eight years old, because I typed in her information."

I said, "I'm listening." I kept eye contact with Alicia, but got up, dipped my cup in the ice chest, and got more bourbon. I hadn't come close to finishing even half of half a fifth, but bourbon's more potent than merlot. Across the cove, the CD skipped, and then someone turned it off. I heard one of those boys say, "Let's make it a little more interesting."

Alicia stared over that way, but she had a look on her face similar to a farm animal lost in thought. "Her name was Ms. Young. Deaf as a railroad spike. I mean, she could hear if you yelled at her, but that was it."

I wanted to ask if the woman drove herself to Hub City Audiology, but didn't. Sometimes Alicia complained that Tony Husband #1 interrupted. And so did Tony Boss the Last. Also, I wanted to say how funny it is for people with the last name Young to get so old.

"She came in right at the end of the day. Dr. McKinney had gone off somewhere and hadn't returned. I kind of think he forgot. I had to call him up and remind him, and he started cussing, you know."

I wanted to say, At one of those schools for the deaf, I guess teachers could get away with cussing all they wanted. I said, "He probably went out to play golf."

"So Ms. Young took a seat in the waiting room, and I yelled out at her that the doctor was with a patient, that he was running behind, and all those other lies I had to tell when things weren't going smoothly. When things weren't going professionally."

I said, "I only met him at those Christmas parties, but I thought right away that he had a drinking problem. I mean, I can't talk," I said, raising my glass. "But I'm not in charge of bringing sound into people's lives. Just light. I guess I'm an eye doctor's worst enemy."

"I don't know," Alicia said. "I never smelled booze on his breath. At least not at work."

My cell phone vibrated a little in my pocket. I'd gotten a text message. I said, "Hold on one second," and pulled it out. Carnell Henderson had sent me a message that read, "I forgot. Flag Day coming up. Please put flag out on pole. In upstairs closet, on shelf."

I texted back, "OK." To Alicia I said, "Hell, I didn't even know why we had a long weekend."

She said, "And there aren't great drugs in the audiology field, unless someone stabs your eardrum with an ice pick, which happens more than you'd think possible."

There were no members of the golf team in this particular fraternity. One of them got so frustrated he pulled out an oversized driver and hit a duck hook that bounced below our deck. I got out the binoculars to see if the guy who gave me the finger earlier might be looking, but all those boys simply turned around and feigned staring at their lake house, as if nothing happened, as if I'd witnessed a golf ball dropping from the sky.

I said, "We should've brought some marshmallows. Hotdogs and marshmallows."

Alicia got up, walked into the kitchen, and came back with four pork chops, but she didn't put them on the grill, just set them on a table nearby. She said, "I said, 'Tell me about yourself,' because I couldn't pretend that she wasn't sitting on the other side of the window, not eight feet away. I yelled out, 'Tell me about yourself, Ms. Young!' and thought I would get back something how she taught school for forty years. Maybe how she taught chorus or band."

My phone vibrated again. I looked down to see that Carnell Henderson had texted, "Don't Tread on Me flag, too. Put below other."

I looked at my wife and wanted to tell her about how we needed to trash this place, but she said, "They had one of those wildlife cameras. Ms. Young and her husband had one of those motion-sensor cameras down their driveway, pointed to the house. In case anyone broke in, the police would have evidence."

It might've been ninety-five degrees. I got up and checked the top of the ice chest to make sure it felt secured. I looked across the cove and watched the fraternity boys give up on Hit the Pontoon. Presently George Clinton and Parliament Funkadelic would blast out of the house, that song about how people should get off their asses and jam. I said, "I've been meaning to get one of those cameras. I want to train it on the back of my truck, because in time someone's going to try to steal my tools and sell them at the flea market."

Alicia shook her head. "This is bad," she said. "This will kill you. Wait—that's a bad way to put it, what with what I'm about to say. This will explain my depression."

Again, I didn't say, "I didn't know you'd been depressed," for if indeed she'd mentioned it a number of times, this would only make it worse, I figured. I looked over at the pork chops and counted eight flies. I said, "Are you hungry?"

"Ms. Young's husband got murdered two years ago. She happened to be visiting her sister in the hospital up in Asheville. She told me that she understood she should feel lucky about it, but in most ways she felt guilty."

I said, "Was he shot?" I said, "Was it at night, and he was shot in bed?"

My wife held up her left palm. "I stood up from my station so I could hear Ms. Young better. She said the cops got the camera and checked things out. Listen, to this. Ted. It went like this. Ted, are you listening to me?"

I said, "I'm looking right at you, honey."

She said, "A deer showed up. Then a possum. Then one of the neighborhood dogs. Then a raccoon. Then that dog again. I might be getting some of this out of order. I know that she said 'neighbor's dog' quite a few times. A coyote showed up once or twice, then a man they didn't know. A cat showed up a couple times. A fox. The Youngs lived out in the country, way out there. The Duke Power meter reader. Then that first man came again, and hung out for quite a while in the middle of the night. He came back the very next night. Then the camera showed Ms. Young coming back home. And then the sheriff's deputy, and a coroner a while later. Like that. And then a hearse taking Mr. Young off the property."

I thought, Goddamn. I thought, None of us are safe. "It was that guy?"

"That man ended up killing Ms. Young's husband, then stealing a wallet, all the silver, a bunch of shit. They haven't caught him yet."

I said, "Did the woman come home to find her husband dead in bed?"

"This is the saddest part. She told me that when one of them was out of the house they had a Dr Pepper rule. They called each other at 10, 2, and 4, no matter what. When Mr. Young didn't answer the phone at ten in the morning, and then again at two in the afternoon, she drove back down from Asheville. And that's what she came home to." My wife got up and walked toward the grill. She said, "We waited too long."

The fraternity brothers came back outside armed with golf clubs. They stood in a line and counted down before swinging at the same time. One of them actually hit the pontoon, and the ball dinged off into the water. I watched through the binoculars as they all did shots from a bottle of Rebel Yell. I said, "We waited too long for what, Alicia? Alicia. What do you mean?"

"You need to put more charcoal on. Or I could just go inside and put these things in the oven."

I sat staring across the cove at young men dancing around, whooping, raising bottles and/or irons. I envisioned Ms. Young sitting in Hub City Audiology, telling her story to a complete stranger receptionist. I said, "Goddamn. Why didn't you tell me this right after it happened? No wonder you quit. Did these kinds of stories happen a bunch?"

I caught myself looking at the soffit and fascia of Carnell Henderson's lake house to see if he'd rightly installed motion-sensor cameras. I looked off into the surrounding trees. "Not a bunch," she said. "But there are stories like that everywhere, every day."

I poured more coals on top of what hadn't quite burned out. From across the water I heard another golf ball hit the pontoon, then another onslaught of battle cries. I said, "I better go find those flags. Now you got me paranoid that we're being watched by a wildlife camera."

At seven o'clock the drinking game stopped and the music came on full blast. It went from those '70s tunes to Lynyrd Skynyrd, with the boys yelling out "Go Fuck Alabama" during the chorus of that one song, which made me think perhaps these scholars did hail from Tennessee. I don't want to say that Alicia and I had turned into the kind of people who eat supper at five and fall asleep by dark, but maybe we had. At least after drinking way too much bourbon and wine. When we got back home and returned to normal routines, I felt sure that we'd eat during the national news, go to bed during the local news, maybe watch reruns in between.

So Alicia put meat on the grill and I walked upstairs to gather the flags. I know I shouldn't make assumptions about wealthy lake-house-owning people, but I walked into the upper-level bedroom to find the two single beds, a lamp, and an old-fashioned Morris chair, plus one bookcase, loaded with hardbacks. Listen—not that I'm a big reader or anything—but I immediately thought, Good on old Carnell Henderson. I kind of envisioned his coming up here between rentals and plopping down to do something besides watching movies and trolling the Internet nonstop. Then I opened the closet to discover no hint of a normal American flag, folded into a triangle. No, there was that stupid Gadsden flag with Don't Tread on Me and the rattle-snake thing, plus a Stars and Bars. Beneath the shelf, dangling off padded hangers, were what appeared to be six genuine Confederate uniforms. I couldn't tell if they were moth-eaten or bullet-riddled.

I said, "Goddamn. He's one of those Civil War reenactors."

I turned and looked up at the crown molding to see if there was a camera, or if there was one of those innocuous teddy bears stuffed with a camera, maybe perched against a pillow. I kept the closet door open, walked to the bookcase, and scanned the titles: *The Rise and Fall of the Confederate Government,* by Jefferson Davis; *Stonewall Jackson's Book of Maxims*; *The Quotable Robert E. Lee*; *Jewish Supremacism,* by David Duke; *Mein Kampf* in both German and English. Then there was a whole shelf of books written by Fox news-casters and frequent guests: Bill O'Reilly, Ann Coulter, the dude with hair growing on his forehead. The shelf below it contained titles like *How Come I'm Paying Taxes So Lazy People Can Live Off My Success?*

and *Send Him Back to Kenya!* and *How Come They Can Say the N-Word But I Can't?*

I bent down closer to find those last three books self-published by CreateSpace, BookSurge, and iUniverse, and all written by one Carnell Henderson.

• • •

I said, "I can't help this guy out," to Alicia. She stood at the end of the porch, staring at the frat boys. I wondered if she flashed her boobs at these kids while I pored over a library and closet of a racist. I said, "Something's burning," and looked over at the pork chops, which at this point could've been used for a tailless beaver's prosthetic device.

Alicia said, "Goddamn. I forgot. Where've you been?"

If I'd gone into further studies in psychology, I would've probably homed in on paranoia, its causes and effects, its importance in regard to evolution. I told my wife all about what I found upstairs, but ended with, "You know, it might just be a test. Maybe Carnell Henderson's a raging liberal, and he set this whole thing up to see how I'd react. Like if he called me over to work on his heat pump in the fall, he might really want to see if I said something like 'Hey, brother, you ought to join my chapter of the KKK,' or 'You want to go out on a lynching with me some night?' This could all be a trap. Or one of those reality TV shows, and we're being filmed by that group of Hollywood executives across the cove, all of them dressed up like frat boys as a disguise."

Alicia picked up my bourbon bottle and said, "You're cut off."

I said, "I'm serious. Hey, you want me to go get out that chicken?"

My wife walked up and hugged me. She set the bottle on a table. "I never finished my story about Ms. Young," she said. "I didn't get to the important part."

The guys across the cove put on that Charlie Daniels song about being proud to be a rebel and how the South was going to do it again. They whooped and played air fiddles, which you don't see that often in polite, sane company. I thought, Where are we? I thought, Did I take a wrong turn and end up at the far western arm of this lake, maybe in Alabama or Mississippi?

I yelled "Hey, shut up!" across the way, knowing they'd not be able to hear me.

Alicia said, "Ms. Young wanted to know if Dr. McKinney could do something about making her *more* deaf. She said she constantly heard her husband screaming. Inside her head. She wanted to know if there was a procedure that could stop sounds from ever entering. Do you see what I mean?"

I looked at my wife and sobered. I thought, Is Alicia trying to tell me something? Is she saying that she wants my voice out of her head? I thought, Is this her way of asking for a divorce?

I was about to say, "Hey, let's go skinny-dipping and we can sober up a little," when out of nowhere one of the orange-clad boys came around the corner of the deck. That meant he would've come through the house downstairs, and so on. I felt sure that I had locked the door, just out of habit. I'll give myself this: I didn't scream like a kid on his first roller coaster. I saw the boy peripherally, turned my head, and said to Alicia, "Anyway, yeah, I brought along the pistol," as if I really had one.

The kid spun toward the other house and yelled out, "Turn that down!" but there was no way anyone could've heard him.

Alicia said, "Who are you?"

This boy looked to be about twelve. "My daddy called and said you need to make sure and turn the light on below the flagpole so anyone driving by can see them." He pointed back to his house and said, "We done got ours up." Sure enough, a Stars and Bars, plus a Gadsden flag.

I said, "You're Carnell Henderson's son?"

He nodded. "I'm Carnell, too. We own this house and the one across the way." He wore one of those baseball caps with the flat brim. "Me and my brothers got that house for the week. Daddy lets us have it twice a year. We put up our car keys, you know, so we don't drive nowhere. Me and Pierpont over there have to run the weed-eater at some point before we leave, to pay for it all."

Alicia—and I'll give her this—said, "Me won't drive drunk, either. Me one time hit a pebble with the weed-eater and shattered a window. Me missed grammar class and missed out on pronoun usage."

He didn't seem fazed. I started laughing. I said, "Y'all have bad taste in music. And it's too loud."

Carnell Jr. said, "From what me and the brothers understand, you're just a regular worker staying here for free. Daddy didn't say you was some kind of music critic. You want to hear loud? Wait till you get that stereo working at this house and then leave. Half of us gonna come over here and crank the music at the same time. We brung us two CDs of everything." Then, in case I didn't comprehend, Carnell Jr. explained how one boy at the other house and one boy here would go one-two-three over a cell phone, then hit play simultaneously. He said, "We gone blow this lake up, cuz. Me and Porter just talking about a way to make y'all leave early so we can crank the tunes both sides." He pointed over his shoulder without turning. "I'm talking stereo-*stereo*phonic."

I said, "Man, go back to your party. I'll get the flag up and turn on the lights."

He nodded sharply once, stared at me too long—to scare me, I assumed—then said, "We gone eat steaks the like you ain't ever seen before, cows raised right there on the college. I know you can't do it, but don't ruin your night wishing you was me." He said, "Ma'am" to Alicia.

Carnell Jr. went back through the house, down the stairs, out the door. From the other side of the cove came another Lynyrd Skynyrd song, the one about someone named "The Breeze."

I poured one more drink, knowing it would be the last for the evening. Alicia grabbed my arm, put her index finger to her lips, and cocked her head. Through all that music she heard one of his fraternity brothers say, "About three in the morning? We gone fuck with them people."

Fifteen minutes later she heard, "Don't he know who your daddy is?"

Someone said, "Steaks ready."

I couldn't make out any of these conversations, but my wife, with her audiology training and expertise, could. She told me one sentence at a time, like a United Nations interpreter.

• • •

Unfortunately it doesn't matter, flying a Confederate flag upside down. An American flag—you can fly that flag upside down to signal distress, I guess like if everyone inside the fort has food poisoning, I don't know. I could've wiped myself with the flags as some kind of statement, like I did with the last check I wrote the student-loan corporation after they defaulted me twice for one-day-late payments.

Besides her batlike sonar, Alicia possessed some mind-reading skills. We piled the rest of the charcoal on the grill, she led me inside, and, whispering, said, "Hoist the flags. Turn on the light. You don't want to appear a troublemaker, so then later on Henderson—or those boys across the way—won't suspect you."

I said, "We should just leave."

"Nope. Go fix the TV and Wi-Fi now. I know that you're a moral person, Tedrick." She meant it, for Alicia rarely used my full name, partly because I asked her never to say it in public. "I know you never think up things like I thought up all the time over at Hub City Audiology. You know how many near-deaf people treated me badly? Every other one. You know how many times I invented some kind of retaliation? Every day. And then there's Dr. McKinney. Some people play solitaire. Or sudoku. They keep a crossword puzzle handy. Me, I started imagining ways to retaliate early on. I guess I started right about the time Tony stood up in the canoe and forced me to swim."

I said, "Let's just go for a swim and clear our heads. I've been thinking about exercising more."

My wife told me again to fix the entertainment center, and to raise those flags. She said, "I'll meet you downstairs on the landing." She looked at her wristwatch, then took it off. "Midnight. That seems appropriate. One minute after midnight."

I could've rigged Carnell Henderson's house so that an electrical fire occurred as soon as someone turned on the dryer, or TV, or stereo. For a racist, though, he'd always treated me fairly. I guess I might not say the same thing if I were non-Caucasian. He wouldn't have hired me in the first place had I been black, Hispanic, or Asian.

I got the TV and stereo connected correctly and turned the volume up on both so that when those college boys came over they'd blow the speakers. I set the place up for Wi-Fi, but couldn't think of how to blow out a computer. Outside, I clipped and rose those flags.

I tried not to think, You are such a pussy.

I tried to think, If this makes Alicia happy, then it's all that matters.

I'm not sure where she found the box of roofing nails. She also held my full plastic bottle of lighter fluid. I met her below the deck where we'd spent the evening. Across the way the music blared louder than ever, the windows and doors to that lake house open. And it started to rain, barely, which kept the boys inside.

"Here's how this'll work," she whispered. "We're both swimming across the cove. You and me. It'll prove that our marriage is better than my first one." Already I foresaw the plan—scatter nails around the base of the flagpole, douse the rope, light it up. Frat boys run out barefoot, and so on. Alicia said, "They have charcoal briquets over there. Easy to pour some on the ground and run a trail of lighter fluid from flag pole to charcoal, right there under their balcony. This will make me happy. It'll make me happy in about three ways."

I said, "How're we going to carry the nails? How're we going to keep a lighter or matches dry?" I thought, We are too old and slightly too normal to do these kinds of things—but figured that her third need for happiness fell into the Let's Be More Spontaneous category, something I rarely achieved, and my wife seemed to attain only when walking off jobs.

I backstroked, with the box of nails and Zippo in one of those re-sealable freezer bags. Alicia swam a one-armed sidestroke. Although we never mentioned it, we both knew not to talk in the water, or on Carnell Henderson's other property, or while packing up and leaving. We understood not to even speak while driving home, late at night, on back roads. We required complete quiet. I wanted to say something about how the army celebrated its birthday on June 14, also, and how we kind of acted like Green Berets I'd seen in one of those movies, way back during my first marriage when I never slept well. Back then, I didn't see myself as an accomplice. Back then, I never considered myself patriotic, either.

Back home, I would install security cameras, and ask my hardware guy about top-of-the-line listening devices. I would not read the newspaper or watch local news for a month.

RESISTING SEPARATION

I never thought about adhesives. Who knew there were so many types? Me, I grew up with Elmer's Glue, and that's what I used if a nail or duct tape wasn't available. My father, years ago, used to talk about glue made out of horse hooves, and rabbit skin. Not that I felt an ethical urge back then to stop the slaughter of animals, even though it might mean I would never fix a broken vase, lamp, or plate, but I tried my best not to use any kind of glue—Elmer's probably had something undesirable in it, or got tested on rats and monkeys. I doubt that I ever made a statement about all this, though. It's not like I took a stand in the same way I did, say, against dope smokers getting sent off to prison, or automatic weapons being readily available because of Second Amendment "rights," or people signing up for snake hunts down in the Everglades. I'd used some nice yellow wood glue at some point, I think when I accidentally pulled two or three kitchen drawers off-track that crashed to the floor, and I needed to clamp dovetails back together. I'd squirted out some useless linoleum adhesive one time in that same kitchen, and it lasted about a year before the single piece of vinyl curled up on a particularly humid day. I should've bought those self-stick tiles. I should've floated some of that laminate. Fuck glue.

"Hey, you remember that time against Greer when I scored a goal with a header? Only goal we scored against them, but it was me," this old high school acquaintance Timbo said to me before I even sat down at the booth there at the back of Simple Simon's diner. I'd not seen him in thirty-plus years until two days earlier. I'd gone off to college in another state, got married, worked until the age of fifty, and lost my job. I'd sent two kids through college for the most part, had my wife Val come down with blood cancer; she died, I got laid off, and I had to tell a Mexican man that I couldn't be his family's landlord anymore after the lease ended. This was a three-bedroom brick where I'd been brought up. I don't want to say that I had foreseen a son and daughter who required full tuition payments, a dead spouse, and unemployment, but after my mother moved to a nursing home I had chosen to rent the place instead of selling it.

I said, "I didn't play soccer, Timbo. I wasn't on the team," and sat down across from him. Simple Simon's looked like a Waffle House, though it had never been one. It had been a Tuddle House Drive-Inn when I was a kid, and then a Sambo's, then something else. The mascot on the sign and menu appeared to be a bucktoothed hillbilly. They seemed to take pride in salmon patties. The waitress came up and asked if I wanted coffee. I said, "Please."

"I know you wasn't on the team, fucker. But you was in the stands, right?" Timbo unflapped the laminated triptych of a menu.

I shook my head no. I looked Timbo in the face—he kept his mouth open—and realized that he'd been talking about this header to anyone who would listen since the day after our graduation. I said, "I've burned up some brain cells, though. Maybe I just forgot."

"We got us a corner kick, and ole Simmy Simms finally got some air and a good English on the ball. Well, I jumped straight up and headed it right past their goalkeeper." He looked at the waitress—her nametag read "BB"—and said, "Last time I drank coffee past noon I stayed up four days. Y'all got any Gatorade?"

She said, "No, we still don't serve Gatorade. We got 7Up, though. It ain't got no caffeine."

I didn't say, "I always thought the soccer players were kind of pussies—they weren't big enough for football, or fast enough for track." I said, "You know what, I'll have a 7Up instead of coffee, now that you mention it. I didn't even know it was still around."

Timbo said, "Two 7Ups." He grabbed BB by the forearm and said,

"One 14Up," and let out a laugh. To me he said, "So. Tell me more about what's going on in your life, brother. I've heard some rumors, you know—stuff about how your wife up and left you, how y'all couldn't have kids and that's why y'all never came to the reunions. Hell, somebody right before I run into you two days ago told me one time that you got brain damage from either a motorcycle wreck or that first war in Iraq. I told some people you had a terrible motorcycle wreck in Iraq, if that's okay." He reached below the tabletop, pulled out a one-gallon bucket of glue, and set it beside him.

I told him most of my story. I left some things out, sure. When I had seen Timbo on Wednesday in Lowe's, he crashed his buggy into mine on purpose and said, "What the hell you doing here in the paint aisle, Morgan David?" It took me a minute to remember his face. Wrongly, I thought he was the brother of a girl I dated in high school. He said, "You 'member me? Say, you 'member me? Say."

Then I remembered that he always called me last-name-first, because he thought "Morgan David" was a type of wine. I said, "Hey Timbo," and "Need to paint my old house" and "I'm thinking about coming back here," but that was it. I didn't tell him I'd been a pharmaceutical rep for twenty-plus years, that if it weren't for people like me some of the best citizens in America wouldn't be addicted to painkillers and antidepressants. There in the paint aisle, I didn't want to have to explain that a pharmaceutical rep's job requires much more than handing over the catalog to a doctor, pushing some samples, then taking an order.

"Hey, if you need any glue, don't go buying it from here. You contact me personally," he had said. He handed over a business card. He was the regional manager of some outfit called Eco-Perm. "I catch shit for this job—people think I give hairdos to women who don't want chemicals spoiling the water supply. Eco-Perm's the only non-toxic adhesive out there. At least that's what we tell people. I don't know if it's true. I know this—it's the best nontoxic adhesive out there. You want to glue two pieces of paper together? Eco-Perm #1.

You need to glue the back bumper of your car back on? Heavy Duty Eco-Perm 3000."

I didn't tell him that my ex-tenant had painted pretty nice murals on my walls that depicted the Alamo, plus portraits of famous Mexicans like Diego Rivera, Emiliano Zapata, Pancho Villa, and Fernando Valenzuela. Then there were cacti, burros, sombreros, piñatas, bottles of tequila, that sort of thing. My tenant either had zero ability when it came to imagination, or long ago decided to live with stereotypes, one or the other. I said, "I'll do that. I might need some glue in the near future," and for some reason I agreed to meet him at the diner on Friday afternoon, three o'clock.

There at Simple Simon's I said, "No motorcycle crash. No military experience. Nothing that exciting."

BB brought over two 7Ups and two straws. She said, "Y'all ready? We serve breakfast all day now. Well, up until ten o'clock when we close."

I said, "I just want a cheeseburger plate."

BB held her order pad out farther than normal. She said, "All the way on that burger?" and I said yes, and she asked if I wanted slaw and fries, and I didn't say, "Isn't that the whole point of 'plate'"? And then she asked if I wanted chili on the cheeseburger, and I said I didn't.

To Timbo she said, "Wha'chew want, hon?"

He said, "I'm good to go. Just this 7Up. I ate over at that new all-you-can-eat barbecue place on Campground Road a couple hour ago." To me he said, "I had to. They bought five five-gallon buckets of Eco-Perm Ultra. Maybe they're planning on taking used pig bones and gluing them back together into skeletons. That would be cool."

Then he pulled a pint of Popov vodka out of his waistband and said, "Say, you 'member that time all us in Junior Achievement went on that field trip to that old potter dude's place?"

I smiled and shook my head. Timbo looked to make sure the short-order cook and BB weren't turned toward us. He splashed vodka in his glass and mine. "I wasn't in Junior Achievement, Timbo."

He unwrapped his straw and stirred his drink. "Well I know that, Morgan David, but everybody still talks about it."

• • •

I tried to think of an excuse—that the Mexican was coming back for some furniture stored in an outbuilding, that Val's parents were showing up to go through their daughter's photo albums, something. I should've lied and said that my kids would show up presently to help out—Amy lived in Oregon working as some kind of intern for a nonprofit that grew organic vegetables, and Mitch kept thinking he might want to go to law school—but I couldn't. For some reason I felt as though Timbo could read my face, could tell that my kids were about as gone as their mother.

He said, "I normally drink this stuff with Gatorade. That's why I asked for it. They got Gatorade at some the other places, but they ain't got these hide-booths where no one can see you."

I turned and looked at the cook. He didn't have anything on the grill. I'd ordered that cheeseburger fifteen minutes earlier. Timbo raised his hand and asked BB, "Can we get a couple more these 7Ups?" I couldn't see her from where I sat. I said, "So. All right. What have you been doing since high school?" Understand that I knew it would lead to a monologue I didn't want to hear.

Timbo picked up a pack of sugar from the caddy, tossed it in the air, and caught it on his forehead. He leaned forward and dropped it into a black plastic ashtray. "Me and Karen got married. We couldn't have no kids, though. She'd be here—I told her all about running into you and all—but she's up at a place I picture in my mind not much different than Simple Simon's. She's up in Burlington, North Carolina, taking samples at this place called Brightwood Inn."

Timbo pronounced his wife's name with a long A—"Kay-run." I wondered how a woman could live with a man for that long, hearing her name mispronounced fifteen, thirty times a day.

BB brought two new 7Ups. She said, "I didn't fill these to the top. It should make it easier for you boys."

I said, "How's my food coming along?" but she had turned her back and walked off.

"When we first got married she got a job working for Pauline Cleans. It's one of them outfits. Started up right down the road, then branched off. It's a chain. Anyway, Karen was so good at what she done, she became a manager. Then next thing you know—maybe about three year ago—this scientist from over at the college says he thinks he can grow another Elvis through that DNA thing. Well, he gets Karen—they had met one time during a Women's Night Happy Hour over at Chiefs Wings, where Karen always took her crew— signed up to travel all over the United States with him, swabbing down stools, benchseats just like this one, countertops, motel carpets. Any place where Elvis once stood or sat or laid down. Sooner or later the scientist says he can locate Elvis's DNA, put it in some kind of little plastic container, and grow another Elvis, just like that."

I took the vodka from Timbo and poured it in. Was he toying with me? Did he know about how, right before Val got diagnosed, I traveled the Southeast with a female pharmaceutical rep? I said, "They grew a human ear on a mouse up in Massachusetts. And there are those test-tube sheep. I don't know how all of it works, but I guess this geneticist professor has some of Elvis's DNA from relatives or whatever." I didn't want to say, "Your wife is having an affair, you fool." I didn't want to say, "Oh come on, did you use some of that special glue to seal your eyelids shut?"

"I guess," Timbo said. "Listen, thank you for not saying what everyone else says."

I took from my drink. "I just moved back here. I don't know what everyone else says, Timbo." I didn't look at him. I could see only the look of Val's face twice: right before she died, and right after she learned of the woman I trained.

Timbo waved the menu like a fan. He craned his neck to look

toward the restrooms for no apparent reason. "Elvis ate in a lot of places, you know. Already they've been to the Western Steakhouse and Lounge in Memphis, plus Earl's Hot Biscuits—or at least the building that once housed Earl's Hot Biscuits."

BB came by and said, "Y'all okay?"

"If we were any better, we'd have to be arrested for having too much fun," Timbo said. To me he said, "That's what I tell my clients— our adhesives need to be arrested for disturbing the peace of mind of all those other adhesive-product salesmen out there."

I said to BB, "No." I didn't mention that I'd ordered food. I said, "Hey, can I get a Coke or Pepsi?"

She nodded hard once. I told Timbo I'd be right back, and went out to my car, where I had a flask of bourbon wedged beneath the backseat's armrest. Understand, I could've gotten in and left. I could've come back with my cell phone in hand and said I had an important call and needed to leave. But I closed the door, not even bothering to lock it.

When I got back to the booth I found a Coke, two inches from the lip, and a plate with one link of sausage on it. Timbo said, "They went to Coletta's Italian Restaurant. I don't know if I made this clear—it takes at least a week for Karen to take out all her swabs, and a special Speedball V-shaped utensil to dig into wood. Think about it, man! Think about all that DNA built up between 1956 or whenever, and today. Karen said the scientist said it wasn't different from when you look at one of those big rock faces blasted out on I-40 between Asheville and Knoxville. Line after line of DNA. Butt-crack DNA, elbow-grease DNA, slobber DNA. Everything DNA!"

I leaned forward. "I got some bourbon." I pulled the flask out of my back pants pocket. "Tell the waitress you want a Coke, too."

Timbo might not have noticed that I ever left. He balanced the salt shaker on the toe of his right tennis shoe. "They been to a place called Johnnie's Drive Inn in Tupelo, Mississippi. A place called the Waffle Stop in Sarasota, Florida. C. F. Penn Hamburgers in Decatur, Alabama. I've been writing them all down, just in case Karen one day wants to remember where she went. Like if she gets the dementia? Maybe this will help her bring a memory back to order."

I took the Coke to the men's room and poured out half of it, refilled with Jim Beam or Jack Daniel's or George Dickel—I couldn't remember what I'd last bought—and came back to the booth. BB had set another plate down, this time with a sausage patty on it. I said, "Elvis Presley probably ate in a lot of places."

"Yeah. Hey, you remember that time we had an away game in Gaffney, and on the bus ride back I ate fourteen square Krystal cheeseburgers and seven orders of tater tots? You 'member? Say. Say."

I remembered how Val craved Krystal hamburgers there toward the end, how she'd ask that I go buy her a dozen, and then when I got home she couldn't finish off one. I said, "I remember."

I told him that one of my problems had to do with never forgetting.

• • •

I started to tell Timbo the rest of my story—how my life fell apart even before Val died, that I'd considered taking a handful of complimentary pills, that my children no longer contacted me—so I didn't notice when BB slid another plate my way, this time four strips of bacon. I got to about, "And then I needed to train this woman named Kirsten," but he interrupted. "I knowed you was a real Jew."

He pointed down at the table. I said, "What?"

"I was testing you. Everybody said you wouldn't come to the reunions because they was on Saturdays. I called up BB earlier and told her to bring you nothing but sausage and bacon, no matter what you ordered. Just to see how you'd take it, you know. Hey, you 'member that time we was in English II with Ms. Herndon and I said I'd had a dream about a earthquake happening and she said sometimes dreams come true, and then I got everybody in class to start shaking their desks at 1:10, right after lunch, like some kind of earthquake took place?"

I didn't say, "I wasn't in remedial English." I said, "That's not why I didn't come to reunions. Or why I'm not eating something I didn't order. You got my name backwards, by the way—is that why you thought I was Jewish all this time?"

Timbo held his hand up to BB. He said, "He just don't like pig, that's all," looked back at me, and started laughing. "It ain't got nothing to do with his beliefs."

The man behind the grill said, "You still want that cheeseburger plate?"

At that moment I hated my hometown more than ever. I thought, If I'd never taken that job straight out of college, if I'd never gotten to feel so big because of all the money, if everyone in America hadn't gotten hooked on Valium, then oxycodone, then Lortab. If I'd foreseen getting laid off after training a woman who probably took my job at half my salary. I said, "Goddamn, Timbo." He had a spoon balanced on his nose.

"I need me a good salesman, Morgan David. I was testing you. You might think we all still rubes around here, but we got computers, and I read about Val's obituary. I mean, after I seen you at Lowe's, I Googled you, and the first thing come up was her obit. That's what this is all about. I guess her people hated you, too, what with putting 'She was predeceased by her husband.' And here you are, not predeceased from what I can tell. On your way, but not yet."

I poured the rest of my bourbon in the glass. I didn't offer any to Timbo. BB came over and set my food down at the edge of the table. I said, "I feel guilty every morning when I open my eyes."

"I know," he said. He said, "Go ahead and eat. I need me some Eco-Perm salesmen who ain't scrawnying up too weak to convince clients that we got what they need. You get you a bunch of obese salesmen? People think, Hey, this shit they sell must be good, selling enough to make people get fat from their big paychecks."

I wanted to say, "But I don't know anything about adhesives. I'm the worst person in the world to ask strangers to buy something that'll keep two things together." I looked at my food—I looked at what I didn't order, too, sitting off to the side—but I didn't feel a hunger at all. I said, "I don't know, Timbo. I'm probably not the right guy for the job."

He said, "Porter House Diner in Weatherford, Oklahoma. Jimmie's in Kingsport, Tennessee. I forget all the rest of them. I got them wrote down, though."

BB came back over and said, "You change your mind? Something wrong?" She turned to the cook and yelled out, "Don't you dare take that hairnet off!" To me she said, "You need you a to-go box?"

"He's my new salesman, girl," Timbo said. "He didn't know it, but I was interviewing him the whole time. Those others I brung in here? Half didn't make the first cut. Know how to drink. Know how to talk. Don't let people surmise your religious or political beliefs—you done all them things just fine, Morgan David. Pretend like you remember some event that happened in your client's life if he or she asks about it." He finished his drink. "Now we just got to get you to memorize some fun facts about the glue."

I didn't say, "I would've worn a tie or something." I didn't ask about salary, commission, or benefits. "It's true that I need a job," I said to Timbo. "I mean, I'm about going broke, to be honest."

BB found it necessary to remain standing by our booth. She said, "Honesty ain't one of the better qualities for a salesman. Good thing you finished the official interview or you might've hurt your chances." She put her hand on the top of my head for some reason. "I got a good feeling about you. I believe you'll help Timbo get back up to one of the best regional managers in the country."

"The proof is in the calculus," Timbo said. He must've picked that one up from someone else. We didn't even have a calculus course back in high school.

BB excused herself to get me a Styrofoam container. I said, "I didn't expect the day to turn out like it did," and only later realized that I had drifted somewhat, that I had been thinking about the day when Val met me at the door with a pair of panties that weren't hers, and the day a few months later when she met me with a stack of papers from her oncologist.

"This is going to be great," Timbo said. "I been hoping to one day hire on somebody from the soccer team. You 'member that time we was down at South Aiken and that old midfielder kept pulling me down by the jersey when the ref wasn't looking, and then I kicked him in the throat?"

I drank my bourbon. I said, "Damn right."

He said, "You 'member that time I stuck my finger up my butt and wiped it on Tappy's nose, giving him a Dirty Sanchez? You 'member? Say, you 'member?"

BB came back with a Styrofoam clamshell box, handed it to me, and said, "Next time you come in here you ought to try our Fish of the Day." I said okay to her, and to Timbo said, "He looked like Hitler."

"Hey, you 'member that time you and me was sitting in the back row of Algebra and you'd just quit dating that girl from the basketball team, and I asked you about if I could date her, and you said, Hey, it don't matter none, seeing as they was girls ever'where? And then I started dating her? What was her name? Shit, man, Vivian? Anyway, I had to take Vivian to one of her family reunions, and that's how I met Karen."

I thought, Glue. I thought, Yes, we are bound, and then there's something that compromises the compounds, and then we spread apart, lose our adherence, and finally dissolve into nothingness. I said, "I remember Vivian. Vivian. Whatever happened to Vivian?"

BB set the check in the middle of the table. I picked it up, then set a twenty-dollar bill down. Timbo asked for my phone number, and said he'd be bringing over a notebook of facts. He asked if I had a GPS. He asked if I had a Triple-A membership. He asked if I needed someone to go out with me on the first few weeks of cold calls.

I said, "I have to be alone, or I won't take this job."

"Don't be ashamed by needing anyone," he said. He asked if I remembered the time he had to get his ankle taped before a match with Wade Hampton High.

I said, "Uh-huh," and got up from the booth. I kept eye contact. Timbo, I felt, tested me. He knew everything about my past. He'd already come to know my indiscretions. I said, "Come on by any time with the glue buckets. My trunk will be open."

In the car I sat wondering why he never followed me out. Did he have other people to interview who didn't know what they were to undergo? Did he have another bottle of vodka hidden away in his waistband? I turned the ignition enough to get the radio working. A woman came on talking about how she'd lost sixty pounds in thirty days. She said her husband told her it looked as though she'd been cut in half, vacuumed out, then sewn back together without any definable stitches. She said that her husband had been thinking about leaving her, but now all was well somehow.

Timbo didn't come out. I turned the rearview mirror until I could see where he sat. He stared forward, squinting, the bucket of Eco-Perm balanced on his head. I thought, Is that what I'll look like in six months, a year? I thought, Was that really Timbo, or a reflection of me? I put my car in gear, knowing already that I wouldn't paint over the murals inside my childhood home. It would be good for me to encounter Pancho Villa daily.

PROBATE

We didn't care, really, about the traveling euthanasia vet's failed marriage. We didn't care about why this woman showed up nine hours later than she said she'd arrive. I can't say all of this for certain. I'll admit that I'm making some suppositions. I'd like to say that I could call Miranda and fact-check this whole night, but she took off two days later without leaving much of a note, and certainly not a new address. Her voicemail's full, so I can't leave a message, saying Call me back so I make sure I don't go around telling this story wrong. I can't even remember the vet's last name, though I remember her showing up, trailing along a rolling hard-shell case of dog biscuits, sedatives, and animal heart-stoppers. She came in, didn't make eye contact, and said her name was Dr. Nancy. She was one of those kinds of vets—like a pediatric oncologist who took one too many humanities courses, or a fearful dentist specializing in adolescent pulpectomies, or a questionably intelligent recent seminary graduate intent on teaching a group why evil, famine, early death, spina bifida, multiple sclerosis, tainted water supplies, dwarfism, cystic fibrosis, asthma, and muscular dystrophy exist in the world (not to mention AIDS, war, domestic violence, neuropathy, club feet, polio in the old days, death by handguns)—who think it necessary to go by first name only. Dr. Nancy. Like Cher or Madonna. Oprah, LeBron. Jesus.

"Hey, I'm sorry I'm so late, but I got stuck on the phone with my therapist," this vet said. Miranda and I stood in our kitchen, where our dog Probate, lying sideways on the floor, panted, squealed, yelped, and practically pleaded "Put me down now." Probate's real name happened to be Max; we'd inherited him when Miranda's mother died seven years earlier. Probate seemed to be a mix of chow and pit bull, he lived to at least fifteen years old, and his hips didn't respond daily. He was so black that no one would adopt him other than us, we knew, what with that fact about black dogs left forever at the pound. He had three tumors on his belly, which meant when I tried to lift him he bit me. I'd do the same thing, I said to Miranda.

Probate had responded to his new name right away. You could say, "Come here, Max," or "Come here, Probate," and he'd do so. That fucker would stare at me nonstop until I finally said, "You want to go to the recycling center?" I'd say, "You want to go see Robin at the liquor store?" I'd say, "You want to drive over to Señor El Perro Caliente and get a wiener?" He loved me, and I him.

A good dog, is what I'm saying.

If Miranda were here, she'd admit that the dog'd quit eating a week before. Anyone with a rational side, or a heart, would understand that it was Probate's time.

My dog Probate!

Miranda's momma died at HospiceCare of the Lakelands, which meant she got lung cancer, didn't want to leave her own house, never told anyone. Nor did she confide to Miranda or me about all the bins of *What Doctors Won't Tell You* and *Miracle Cure* pamphlets and books she kept shoved beneath beds. She never let on that she possessed hoarding tendencies. It's not like Miranda and I visited, then found it necessary to open closet doors to find stacks and stacks of Bradford Exchange "limited edition" collector plates; post-1992 Donruss, Topps, Upper Deck, and Leaf baseball cards from when the market got flooded; Beanie Babies; electroplated "coins" produced by the British Royal Mint in conjunction with the Columbia Mint in Washington, DC; every canceled check since 1965, and so on.

We visited often, but didn't go snooping around, I guess. And Miranda's mom came to live with us on a number of occasions. We lived ninety miles away only. Miranda's mother showed up after hip surgery, and after that time when she fell down and dislocated her shoulder, and the ER doctor said, "I can pop this back in," and then he sheared the ball right in half. Miranda's mother—her name was Evelyn—came to live with us that time when she thought she might want to hurt herself with the drugs she held left over. She brought poor old Probate with her. He lifted his leg on the dining-room table, on end tables, on both couches. He walked right up to the front door and lifted his leg, then trotted to the back door and did the same. He went up the stairs, jumped up on the guest mattress, and licked himself in ways that ruined the queen-size bedspread.

Probate!

"He's the only thing my mom had to love," Miranda announced more than once. Personally, I think it was a slightly passive-aggressive thing for her to say. I mean, I guess I should've gone ahead and blurted out, "No, she had you, Miranda," but I rarely followed through. Sometimes I got out, "She had the entire Atlanta Braves lineup, in order, stacked tightly in those little boxes, or in plastic-sheeted notebooks, from about 1990 until her death."

Her momma sank and fizzled and occupied our time, then she died, and then we went through probate. And we got good Probate, who put up with us until we needed to call the traveling euthanasia woman.

As an aside: Miranda hired out an auctioneer. Me, I didn't care about the estate's worth, but my then-wife seemed upset that her mother's collections didn't bring in more than two thousand dollars, after the 25 percent, after the thousand dollars charged for sending out mailing-list postcards to people who, obviously, didn't care to clog their homes with Beanie Babies, baseball cards, collector plates, or fake coins. Even the Hospice Thrift Store people didn't seem all that excited about garnering the leftovers that no one bid on: a console stereo, circa 1968, that weighed about four hundred pounds, for example. That Hammond organ with the special piccolo/flute/ timpani keys. Maybe thirty stuffed vipers, all coiled in a lifelike way, that Evelyn kept after her husband—an amateur herpetologist—took off for one of the southwestern states when Miranda went to college.

As it ended up, we filled most of our attic with useless "collectibles."

• • •

Besides not making eye contact, Dr. Nancy showed up dressed in what appeared to be some kind of damsel-in-distress costume. I'd never met a traveling euthanasia veterinarian in the past, so it didn't occur to me that, perhaps, he or she should wear scrubs, or at least blue jeans if the euthanasia involved a horse or goat. I'd left the back-porch lights on and had told her—some eleven hours earlier, when she said she'd show up at noon—that the driveway would lead her to the back of the house. I heard her big Suburban growling onto our property, spitting pea gravel, and went to the door.

I should mention that Probate had howled, probably in pain, for all this time. Miranda spent most of the hours petting the dog's head, or crying, or finding ways to go outside and perform tasks that could've been accomplished later: raking pine needles, filling the Yankee feeders with sunflower seeds, cleaning the gutters, checking the tread on our two cars' tires with a Roosevelt dime.

My wife started digging a grave in the red clay that might've measured six inches deep until later I went out there with a real spade, and an ax to cut through roots and tendrils. I rifled through every drawer we had, but could only find aspirin, Benadryl, and half of what I figured might be Lortab from when Miranda suffered her last bout of kidney stones. I discovered a sliver of what might've been oxycodone, and residue from about six separate one-hitters I'd stashed on the bookshelf behind *The Confessions of Jean-Jacques Rousseau*. When the vet hadn't showed up by two o'clock, I placed a speculative concoction on a glob of peanut butter, lifted Probate's flews, and scraped the homemade sedative behind his upper back teeth. He bit at me, sure, and then continued his horrific howl-whine.

It just occurred to me that "howl-whine" sounds like "Halloween." Maybe there's a reason. Add that to Dr. Nancy in her costume, at our door. She wore a corset, a floor-length dress made of velour-like material, lace sleeves, the whole getup. Dr. Nancy sported a Robin Hood hat with a feather spouting out the side, which I thought, in retrospect, kind of veered from the rest of her attire. I don't know what kind of brassiere she sported beneath, but it influenced her décolletage mightily.

She dragged that suitcase and said to me, "Please tell me you're the Stinsons."

I nodded. I said, because I wanted to know, "Does your therapist have a dog that needs putting down?" Of course I knew the answer. Dr. Nancy harbored unrelenting neuroses and spiteful daydreams and more issues than the Library of Congress's newspaper and magazine stash.

"No," she said. "No. I just need to talk to her when I'm spiraling. My husband left me after nineteen years. You ever have any foot problems, Mr. Stinson?"

I said, "Call me Charlie." I almost said, "Call me *Mr.* Charlie." I said, "I'm Charlie, and this is Miranda." Probate lay on the kitchen floor panting, whining, yelping. I said, "I've never had any foot problems."

"My ex was a podiatrist. You probably know him—Walker Posey. I think he's been named Best Podiatrist in the County going on about ten years now, according to the *Spinning Around* Readers Poll." That was the local newspaper's weekend supplement that came out on Fridays so people would know all about the crummy things people like Miranda and me wouldn't do on Saturday night. *Spinning Around*'s readers named Olive Garden as Best Italian restaurant, Wal-Mart as Best Sporting Goods, Subway as Best Ethnic Food because the place offered ciabatta bread.

Miranda said, "Probate's got all his shots. Our regular vet's Dr. Gagliardi. We couldn't get Probate into the car, so we called you."

"I know Dr. Stefanie," Dr. Nancy said. "I think I used to work there, maybe about ten or twelve years ago." She pushed up her boobs with both hands. She pulled back some kind of near floor-length cape that accented the costume.

Who doesn't remember where he or she worked at some point? Me, before I signed on with Piedmont Consumer Pulse because the previous vice president lost it altogether and quit—which *hadn't* gotten voted Best Marketing Firm in the County—I had a number of both full- and part-time jobs throughout high school and college, then afterwards. I worked at a pharmacy (mistake on their part), drove a water truck, washed dishes as part of work-study, spent six days as a roofer, worked at a Budweiser warehouse (another mistake on my employer's part), waited tables during that one semester of law school, delivered newspapers in the middle of the night, cut and delivered firewood from my daddy's tree farm, sold Christmas trees from my daddy's tree farm, married Miranda, worked for *her* father's Consumer Pulse of the Carolinas, then went out and took the VP job with the competition. Who doesn't remember jobs?

Probate let out a noise that almost sounded like "Help," I swear to God.

Miranda said, "You can just call up your therapist like that? Does she charge you by the hour even over the phone?"

I kind of wanted to know the answer, too. Dr. Nancy said, "It's okay. It's okay, buddy. It's just your soul trying to leave your body."

It took me a second to realize that she talked to Probate, not me.

Miranda said, "Probate's real name is Max. Charlie renamed him Probate."

Dr. Nancy had been stooped down in her damsel-in-distress costume until this point. I'm not proud, but I could look down and see her boobs easily from where I stood. I'm not proud, but I kind of wanted Probate to stop whining and breathing erratically for an hour, just so Dr. Nancy could remain crouched, considering her options.

"Oh," Dr. Nancy said. She stood up. "How old did you say Max is?"

"Fifteen," Miranda said. Maybe I should mention that Miranda wore those Spandex things I see more and more running women wear, plus a T-shirt that didn't go much past her navel. She said, "Well, we don't know. Probate came from the Humane Society, and then my mother had him for about eight years, and we've had him for six or seven. I'd say he's between fifteen and seventeen, really."

"There's no telling," I said, because I couldn't think of anything else to offer. "We never fed him onions or chocolate! I pride myself on knowing what dogs can and cannot consume. We made sure he never ate pork, or any of those other things that make dogs sick or poisoned!"

Dr. Nancy said, "Renaming animals can be very confusing for them, and make them feel worthless. Some scientists speculate that that's what happened to the dinosaurs."

• • •

So the vet shot my dog up with a sedative, Probate went to sleep, the vet shaved a spot on Probate's left foreleg, then she swabbed it with alcohol. I didn't say, "Why did you sterilize the spot on my dog's leg? It's not like an infection's going to bother him later."

Miranda shook her head sideways as if she underwent a petit mal seizure, held her mouth wide in a stifled cry, and excused herself to the bedroom.

The vet injected pentobarbital, I stroked down Probate's spine, and his pains—the cancer, the failed hips, the probable long-term mourning for my mother-in-law—vanished within a minute. Dr. Nancy got up and, without asking if I possessed any allergies, pulled a stick of incense from her bag, lit the end, and waved the smoldering thing over my dog. She held a stethoscope to Probate's chest, then pulled back and said, "Okay. His spirit has lifted. This is just your dog's body. His spirit has risen." She spoke calmer than a golf announcer on CBS, or someone trying to coax fish toward the shoreline.

I feel bad, but I started laughing. I mean, I bent over and slapped my knee. I said, "Is that sage? What's that scent?" But I tell you, I couldn't stop laughing. I said, "Oh my God. Oh, Jesus, you're something. Hey, do you go to Burning Man every year? Oh man oh man oh man. Hey, what's with the getup? *Spirit has risen.* Goddamn."

Dr. Nancy saw no reason for my humor. She said, "Do you have any other animals living in the house who need to say farewell to their friend?"

That made me laugh even more. I yelled out, "Miranda! Miranda, get in here!" I looked down at Probate, whose eyes were open, staring at that little vent at the bottom of our refrigerator. I said, "Myrrh? Sandalwood? Frankincense?"

Miranda yelled back, "I can't!"

I said, "No, we don't have any pets who need to offer their bon voyages." Then *that* made me laugh. I said, "'*Bon voyages*'! Like we have a cadre of *French pets* upstairs. Miranda!" I screamed out too loudly. I said to the vet, "No, no pets. Probate had a special relationship with some squirrels and chipmunks out in the yard, but I don't think that they held the same feeling of camaraderie."

"Will you be wanting me to take the body to get cremated? Do you want a paw print cast? Now would be a good time for me—or you, if you feel strong enough—to cut some of Probate's fur off, for a keepsake. You can put it in a jar. I've had clients frame their dog's fur."

The vet's eyes went all cockeyed at this point. She looked all over the house. I thought maybe she'd made up stories about an ex-husband, and she would come back later with her spouse and rob us. "You could put Probate's hair in a little amulet and wear it around your neck."

Like I said, Probate was part chow and part pit bull. He kind of shed. I looked over at the corner and saw a swirl of his hair gathered. I said, "No, that's okay."

"That's okay to not get cremated?"

I said, "How much do I owe you?" and pulled a checkbook out of my back pocket. "I already dug a grave, right beneath a tulip poplar. It was Probate's favorite place to sit and listen to the songbirds on crisp spring mornings."

And then I bent over and started slapping my knee again. I leaned down and pet my dog over and over. I got out, "Songbirds!" I got out, "Your spirit has lifted!"

I got out, "God*damn* it, Miranda, grow up and *get out* here."

"Some of my clients have been fiber artists. They've incorporated their pets' fur into works of art," the vet said. She stared up at the ceiling, and at the floor simultaneously.

I glanced down at her boobs, one of which had kind of fallen out of the weird, encumbering costume. I caught myself thinking of moats, and flaming arrows, of Trojan horses, and then Trojans. I said, "It's weird that your ex-husband is a podiatrist, and his name is Walker. Did he always know that he was going to be a podiatrist?" Maybe it was the marketing side of me, but I thought it necessary to say, "Did your ex-husband ever think he might want to go into physical therapy?"

"I'll help you carry Probate to the grave," the veterinarian said. "Let me help you. Probate's going to be heavy and cumbersome."

"No. I need to do this myself," I said.

Miranda opened the bedroom door a crack and said, "Is it over?"

I looked back toward my wife. For some reason Dr. Nancy thought it necessary, at this moment, still holding the incense, to hug me hard and stuff her face sideways into the nape of my neck. She kind of wailed a little, too. She made a noise that didn't sound unlike a dry heave. I didn't think Miranda could hear it, but I'm pretty sure the traveling euthanasia vet said, "I wanted to meet a knight at some point tonight."

I waited about two seconds before saying, "That rhymed."

She said, "It has come to this."

Miranda opened the door and strode toward us. I held my arms out in that way that people do to prove they're not hugging back. I held my arms out sideways in the international sign for, Hey, This Isn't Me Doing This. My dog Probate lay dead—or at least his body was there, seeing as his spirit had scrammed the entire scene. Dr. Nancy said, "It is all for the best," and "He is in a better place now," and "We are not supposed to understand the meaning of Death, or of Life, for that matter."

My wife—now ex-wife—said, "Do you have any more of that drug by any chance?"

• • •

The eleven o'clock news came on. Dr. Nancy stubbed out her incense in the sink, then put what was left over into a special pocket of her suitcase. She took out a bottle of spray Clorox, got down on her hands and knees, and encircled Probate's body with disinfectant. I got a roll of paper towels off the counter and handed them to her. She said, "Probate might've emitted invisible microbes, and I don't want y'all breathing them in."

I shrugged. Miranda started crying again, covered her face, and went out on the back porch. I said, "Do you have a regular clinic, Dr. Nancy? I mean, in case we get another dog, can we bring it to you for rabies shots?"

She shook her head. She said, "I couldn't take it anymore. Too sad."

Too sad? I thought. Sadder than traveling to strangers' houses and putting their pets down daily? Or nightly? I said, "Huh." I said, "Look. I'm not going to let you leave here without telling me why you're dressed up in such Renaissance festival attire."

"Corpse-dew. I believe that I have eradicated any possible corpse-dew."

I said, "Good. Maybe I'm wrong. Do you dress like this every day?"

From outside, I could hear my wife sobbing uncontrollably. I heard her call for her mother. In retrospect, maybe I should've gone out to comfort her.

Dr. Nancy said, "It's my therapist's idea, really. She says one of my problems is that I wish, too often, to conform. She says my ex-husband drilled it into me I should conform, and before that time my own parents wanted me to be a debutante, and before that time I needed to be a cheerleader, and before that time I had to win the spelling bee. Spelling bee, cheerleader, debutante, wife who acted stupid in front of her husband's friends." She kind of let out a heh-heh-heh. "Do you know how much harder it is to graduate from vet school than med school, or at least med school to end up a foot doctor?"

Again, we stood there right beside my dead dog. I didn't think it was right. I said, "I have to work in the morning. I better get Probate in the ground, then cover the grave with a big piece of roofing tin I got out earlier. And some cement blocks."

Miranda sounded like she had dry heaves. She couldn't hear the veterinarian, I didn't think, but I thought about how she'd shown me photos of her own self winning a spelling bee, being a cheerleader, being presented to society the summer after her first year of college. Did she think that I made her act stupid in front of my friends? Did I, unintentionally?

The vet placed both her hands on Probate's chest, held them there ten seconds, stood up, and said, "The spirit has definitely lifted." She said, "On my way out I'll talk Miranda into coming back inside while we bury your friend."

I said, "No. I mean, yes, talk her into coming back inside. But like I said, I want to bury him by myself."

"He's heavy," the vet said. "You're going to need my help."

I said, "I can handle it." I still held the checkbook.

She said, "It's five hundred dollars, made out to Dr. Nancy, DVM."

Finally, I stood above my dead mother-in-law's dead dog for five minutes before Miranda came back inside. She walked straight to the bedroom and, without turning her head, told me to get the sheet she'd set aside earlier to wrap Probate's body. In another five minutes I heard Dr. Nancy's big Suburban crank up, and she backed out of the driveway at about forty miles an hour.

I don't want to admit that the traveling euthanasia vet held some knowledge in the situation, but Probate's corpse didn't feel like any fifty-pound bag of dog food I'd ever hefted over my shoulder. It felt like what some of those He Man competitors endured. I don't know what the spirit weighs, but it couldn't have been much.

I could've plain dragged my dog out the door, down the couple steps to the pea gravel, then continued toward the tree where I'd fashioned his deep red clay–walled grave. Or I could've gotten a flashlight, roamed around the backyard, found the wheelbarrow that I never kept in the same place two days in a row, returned, and so on. But in the end I bent down, remembered to use my thighs instead of my lower back, and cradled my now-ex-wife's still-dead ex-mother-in-law's mixed breed after I wrapped him tighter than a specialized burrito in a bedsheet Miranda used only when my friends from college showed up needing to spend the night.

Anyway, I got the dog out there and set Probate down on the edge of his final resting place. Hours earlier I'd had the foresight to leave my spade against the tulip poplar—I'll go ahead and say that the tree died within a year, maybe from my having to cut half its roots. I picked up Probate's body in two clenched fists of Percale, leaned over slowly, and eased him into the ground. I'm not one to be religious or spiritual, seeing as I'll go to hell for misleading people in the ways of marketing and advertising, but I thought it necessary to say aloud, "You were a good dog, Probate. You were good as Max, and you were good as Probate. I hope we meet in the afterlife, buddy."

I shoveled hard clay on top of his body, then shuffle-stepped a few times to tamp it down, then placed that piece of roofing tin over the bruised and tender earth-breach, plus six cement blocks I'd sequestered over the years for such a moment.

At this time I cried.

Maybe I stood out there and looked through the branches toward the sky for thirty minutes. Maybe I wondered if it was too early to consider driving down to the Humane Society at some point within the month, picking out a young stray, and naming it for the first time. I can't remember. I sat down on a compromised wood-slatted bench nearby and tried to imagine a traveling euthanasia veterinarian's nighttime dreams. I thought of Miranda inside, and envisioned her opening and closing drawers, in search of pain medication. Somehow this would all be my fault: Probate's demise, the vet's tardiness, the inappropriate cleavage. The long-buried reminder of Miranda's own life-filmstrip: spelling bee, cheerleader, debutante, unhappy spouse. I envisioned my wife pulling open our filing cabinet upstairs, finding our wills, making a note how she needed to change hers. Or did she ricochet around our house, gathering useless mementos, readying them for one of the local thrift stores so that, later, we wouldn't encumber each other with needless keep-or-trash decisions?

I returned the shovel. On the back porch, after standing too long trying to compose myself, I turned the knob and tried to remember if I had locked the door behind me, out of habit.

ECLIPSE

I might not've earned an associate's degree in culinary arts from an accredited junior college, but I stood there, tongs in hand, contemplating undercooked chicken. The shrimp appeared rubbery and the pork questionable. Who knows why we didn't have regular hamburger meat available? I couldn't blame our chef. She got bombarded with five separate Cinco de Mayo catered parties. I might not've earned a Ph.D. in clinical psychology from one of the better private universities on the Atlantic coast, but I'd've bet that Alvarita suffered from depression on this nearly nonexistent holiday back in her homeland, or that she became preoccupied with visions of her relatives duped and stranded by cavalier and unscrupulous coyotes just this side of the border. Alvarita—normally responsible and inventive, cheerful and brave—became overwhelmed, and so there I stood at the taco station, ready to serve salmonella-worthy entrées to members of No Stigma, one of the nonprofit mental health outfits sprinkled across the county. They'd evidently undergone such a year as to warrant a catered celebration.

"There's no guacamole," my coworker Leon said to me right as the door to the Willie Earle Community Center—which used to be Willie Earle Elementary School from right after Willie Earle's lynching in 1947 on up to integration in 1971—opened, and a swift-striding knot of mental health–concerned do-gooders focused on me. Gator the Caterer always insisted on setting the taco selection right in the middle. Plates and plasticware, salads and condiments—then the tacos—followed by, on this particular afternoon, iced tea, water, and margaritas.

My boss Gator attended the University of Florida. His real name was Randall, but he came home insistent about his new moniker. Gator didn't make it long enough to qualify for one of those associate's degrees. His daddy owned a car lot and a meat-and-three place supported by insurance agents, road crews, his used-car salesmen, anyone driving a step van, and retirees. Gator learned how to scrub pans and chicken-fry steak after flunking out, then asked his father for a loan.

As an aside, the meat-and-three's called Periodic Table and Chairs. Gator's father flunked out of college when he couldn't hack a chemistry major. One day Gator will inherit both car lot and diner. There's no justice. It might contribute to how I became, probably, the only atheist serving undercooked meat at a catering service in this tri-county area.

"That's not our biggest problem," I said to Leon. "Take a look at the chicken."

Someone from No Stigma plugged in a boombox. "Low Rider" came up as the first song. Leon pulled his eight-pearl-button chef's coat up over his nose. He said, "I bet you a hundred pesos there's still asbestos in this old building. I'm going to contact one of those TV lawyers, first time I let out a dry raspy cough."

Like me, Leon'd nosedived. He'd lost jobs in a number of sectors, from textile supplies to real estate. Then he discovered OxyContin after injuring his back while post-hole digging one of those heavy L-shaped FOR SALE signs made from 4×4s, big enough to crucify half a martyr. Me, probably booze, then Lortab, then worse—from bad hips, caused by hiking, caused by taking my Geology 101 students on excursions that, I've come to understand, didn't matter. This was at a college made up entirely, it seemed, of entitled boys and girls who later in life needed only to recognize marble for their countertops and pea gravel for their long serpentine driveways. Since I've left, I've heard that the students now set the curriculum, for courses they want to study. *They* set the attendance policies. *They* have somehow talked the Board of Trustees into approving a No Grade policy.

The door to Willie Earle continued to open. Alvarita'd "cooked" food for a party of fifty. "Low Rider" turned into "Feliz Navidad," which meant—though I might've received a doctorate in geology, and not a bachelor's in music appreciation or sociology or logic—that someone in No Stigma plain Googled "Spanish songs" or "Mexican songs" or "Songs with Spanish words in them." I awaited Charo. I tried to not think of my hips throbbing. I tried not to think of how I no longer had great insurance in terms of deductibles, and not enough money saved up to become a Canadian, British, or Japanese citizen where I could get double hip replacements for under a grand. *No matter how hungry you get, don't eat the pork or chicken,* I tried to think, instead.

No one, yet, came up to any of our stations. I lit three extra Sterno cans each and placed them under the chicken, then the barbecue, hoping it might deter gastrointestinal maladies. Not that I have a degree in anatomy with a concentration in internal organs.

"I don't think this is going to be much of a tequila-drinking crowd," our margarita maker, Marianna, said. She said, "Y'all sure y'all can't drink? There's going to be so much left over. Gator won't know."

"I'm on antibiotics," I said. It's what they taught me to say in re-hab.

Leon said, "Me, too. Bad infection. All over the place."

"More for me, then," Marianna said. She'd flunked out of college, but spent enough time in her sorority parties to work as a bartender. Gator's niece. Gator's wife's sister's daughter. Which meant that she couldn't be trusted, seeing as how if Gator, his father, and everyone else died, Marianna would inherit everything, though she thought Washington State and Washington, DC, were the same place. She'd been my student, a few years earlier.

One day, toward the end of my tenure as an associate professor, I joked that South Carolina's official state mineral happened to be

Bondo. Marianna wrote, "Bondo's our state rock!" at the bottom of her final exam. "Can I get extra credit for listening?"

• • •

"Hello!" a woman from No Stigma came up and said to me. She stood behind a young black man who might've been twenty. He sported a mustache, wispy, which consisted of about eighteen hairs total, plus a soup-snatch goatee not thicker. The woman held onto the boy's shoulders. "This looks so good! Doesn't it look good, William?"

William didn't answer. He kept eye contact. He looked like he might pull a piece of rebar from his tube sock and knock me upside the head. I understood. I didn't like white people most days, either, do-gooder or down-on-their-luck caterer's helper.

"How about a nice chicken taco, William?" I said, slowly, as if speaking to a wild squirrel I wished to tame. Man, I didn't know that No Stigma would bring along their "star pupils" with them. I said, "Eat a barbecue pork taco and a chicken taco, and if you can identify which is which, I'll throw in a shrimp taco."

This woman said, "It looks so delicious. I'm Samantha Gowdy-Bright." She stuck out her hand for me to shake. That meant taking off a disposable glove on my part, shaking, putting hand sanitizer on my palms, and lifting two more gloves out of the cardboard dispenser. She said, "You look familiar."

When I taught geology I got asked to speak at a number of garden clubs, public schools, and the like. Never one of those private white-flight Christian schools—those science teachers and administrators understood how difficult and uncomfortable it might become explaining to students how a chunk of coal emerged from millions-years-old peat on a planet barely six thousand. I figured that Samantha Gowdy-Bright either attended one of my show-and-tells or gave money to the college.

"I'm just an employee at Gator Caters, ma'am," I said. I handed over two tacos to William. "Maybe you attended another function where I served." Hardly ever did a catered event require my attendance, to be truthful. Maybe two a month. Normally, Leon, Marianna, and I just went to someone's house, set up, then returned the next day to pick up serving trays, used Sterno cans, and any nonplastic utensils.

Samantha Gowdy-Bright shook her head no. "What is your name?"

I said to William, who held his taco as if he planned to eat it down the middle instead of from the end, "Go ahead. Eat." That song "Tequila" came on, this the version sung by Bert Parks in the movie *The Freshman*, starring Marlon Brando and Matthew Broderick, a film that my ex-college always showed at their three-week-long orientation, the movie about people paying incredible amounts of cash to dine on what they think are endangered species. I don't know the ins and outs of moviemaking, but after viewing this particular film ten times I'm pretty sure it deserved an Oscar, or at least one of those People's Choice awards.

I said, "Does No Stigma stand for anything? I mean, I know y'all stand for people showing a little more compassion toward people suffering from invisible illnesses, but is it an acronym? I've always been an acronym fan."

What the fuck was I saying? I tried to think of *one* acronym, but couldn't.

Leon yelled over, "Line's backing up!" in order to get Ms. Gowdy-Bright and William shuffling off to the drink station.

Samantha said to me, "We'll talk later."

I said to the next person at my station, "What would you like?"

This was a man, wearing a blue-striped seersucker suit, his thinning gray hair combed over from left ear to right. He said, "How's about that William?!"

I said, "Uh-huh."

He said, "Y'all spend enough time together to get his entire story?"

I looked over at William. He threw both uneaten tacos in a blue Rubbermaid trash can stationed by a water fountain.

I said, "Chicken, pork, or shrimp?" This guy had hair sticking out of his left ear, too, kind of combed upward, like a mini-tornado coming out the side of his head. "You can have one of each, I suppose. Hell, maybe all three." I looked at Marianna and noticed how both Samantha Gowdy-Bright and William requested margaritas. Maybe he was twenty-one, and not taking medications.

"They say *60 Minutes* is coming down here to do a special report on William. *60 Minutes,* or *Nightline.* Or the *Today Show.* Hell, maybe all three." Now I couldn't tell if he was a volunteer or a client. He might've had echolalia.

I said, "I like barbecue tacos. You should get some jicama, too. It's a bulbous root vegetable from Mexico, so what with it being Cinco de Mayo . . ."

"William was born blind. *Born blind.* Then we had one them solar eclipses and his foster mother took him out and made him stare at it." The man held his hand up to his mouth, either burping, or hiding crooked teeth.

I said, "There's a fifty-acre limestone quarry over in Gaffney."

"They say he stared up, you know, and by the time the eclipse ended, he could see! You understand what I'm talking about, don't you? Regular people look up at a eclipse and *go* blind. Blind William looks up and sees. It's the new normal. It's what can't be explained by scientists, medical professionals, or the clergy alike. William is kind of No Stigma's mascot. If we could figure out what he needs to stare at to stop his other troubles, we might come up with a whole new tourism industry for the entire state."

"You seem to be the kind of man who'd appreciate a one-to-one mixture of chicken and barbecued pork in a soft taco," I said.

Seersucker man leaned into me. He whispered, "When William was totally blind, he showed no visible angry, panic attack, urgent, threatful tendencies. He'd been totally passive, is what they say. Then things happened. Old days? Salamander."

I said, "Hematite's one of my favorite oxide minerals."

• • •

Willie Earle got lynched on February 17, 1947. He'd been accused of stabbing to death a white taxi driver named Thomas Brown two days earlier in Pickens County, South Carolina, and police followed footprints for a mile, entered Willie Earle's mother's house, and supposedly found a knife, plus twelve stolen dollars. A lynch mob of thirty-one white men—twenty-eight of them cabbies from Green-ville—threatened the jailhouse guard, extricated young Mr. Earle, took him back across the county line, beat him, blew his head off with a shotgun, told on each other during a trial, then all got acquitted.

So I served undercooked food inside the ex-gymnasium of an ex–elementary school–turned–community center now rented out to celebrate the travails of those fighting mental illness and/or the miracle of reverse eclipses.

During a lull, while José Feliciano sang his version of "Light My Fire," I set down my tongs, took off my disposable gloves, and looked at the line forming at the two restrooms. I walked over to Leon and said, "I want a drink something bad, man." I said, "This is too much for me. One time I took some students out to look at clay deposits, and it ended up being the spot where Willie Earle got killed."

William wandered back over in front of my station, alone. He held a margarita in each hand. I stepped back behind the tortillas and donned new disposable gloves. Maybe I'd focused on Samantha Gowdy-Bright earlier, for I'd not noticed two healed wounds on Wil-liam's face, both slightly covered by sideburns. It looked as if some-one—maybe William—had taken a red-hot cigarette lighter and held it right below his temples. Perfectly round as the Carolina Bays south of us, where meteors pockmarked the land like so many perfectly round shotgun pellets sprayed from the gods.

I looked at one scar, then the other. I thought, Jesus H. Christ, there's more going on here than the miracle of sight. I thought, Do not drink, Tommy. Do not drink, which will make you think, which will lead you straight back to the opioids.

William drained one margarita, then cleared his throat twice. In a voice that came out holding ancient rhythms known only to Negro

Delta blues singers brought up dealing with Jim Crow laws and cat-fish stew, Old Crow bourbon and the double calls of eastern brown thrashers, he croaked out, "You don't look so happy, mister." He swiveled his young, damaged head a few times and rolled his eyes. "I can tell you smarter than your station in life."

Listen: there were a good fifty people, indeed, attending No Stigma's annual fête. None of them approached the food area. Peripherally, I witnessed them back up—zoom—like in a movie when the director wants to show some kind of solipsism taking place, a character feeling all alone in the world, aware of secrets no one else understands.

Not that I have a degree from the University of Chicago in philosophy, with an emphasis on Cartesian studies. I said, "I saw you throw away those first two tacos, my man. I didn't poison them or anything." I said, "Some guy came up right after you and said that you'd been born blind, then underwent some kind of solar eclipse transformation."

William said, "That's what they say."

I said, "Do you like seeing? Hot damn. That's got to be different." I thought, Who says such a thing?

"Sometimes," he said. "Not really."

I said, "The shrimp's rubbery, but it's not undercooked. Over-cooked shrimp might not be great, but it doesn't cause gastrointestinal pains and their attendant problems."

"I could've escaped rocks," William said. "I could've dealt with rocks. Anyone can deal with rocks, right? You know what I mean? Rocks is different than guns. Sticks and Stones, but not Guns and Stones."

I said, "Uh-huh." I thought, Did I say anything to him earlier about my ex-profession? I thought, Was he at one of those required meetings at some point when I had to say my first name and explain my downfall?

"Man shows you a rock in his hand and says sit in the car, you just run."

I said, "My father wanted me to study business, then go to law school. He said that if I studied geology then I'd have rocks in my head all the time, ha-ha. That's what he said. My father said I'd spend too much time in the sun, then drink too much, then turn out exactly the way I ended up turning." I said, "What's your last name, William?"

"I play along. I pretend. It makes the old lady and her friends feel better about themselves." William looked left and right. "It don't matter the truth, you know. They ain't no Truth with a capital T. Stories, sure. Rumors and conjecture, but no Truth."

He said it like "Troof." Troof!

I said, "I got you," though I didn't. Instead, my head raced toward everything I'd ever read concerning hallucinations vis-à-vis overindulgence and wet-brain.

William stood up straighter. He turned rigidly, to one side, then the other, as if posing for a mugshot. "Why do we bury the dead in the ground? Souls can still escape soil. That's why 'soul' and 'soil' sound so much alike."

I said, "Marianna might be pouring the tequila a little heavy. She was in one of those sororities."

"I'm keeping up for when there's another solar eclipse. Nothing against my foster mom, but I'm thinking about reblinding myself. Seeing these kinds of things I've been seeing, I ain't so sure it's good for my mental health, you know what I mean?"

I said, "Back when I taught college, I took students up to North Carolina to this place called Ronboy's Ruby Avalanche. We'd buy up buckets of nothing, then hope a ruby'd show up. It was a two-day hike. It was a good flask walk up, and a flask walk down. Sometimes a student made some money. Mostly, not."

William said, "There's no need to stare at my scars. Look at them once. They'll still be there. Scars won't jump out and attach themselves to you, at least not physically."

I clapped my tongs as if I wished to summon lobsters. Then I caught myself clicking away, unconsciously, S-O-S, something I'd learned in Boy Scouts, then in graduate school. Then maybe sitting there a couple times in rehab, in a circle, wanting to escape.

I looked at those two scars again. I couldn't not look. I said, "You're Willie Earle, returned from the grave."

•   •   •

Did I emit some kind of mostly antidepressant-caused odor from my pores? Did I hold one eye squinted almost shut, the other wide open and roaming like a damaged ship's compass? Was I twitching in a violent, uncontrollable manner? Could these people read my mind—that they should've held this little party on MLK Jr. Day, or the birthday of Harriet Tubman, or on February 17, when Willie Earle got lynched? At least it would've been Black History Month. What the fuck did mental health have to do with Cinco de Mayo?

People came to the condiment station, skipped me, and veered straight to Marianna. Oh, earlier they'd gotten undercooked pork and chicken, and then some kind of autoimmune sufficiency gene kicked in and urged "Eat salsa/drink tequila."

I figured this out just as "La Bamba" came on by Los Lobos.

Samantha Gowdy-Bright returned to my station and said, "Are you all right?"

I came out of my daydream. "Yes, ma'am."

I didn't remember her wearing an old-fashioned fox stole earlier. She said, "I saw William over here talking to you a few minutes ago."

I said, "No one's eating the tacos. I hope they're not bad."

"He's quite a young man. You know, he's done quite well at twenty-one up at the casino in Cherokee. He's like that man in that movie, being able to predict what's coming. In cards, at least."

I said, "Oh. You mean blackjack." I thought she had talked about his age.

"But you have to watch out for him. He's a sly one. He'll tell some stories. He'll veer you into believing some other things. You don't want to take William very seriously. He was blind, and then he wasn't, basically. And he holds some anger-management issues." Samantha Gowdy-Bright stroked her dead fox. For a microsecond I thought she looked down at my crotch.

"Uh-huh," I said.

"Later on we're going to be giving out awards, you know, for Volunteer of the Year, and Most Improved. 'Most Improved' can go to either a volunteer or a client." She leaned in and whispered, "It's a tie this year. We have one of each."

"Quartz. Limestone. Sandstone," I said. "The Carboniferous Period. The Silurian Period. Cambrian. Devonian."

She said, "You should be proud of yourself. You've done good."

I said, "The Oxford Period," even though it wasn't one, just a joke one of my old English professor colleagues used when students accidentally added an extra dot at the end of a sentence. Not that funny, except around grammarians.

"William's a special case, when it comes to humans and their pasts."

I nodded. I was on to these folks, with the exception of not being able to discern the healthcare volunteers from the needful. I said, "There's so much chicken left, it ain't funny. Please take a sack of chicken home. Eat some now, then take a sack home."

Samantha Gowdy-Bright said, "My husband's an attorney."

"I figured that," I said.

She said, "He told me that we don't need to bring the past up if we want to reinvent our town into the kind of place where open-minded people would want to move, and have families of children."

I felt my old paranoia rising. "It's a complicated economic, sociological direction we're all taking." I wasn't sure how that got out of my mouth.

Samantha looked around the ex-gymnasium. I did, too—I saw William with one foot out the door. She said, "You're not welcome here, Tommy. You're just not welcome here."

For a second I unreeled my memory right up from entering the Willie Earle Community Center until this moment. Had I said my name to her? Did she ask Leon or Marianna? Then I remembered that everyone from Gator Caters wore name tags. "Really, really, not welcome here."

I thought, Man, I can't lose another job. I thought, What did I do in a previous life to deserve all this?

· · ·

"I'll take care of everything," Marianna said. "Go on. Take off. I'll clean up. You can let me go early after the next gig."

I said, "I lost my good job. My wife left me. People like Willie Earle got lynched. A lot. People lynched people. America."

Marianna said, "I'm not going to let you drink. You go on back home. Leon and I can get all this back in the van. Get out of here."

I said, "I can't fucking take off. If you remember, we all drove together. My car's back at the kitchen."

Leon took off his toque. He stared at a full bottle of mid-shelf tequila. He pointed at the door, and I imagine he was about to tell me I could go sit in the van and wait. The man who won Volunteer of the Year came up and said, "Thank y'all for everything." He raised a miniature trophy, maybe four inches high.

Samantha Gowdy-Bright reappeared. She exuded a manner 180 degrees from when she said I wasn't welcome, not twenty minutes earlier. Of course I could think it had been my imagination, that I'd misinterpreted what she said to me, and how she looked when saying it. Now she came off all smiles, all good-hearted humanist. She'd shucked the wrap, and carried at her side an old-school boxish Samsonite normally used for toiletries and makeup. "Do you have any granddaughters?" she asked me. "Do you have daughters?" she asked Leon and Marianna.

We all said no, and she unlocked the spring-powered metal clasps. She said, "Never overestimate someone totally insane giving meaningful attention. Maybe that's what No Stigma stands for."

Marianna, evidently, found it necessary to lug her two galvanized steel tubs filled with melting ice, one at a time, in order to pour them out in a locker room once used by now-dead black kids when they attended a segregated elementary school.

I didn't connect what Samantha meant—by this time I'd forgotten all about the acronym conversation. I said, "I don't even have a kid. I guess I'm old enough to have grandchildren here in South Carolina, now that you mention it. Have a kid at eighteen, kid has a kid at eighteen. Thirty-six, thirty-seven. Grandpa."

She didn't respond. Ms. Gowdy-Bright hefted her toiletry case to my table station, lifted the lid, and began extracting tiny chipmunk pelts. She said, "I make miniature furs for Barbie dolls. A chipmunk's the perfect size for a full-length coat." She pulled out one of those collectible Barbies, like from the late 1950s, lifted the doll's arms out like a zombie, then slipped the chipmunk coat on her. "I do it all myself, from trapping, to curing, to sewing."

Leon yelled out, "Let me help you!" to Marianna, and he disappeared.

I said, "Good God."

"I bet you've never seen anything like this," Samantha said.

I shook my head. For more than a second I wondered if maybe William worked for No Stigma, and *he'd* brought Samantha Gowdy-Bright along as a potential Client of the Year. "I hope PETA never hears about this," I said.

"Things were so much better down here fifty, sixty years ago. In every way. There's a little thing called 'survival of the fittest.' Have you ever heard of this term, Tommy? If chipmunks happened to be more fit than women, then they'd be wearing coats made from human skin."

I said, "I need to call a cab." I said, "I can't wait around for Marianna and Leon to finish cleaning up."

Again, maybe I'd dipped straight into wet-brained, painkiller-induced delirium tremens and hallucinations, but this woman kept eye contact, holding a skinned chipmunk, and said, "Negroes often self-invent temporary insinuations, grasping momentous anecdotes.

I have a hundred of these things. Usually when I'm sewing little fur coats, I think up words standing for where I volunteer my time."

She didn't use the word "Negroes," of course.

This woman, I thought, worked directly with Lucifer. I pulled out my cell phone, pretended to make a call, and walked outside the Willie Earle Community Center, confused, surely, but filled with intentions I'd not undergone since trying to explain Earth's age to the idiot rehab counselor, who kept talking about that higher power.

When I tell people this story now—and understand that I must gain a lot of trust—almost all of them blurt out, "Of course there was a cab in the parking lot!" These people range from twenty to seventy years in age, all coworkers or regular clients at Southwestern Numismatics. I got a job here soon after the catering gig, only because I talked the owner into believing he needed an ex-geologist to identify gold, silver, copper, platinum, and non-ferrous, over at the precious metals side of the coin shop, way out here 1,600 miles from where I had always thought I felt comfortable.

"Need a ride, partner?" the cab driver asked me.

I didn't say, "How did you know someone would be here needing a taxi?" I didn't lean down, study his white face, and think how, the next day, I'd do a morning's worth of Internet research poring over photos of Thomas Watson Brown, the driver stabbed by someone other than Willie Earle, who—I'd find out later—had indeed taken a cab that particular night, but driven by one of the lynch-mob defendants.

I said, "I guess it might be good for me to walk, now that I think about it."

"Get on in," the man said. I didn't know how to ask if he'd turn on the inside light so I could see his face better. "I got past-life sins I need to make up for. Nothing new. Every night before I go home, I throw in a free ride. Makes me feel better about myself."

I got in the backseat and thought about saying, "Virgin Valley, Nevada," or "Peridot Mesa, Arizona," places I knew still hired on rock hounds, just to see if this man might enable my need for a geographical cure. I said, "You can plain let me off in town. I live near the corner of Jackson and Hampton, there at the apartments."

"I know the place well," he said. "Not far. Hell, I might have to give two freebies tonight."

I didn't think about how I needed my car. I didn't think, until later, that if I had said, "My car's parked at Gator Caters," we would've taken a route in the opposite direction.

And then there stood William, thumb out on the right side of the road, smiling—and I don't want to come off as politically incorrect—like the quintessential late nineteenth-century minstrel, like either Amos or Andy, like any of a number of advertisements featuring black customers in 1947.

The driver slowed and put his blinker on.

I said, "No, no, no, no, no." I reached up and pulled the back of the cabbie's headrest.

He said, "What do you mean, No? You're getting a free ride. This ain't like old times, Bubba."

William had his right thumb out, but his left arm stayed behind his back, as if he held a gun. Or knife.

He got in the cab beside me. William said to the driver, "Thank you, sir. I got money."

I said, "Willie Earle."

The cab driver turned off his blinker. He pulled back onto Lee Road. "Where you headed, son?"

"Oh, I don't know. About one block past this man's place will be good enough, I expect."

If I'd been drinking I'd've never been able to think this through: Willie Earle's ghost plain wanted to see where I lived when I got dropped off. Then he'd get out, thank the cabbie—maybe kill him— and walk back to find me.

I might not've ever received a certificate from the L.A. Stunts Training Center or International Stunt School or the Rick Seaman Stunt Driving School, but I understood that I needed to open the back door at some point when we cruised beneath thirty miles an hour, and roll myself into a drainage ditch. Then, before any pain set in—though, again, I possessed no official training in pain management or chiropractic studies—at least to find a worthy hiding place.

Once-blind William said, "I don't know about y'all, but I'm tired of seeing nothing but bad, bad, bad. Poverty. Killing. Illiteracy. More poverty. Next eclipse? I'm going to stare right up into it, get rid of what I don't want to witness."

I don't know if I said, "Yeah, you told me that a couple hours ago," or if I just thought it when I jerked the handle, gave the door my best shoulder, and rolled out of the vehicle. Oh, I rolled and rolled, my eyes shut tightly. Nowadays I probably exaggerate—we'd come to a stop sign—but I know this: The driver didn't stop. I took off running straight into a large elaeagnus bush in someone's side yard, and felt hidden enough to crouch there.

I heard two shots presently.

I stayed in town one more week—long enough to read the newspaper every morning, check the police blotter, scan the obituaries, find nothing new. Then I came out here, where men and women wrap themselves in semi-precious stones. They pride themselves on keeping chickens, and talk behind the backs of women who look similar to good chef Alvarita still living quietly there in my homeland.

RINSE CYCLE

Tyler Fort would still be alive these thirty-plus years later had my father not thrown away the cheap Zebco rod and reel, if my best friend Arlie Capps's father hadn't beaten him after we got caught, if Mr. Fort had learned how to read and been able to get another job after the mill closed, if new owner, Mr. Patel, had drained the swimming pool after Labor Day behind the twelve-room Hilltop Motel like old owner, Mr. Liner, always did, if Tyler Fort's father hadn't been so poor that he couldn't afford even a used Maytag, if Mr. Fort hadn't been so racist as to not want his grease-tattooed work clothes swishing around in a drum where black people's clothes might've been previously, if my mother hadn't agreed that Tyler might've gotten injured by a mis-cast, if my father hadn't pointed out that I could've gotten pulled in to the deep end of the pool, if Raj Patel had installed a higher fence or security cameras to let him know when two fourteen-year-old boys jumped a split rail in order to harass a boy pummeled by an unhinged father, if the town of Poke could still afford a single cop to work third shift driving around with a spotlight, and—to be honest—if Tyler Fort possessed the ability to say, "I don't want to wear dresses every Sunday night." But he's long dead. Mr. Patel found him at the bottom of the eight-foot deep end one Monday morning and, not knowing rational, proper American procedures of calling the fire department or 911, ran back to his landline and called Piedmont Pools and Spas, which happened to be some fifty miles away. It might be revisionist history, but the rumor was that Mr. Patel said he had an emergency clog. It might be rural myth, but some people said that Patel first called a number for pest control, saying he had something trapped in his pool, but no one answered. Then he called a Pentecostal minister asking if he'd left someone behind at a recent baptism. But he called the pool people, and they showed up. They say that Mrs. Patel—who wore what we all considered a loud floral bedspread and kept that bindi between her eyes, though all of us called it a plain "dot"—went back to India within a week of this, claiming that America held nothing but bad luck and that she'd rather drink nasty water from the Ganges twice a day than deal with Pokers. People from Poke called themselves that, Pokers, not Pokites or Pokists or Pokians. You'd think that a clan of such upright folks wouldn't align with a card game or fireplace implement, but they did. Mr. Patel claimed that his wife, who ended up being named Sukh—which meant something like Happiness, I learned later—returned to Mumbai because she tired of the woman at Poke Drugs pointing out where they shelved the pimple cream, or mosquito-bite itch-relief tincture.

● ● ●

For two years after his father lost his job as a doffer, Tyler Fort took a duffel bag of dirty clothes—his parents', his older sister's, and his—to the Hilltop Motel on the other side of Denim Street, maybe a half-mile from Poke Cotton Mill. Tyler and I had been in school together since the beginning. I don't want to come off as superior, but my father had gotten a degree in Art History with a minor in Poverty Studies, then gone to this place called the Penland School so he could learn glass-blowing. He married my mom—she was a jewelry-maker—and they moved into the two-story farmhouse in Poke where my father'd grown up. I got born. My parents made me read. In his spare time, when he wasn't ruining his lungs with silicosis, my father volunteered at a literacy association, teaching mostly ex–mill workers how to read, and how to write up résumés should they move to towns with actual employment opportunities. Tyler's father said he knew how to read the Bible, and that's all he needed to know. The same with my friend Arlie Capps's father. Know when to reference the Bible, know how to talk people into believing that your decisions shouldn't be questioned, know how to make people fear you just by keeping a crazy look in your eyes, and say "Believe me" after every sentence: That's all one needed to succeed. I hate to admit it, but here thirty-four years later in an even smaller Poke, it seems that Mr. Capps and Mr. Fort might've been on to something. My own father said I should never listen to those men, and no one in their extended family. He wasn't being holier-than-thou, really—he said I should stand there making eye contact with every human being no matter what, and to nod occasionally, but to never let anyone think that I agreed with him or her. That's the way with glass-blowers, evidently, or art historians. Anyway, Tyler took his families' clothes to the motel pool, donned the dirty dresses, pants, T-shirts, blouses, boxer shorts, and panties, and swam laps back and forth in the overchlorinated water. He dove in the deep end, and swapped between Australian crawl, breaststroke, backstroke, and—toward the end of the cycle—dogpaddle. Back and forth. I don't think he ever ventured into the butterfly, just those more popular three strokes. But I wasn't there every night to witness. Maybe there'd been a particularly deep stain on a blouse or shirt that required his plowing a fly through the water. I don't know. I only know that none of us was old enough to drive legally, and most of the time Arlie and I met up—he lived in the mill village that's now mostly vacant and corrupted, and I through some woods where my ancestors settled long ago after leaving Ireland—right there on Denim Street, near the laundromat, Poke Diner, the one-room post office, an archery/pawn shop called All Bowed Up, or Poke Gro. We met without having to call each another, and we walked back and forth like we owned the asphalt. We continued past houses, got to the Hilltop Motel, and after we figured out Tyler Fort's ritual on Sundays, we brought along our fishing poles and top-water plugs.

Sad, unknowing, cursed Tyler Fort—he told me one time there in homeroom seventh grade that his last name stood for "strength" in one of the languages we never learned at Poke Middle or Poke High—would've never been discovered emasculated in his mother's nightgown had Arlie and I had girlfriends, or if we went to Sunday services, or if our parents told us we couldn't leave the front door after dark, or if Arlie and I had gone in the opposite direction to fuck around at a real farm pond we knew that had bass surfacing for bugs that hatched, or if we walked even farther to a family named Knight that wasn't much unlike my mom and dad who left Poke and returned after getting so much hippie lifestyle that they named their daughter Friday—Friday Knight—so people would say things like "I can't wait till Friday Knight," or whatever other double entendre they might say, or if we just stood around like idiots looking upward at the occasional jet flying from Atlanta to somewhere else, or a cyclone of bats emerging out of the mill's old smokestack. At least that's what I've beaten myself up about all these years. As I figure it, Tyler feared that Arlie and I'd show up once again, he tried to swim faster than normal, he tired, and he sank weighted down with too many layers of clothing to the bottom of the pool, his lungs filled with water.

This was after the first weekend in September. As a matter of fact, it was closer to Halloween, and although the air felt warm most days, I doubt Mr. Patel's unheated pool's water reached anywhere near a comfortable temperature, even if one wore two pairs of panties, a couple slips, a pantsuit, and overalls.

The Sunday night before Tyler Fort drowned, Arlie and I snuck out with our fishing poles and maybe a dozen good lures. We'd been doing this, I'd say, for the previous three months. We'd wait on the other side of the fence until we heard Tyler swimming in the opposite direction, jump over, then cast out hoping to snag a hem, a belt loop, or a collar. It wasn't difficult. Then one of us—or both—would scream, "I got a big one! I got the world record!" and so on, while Tyler churned his arms faster. It looked like he swam in place, like maybe how Olympic swimmers trained in a high-tech cylinder of oncoming waves.

In our defense, the shallow end of the pool stood on the opposite side, so when we hooked Tyler the only thing he needed to do was stand up, turn, and give us the finger. He would say, "Goddamn it, Dale, you're going to rip my momma's sundress." He would say, "My sister ain't gone be happy if her bra strap's broken," and so on. I hope that Tyler Fort doesn't come off as stupid—just unlucky by birth—because by the second time we showed up to reel him in, he'd brought along a pair of scissors to cut our lines. That's when we—not stupid, either, and both of us skilled in loop and blood knots—started bringing a tacklebox of Rapalas, buzzbaits, and poppers to tie them up again.

I'll give Tyler this: He never told on us until Arlie accidentally snagged his face and Mr. Fort thought his boy got one of those eyebrow piercings.

• • •

I returned to officially take over the house three decades–plus later. My father had died during a coughing attack years before to no Poke fanfare, and then my mother, finally, in a nursing home. By "finally" I don't mean that I wished for her death whatsoever. She'd suffered early-onset dementia for a half-dozen years, first at home, then with us, and finally with a nursing home that didn't deserve or pretend to be a "retirement facility." This was on the outskirts of Poke, in an L-shaped building that, until 1970, had been a black elementary school. Some of the caretakers had actually gone to Phillis Wheatley Elementary. Whenever I visited—my wife and I lived a hundred miles away, but for four years one of us traveled down and spent a night or two per week in my old house and visited with Mom, checked on her needs, did what we could—I wondered how the black staff members withstood what they heard. I don't pretend to know anything about human memory or lapse of judgment or deep-seated, atavistic prejudices, but it seemed as though a number of the white residents there with my mother found nothing wrong with using racist terminology toward anyone needing to roll them over or change their soiled sheets.

Luckily, soon after my dad died, my mother had driven fifty miles to deal with an attorney who paid attention in law school, and she set everything up in her will so that I could write out checks on her account and not deal with probate court. I could sell the house within a month after her death, could auction off the belongings, could take out all the jewelry she'd made over the years, and the blown glass left over from my father, and not deal with trifling long-lost cousins who wouldn't know a Roman chain from a chain letter.

I am sure I'm not the only son who has felt grief and relief simultaneously. My mother hadn't spoken in a year, and for a couple before that her communication skills played out on the lines of "Hey, Gypsy!" when she saw me, which was the name of my childhood dog, or "I need to get to Hale's and lock the door; I forgot to lock the door!" Hale's was the name of a jewelry-store chain that my mother detested. Then there were her frightened-eyes looks—much like what I bet Tyler Fort looked like right before he submerged—before pleading, "When are we going home?" Or when she yelled at me, "Why did you send me to a nuthouse?" Or when she looked at my wife, Cecelia, and whispered, "You were never the pretty one."

My mother's wishes, set out in the will, were for us to cremate her body and throw it atop my father's ashes, which happened to be in the mound of sand he kept off to the side of his studio, which had, at some point, been a barn. We were to hold no funeral, only a remembrance of sorts, there in the living room and kitchen. I was to have RC Cola and Moon Pies available for local Pokers, and champagne and foie gras for her metal-arts comrades strewn throughout the Southeast, plus collectors. She pointed out that I could start off the evening with Chopin's funeral dirge, but by God I better move on to Bob Dylan and

Neil Young, to Howlin' Wolf and John Lee Hooker and the Allman Brothers Band.

. . .

She'd made her own funerary urn long ago. It looked not unlike one of the better golf-tournament trophies, all silver and etched and inlaid, handles to each side, a lid that looked part beanie, part dunce cap. As some kind of joke, down on a nameplate of sorts, my mother engraved her full name and date of birth, and below it "Uh-Oh." I didn't know if I was supposed to get someone to etch her death date below what I guess she thought her final words would be. I didn't even know why she spent all that time and money on such a container if she really wanted me to dump the contents out. I tried to remember if she'd fashioned such a vessel for Dad, of if he plain got dumped out from a plastic bag.

"She lived a full life," Cecelia said to me as we waited for mourners to arrive. This was a Monday evening. I'd brought along my computer to play all that music, not thinking about how Mom never had reliable Internet. Cecelia wasn't as distracted, and brought along a boombox, CDs, and—seeing as Duke Power offered little reliability, also—a gross of D batteries.

I said, "I guess." I said, "Nothing against Dad, but she should've moved to a city after he died. She seemed to wither here. I always felt she could've done better in a number of ways had she moved to a place big enough to offer a gallery or ten."

Someone knocked on the door. Cecelia got up from the chair— we had been sitting across from each other, the gigantic loving cup between us on a table, for a couple hours. My wife said, "I bet that's the food."

My mother instructed that her celebration of life be a catered affair, and she'd already, years before her mental deterioration, contacted the owner of Halfway Barbecue, not six miles down the road from desolate one-row-of-buildings Poke. She'd given him a down payment and another blank check. I didn't care. I wasn't going to squabble.

Arlie Capps walked in carrying a foil-covered baking tray of pulled pork and said, "How you been, Dale?"

Listen, like I said, I'd been back to the house of my training once or twice a week for a few years, stayed there and—I guess—brought my own food. Surely I'd ventured over to Halfway Barbecue, about the only place making any money in a thirty-mile radius. I said, "God-damn, Arlie, what're you doing here?"

"You 'member that time I caught you peeping-Tomming in my sister's window and you thought she had twenty nipples because you seen her wearing a polka-dotted nightgown?"

I said, "This is my wife, Cecelia. Cecelia, this is Arlie."

He set the barbecue down right next to my mother's ashes. He said, "You 'member that time my father put a big glass jar in Poke Gro. saying I needed a eyeball transplant, and me and you'd go in there to collect the money, but one time someone put a rubber in there and a note telling my daddy to never have kids again?"

Arlie hadn't grown. This sounds mean, but Arlie hadn't grown much mentally, it appeared by the way he talked, and he couldn't have stood over four-eight. He kind of looked exactly like he did when we cast lures at Tyler Fort. I said, "If I'd known you were still in town, I would've looked you up."

Cecelia said, "Dale's told me a lot about you," which wasn't true. She leaned down and hugged him.

He said, "I got cole slaw and cornbread in the truck." He said, "I got iced tea and sweet potato casserole in the truck." But he didn't move. He looked up at the ceiling, then slowly rotated his head to the ashes and said, "Hey, Dale's momma."

• • •

I guess it matters who showed up—the people my mom expected, basically—but what I'll never forget, or find a way to quit talking about, is when Tyler Fort's father, maybe seventy, seventy-two at most, came through the door, alone, wearing the same black suit that, I felt certain, he wore to his son's funeral. I am not exaggerating when I say that he focused on me and strode over as if on a mission. He didn't limp. I turned to start a conversation with a woman from up in Asheville that my mother knew, a woman who manufactured rings out of glass eyeballs, but she turned and walked toward the barbecue. I looked down at Mr. Fort's shoes, old tan wingtips that didn't match his suit.

"Little Dale," he said to me, for my father was known as Big Dale.

I smiled. I felt tears form in my eyes, out of either fear or embarrassment. I said, "Thanks for coming by, Mr. Fort."

Cecelia walked up and said, "You want me to make you a plate?"

Mr. Fort said to me, "I'm sorry to hear about your momma. I'm sorry you got to go through such. I guess that's something Tyler won't ever have to do."

I could see Arlie and me casting those lures toward the boy as he swam awkwardly in a dress bought at Kmart or stitched handmade from one of those paper Simplicity patterns. I said, "I don't know what to say, Mr. Fort."

He said, "I do." "Smokestack Lightning" ended, and "Whipping Post," of all songs, began. Mr. Fort said, "I do," but then didn't continue.

Arlie came over and said, "Hey, Dale, you 'member that time my daddy rode up on his minibike all mad because I wasn't cleaning the gutters and I punched him in the mouth and his false teeth flew out and then the minibike fell over and broke the things?"

I said, "Dale, do you remember our friend Tyler's father, Mr. Fort?"

Mr. Fort said, "Boy, you ain't right," and started laughing at Arlie. He popped him on top of the head. To me he said, "I guess when you left Poke, you left Poke, Little Dale. I guess you left Poke and took all your memories with you. Everybody said you took off all better-than-everyone, went off to that college, erased the past. Never even bothered to take care of your momma."

I didn't say, "Whoa, now, come on." I didn't go through how my mother lived with Cecelia and me for a time, that I came down to visit as often as I could. In a way, I knew that Mr. Fort spoke some truth. I said, "I'm missing something, right?"

Arlie said, "You 'member. I moved in with the Forts a couple years after Tyler drowneded. 'Member?" I guess from the look on my face he could tell I'd forgotten. I should mention that my parents took me out of the Poke school system and had me go into some kind of homeschooling Great Books program, that perhaps I never noticed that I'd become sequestered for a few years after the tragedy. Arlie said, "My daddy broke my arm and tried to strangle my momma, and then he got sent to prison. My momma had to move down to Bishopville and live with her parents. She took Wanda, and I moved in with the Forts, seeing as they had a spare bed. Goddamn, boy, you don't 'member all this?"

I thought, How can none of this sound familiar to me? I thought, Was my childhood some kind of dream that I've rejected? Was everything somehow washed away? I said, "I remember when you pretended to need an eyeball transplant," but that wasn't quite true, either.

Cecelia came up and said, "This barbecue is the best thing I've ever had. We might want to think about moving back down here and staying in the house. It's not like we're committed to Asheville." She handed me a plate of food. I took one forkful, spilled it all over the front of my shirt, then tried to wipe it off with my index finger. Cecelia said, "You missed a spot."

"Whipping Post" ended, and then Neil Young started wailing about that old man.

I watched as some of the poorer Pokers pulled Ziploc bags from their purses or pockets, filled them with food, then walked out of my childhood home.

Mr. Fort said, "Arlie and me started up a appliance repair business. He can crawl back behind washing machines and refrigerators good. When he's not slinging hash."

Arlie said, "It's probably 'cause I wouldn't swim in that pool for him, even if he did take me in."

Mourners drifted away. They missed hearing Cream's version of "Crossroads."

• • •

I would've stayed in the Poke school system had not Tyler Fort drowned and my parents thought it necessary for me not to be tabbed the kid who inadvertently killed a boy who wore his parents' and sister's clothes while plunging into the overchlorinated waters of the Hilltop Motel pool. I wouldn't have taken the SAT, done okay, and gone off to a college up North that felt it necessary to admit someone from South Carolina only because they needed to brag about "students from all fifty states and fourteen foreign countries," or whatever. If Tyler Fort hadn't drowned, I would've graduated from Poke High, gone to the closest public college, studied something as banal as accounting or business administration, returned to Poke, and established some kind of H&R Block–type situation. If I were lucky, I would've married a local woman who taught kindergarten and said things like "I before E, except after C," or told me all about how she had to wipe a kid's butt. I owed Tyler Fort, basically.

My mother didn't move from the dining room table. Her urn held fingerprints doused in mustard-based barbecue sauce. Everyone touched her—Pokers and competitive jewelers alike. Arlie took the trays away at the end of the remembrance and said he'd come back by to check on the house if we wished for him to do so. I thanked him, though I knew the future of this particular abode, that I would give up my job at a nonprofit called Shod America that's mission was to offer needy Appalachians shoes, and that beautiful, kind, and committed Cecelia—who worked for a nonprofit called Bless Immigrant Kids Every Second and gave them donated two-wheelers so that one day they might enter the Tour de France—would relocate with me to Poke. We could work anywhere, really, as long as we held consistent internet services. And if that didn't work out, I could maybe use my father's old glass-blowing studio as a place to make furniture, and Cecelia the jewelry that she'd always wished to concoct out of typewriter keys. That's what Cecelia said to me when we first met, in a slightly experimental class called Outsider Art, Blues Music, and Foodways of the Poor.

Afterwards I had no choice but to take my wife by the hand and walk her through some darkened woods to where the rec center once thrived. I said nothing. My mother's ashes remained on the table, surrounded by compromised paper plates and fouled napkins.

We got to a place that had been filled in, a place that looked nothing like I'd remembered. I said to my wife, "There used to be this poor idiot who swam on this spot, cleaning his family's clothes."

She said, "Shhhh."

I said, "Arlie and I were assholes, casting toward the guy, this guy Tyler."

She said, "Shhhh."

"He drowned," I said. "You met his father there at Mom's funeral."

Cecelia said, "Come on, Dale. Come on."

I might've mentioned how this particular spot thrust my life a direction that it would've never taken otherwise. And just like at the end of too many sorrowful movies, I looked forward in our life together, unintentionally. Sure enough, I saw Cecelia going on various pilgrimages to find manual typewriters, disassembling the things, then turning keys into spoken-word jewelry of a sort. Me, for some reason I watched myself entering the Poke County School District warehouse, buying used oaken desks by the gross, then scouring over every etched and graffiti-ridden brown-stained desktop for signs of a radical, unencumbered, disobedient, reckless Tyler Fort that no one met. I might make square paneling out of all the others, or flooring tiles. I might make wall-hung triptychs, there in the workspace my father once occupied, always knowing that I'd come full circle.

ONE MORE

I arrived two days early, without telling my newly widowed aunt, Maura, or my special-needs adult cousin, Jerry, who lived at home. I'd promised to show up Saturday, but here it was Thursday after a six-hour drive, seven counting the time change. My uncle—this would be my dead mom's only brother—died in front of his computer, trying to figure out, evidently, how to play spider solitaire. His name was Spence, a middle name actually, but what everyone called him, at his request. His given name happened to be Willard, and that's how everyone addressed him until that movie about rats showed up nationwide. My uncle asked people to call him something else right after. What's wrong with that?

I checked in two days early for a couple reasons. My ex-wife had gotten a job one town over. We'd always gotten along, and I thought I might ease by her house. I promised myself that I wouldn't ring the doorbell. If she happened to be out in the yard, I'd pull over. Maybe she'd believe I'd merely gotten lost, driving by, unable to follow my GPS to Aunt Maura's house ten miles over. Like I said, she and I got along better. The divorce wasn't even much of a mess, half and half, she wanting to start over, me mesmerized by a new woman hired on over in Building Permits, just down the long hall from where I worked in the Office of Appraisal and Reassessment. My ex-wife and I sold the house, split what was left over after paying off the mortgage, and she ended up—I'm talking ten years later—not far from where Maura and Spence lived, though they never knew each other.

Maura and Spence didn't drive up for the wedding, long ago. It was small. It was one of those weddings wherein the bride would have a baby six months later. We never talked about it. I never said anything like, "You railroaded me into marriage, pretending to be pregnant!" Maybe that's what led to the amicable divorce.

I planned on driving by Gina's house. It wasn't hard putting her name into the computer, then trying her maiden name, then her second husband's name—checking out one of those Who Lives Here sites to see what the place was worth, when it last sold, et cetera. There was a photo on Zillow—nothing special, though better than where Gina and I had once lived, if I want to be objective about it—a ranch-style house, 2,200 square feet, half-acre lot, there amidst another fifty or sixty houses, some Colonial, some Cape Cod. Gina's house could probably go for $162,350 in my opinion, though Zillow had it for only $159,800. Zillow. Trulia. I've applied for jobs at both places, and never got a response.

It's not that I'm weak of spine or commitment, per se, but I checked into the Marriott and didn't even take my luggage out of the car. I went straight to the bar while they still ran a Happy Hour. Back when Gina and I lived together, which lasted exactly one decade, one year, one month, a week, and a day—I figured this out later while staring at a computer and not playing a game such as spider solitaire—she and I liked to drink vodka tonics from the first day of spring until Labor Day, then Manhattans from September until March. It's not like we were alcoholics, I don't think. We didn't shake around if we missed a day. It's just what we slid into. Gina and I went to bed afterwards, no matter the season, and tried to have a real kid instead of the fake one that got us married. Nothing took. As I've gotten older, it seems like a special godsend: We didn't create another bad carbon footprint, we didn't bring into this world one more biped plagued by attention deficit disorder, not one more person who might buy a semiautomatic weapon and kill off parents and professors and strangers, not one more person who thought it necessary to need a

trophy a day, and so on. We did the right thing, maybe unintentionally. We didn't bring into the world someone who might be swayed
by crazy-talk, then vote.

Aunt Maura had said on the phone that she and Jerry moved to
a KOA campground temporarily, somewhere down on the coast, until I'd done my job. She said, "We can't go back there, Paul. It's too
much for both of us. If you could just go in and tag things as to what
you think they might fetch, we'd be appreciative. And listen—get
what you want. I mean, to a certain extent. If you want the TV, take
it. You're the only person I can trust as to what things are worth, what
with your job, you know. If you want that painting in the den, take it.
Your uncle would want you to have it. The hide-a-bed down in the
basement? Take it. Spence would be proud to know that you used it."

I said, "Are you sure about this, Aunt Maura?"

"My mental health couldn't handle anything unsuspected or
tragic. If you could get out his clothes and take them to Goodwill or
the Salvation Army or the Hospice House, I'd appreciate it. Anything
you think I would never want to see, get it out of there."

Why didn't she tell me that I could spend the night there, instead
of spending money on a hotel room? I didn't ask. Maybe she figured
I'd be spooked alone in a place where my uncle died playing online
games. I tried to think of Aunt Maura and my cousin Jerry in a campground. During the day, Jerry spent some time in a place for special
people. I think he put beads on string, or something like that. He was
forty-eight years old, same as me. As a kid I remember his hitting
himself on the head, hard, when we played Old Maid, down there in
the same basement.

I had said, "To be honest, Aunt Maura, I'm only qualified to assess
property values, not things like furniture, or stamp and coin collections. I remember your having a slew of plates on the wall. I hate to
tell you, but I think those Bradford Exchange things are pretty much
worthless."

Aunt Maura had said, "You take what you want. And listen. I want you to take out whatever you think I don't want to know about. That's what you can do for me. That's what your mother would want you to do for her brother. It's what your father would want, too."

All this had to do with a porn stash, I could tell, unless he was some kind of secret member of the KKK and kept a robe and hood crammed in the back of his closet. Or it had to do with a diary that Aunt Maura didn't want to find.

• • •

What kind of over-seventy man even owned a computer, I thought as I walked into the Marriott's bar, a place called Sparks. There were four TV screens on the walls, three of which were tuned to Fox News. Windows looked out toward a wide side road. It kind of looked like an airport bar. The other TV showed one of the ESPN networks. It showed women's softball.

"I wouldn't want to run into that pitcher in an alley," this guy two seats down said. "Goddamn. Way she wings her arm down hard, your balls wouldn't have a chance."

My hips hurt bad. I hadn't driven three-hundred-plus miles at one clip for a while. I'd read something about how keeping knees above hips wasn't good, and evidently the writer knew what he or she talked about. It felt as though someone had taken a chisel to the front of my hip bones, then tapped them lightly with a ball-peen hammer. There at Sparks I pulled my seat back, but remained standing. The bartender said, "Hey," then flipped out a paper napkin on the bar. "What'll it be?"

I thought about saying "Manhattan," seeing as it was that time of year, but decided against it. There was something wrong with ordering a Manhattan alone, I thought, especially here. I said, "Wow, I don't know. You got any hip elixirs? How about just bourbon, a little water, on the rocks. You got any PennyPacker?"

The bartender said, "No."

"Four Roses?"

He said, "No."

"Jesse James?"

The bartender shook his head. He pointed behind him at the bourbon row.

I said, "You got any Bulleit or Booker's?"

He shook his head.

The man next to me started laughing. He said, "Oh, man, goddamn, it was perfect. Perfect! I can't believe they pulled it off. Goddamn those idiots deserved it!"

I said, "I don't like Jack Daniel's, unless it's the last choice. You got any Knob Creek? Old Crow, Evan Williams, George Dickel, Maker's Mark?"

"We got Jim Beam."

The man next to me start laughing again. I looked over. He wore what appeared to be a leisure suit popular circa 1971. He wore a suit that men might've worn while going on a date to see *Willard.*

"Well, okay," I said. "A little water and ice."

The bartender turned to look for the bourbon. He wore what I figured to be a mandatory Marriott bar uniform, black pants and red shirt. The shirt was buttoned to his Adam's apple. It might have been the style for this part of the United States, for all I knew, for the other patron kept his buttoned way up there, too. This other guy, drinking in a hotel bar before three in the afternoon, said, "I overheard you saying your hip's hurting, which makes me think that you been on the road all day, which means you probably ain't heard the news around here."

I turned to him. "No. I got relatives around here, though."

The bartender said, "You want me to charge this to your room?" He said, "My name's Gregg. Don't believe the nametag. They misspelled me." I looked at the gold rectangle pinned to his chest. It read GRGG.

"Grgg," I said. "That's kind of funny." I said it again a few times, one after the other. I imagined my cousin Jerry saying something like *Grgg* over and over, for no reason, maybe after he heard a truck going down the road.

"Sounds like what might come out of that softball pitcher's mouth every time she grunt- pitches," the other guy said. I thought, It's always been my luck to drive six hours—seven counting the time change—and end up next to a guy like this.

I said, "Let me just give you my credit card. I haven't even checked in yet. I need a couple drinks in me, then I'll go check in. I've been driving six hours—seven counting the time change," like a fool. I handed my Visa to Grgg. "They said I couldn't check in until four o'clock anyway, so I got an hour."

Grgg took my card, slid it through the machine, then handed it back. He set my drink on the napkin.

The other guy said to Grgg, "Hey, get me another scotch when you get a chance. I'm Lewis. Put it on Lewis's tab."

Grgg said, "I know you, Lewis. You don't have to tell me who you are, Lewis."

Looking back, I realize that this guy just wanted for me to hear that name over and over, like sending me down some kind of shrew hole, so later on I'd send the police looking for someone using an alias.

He stood from his seat and leaned his arm on the counter, like me. He said, "Brilliant!"

I looked up at the closest TV. Someone being interviewed went on and on about how he thought the president was an alien. To Lewis I said, "I can tell that you're about to burst telling me something."

He offered his hand to shake. He said, "Lewis."

I shook and nodded. I said, "Paul."

He raised his glass after we shook hands. He said, "So here's what kinds of things you're missing around here."

I said, "What's that?"

"Well, it seems this old boy duct-taped a tripod on top of his car. On top of the tripod he had a regular old Nikon or Canon camera, you know, nothing special. Certainly not a video camera or whatever they got out now. Not something professional. Hell, they might've had an old Polaroid One-Step, for all I know."

I started thinking about how Gina and I had a Polaroid One-Step. We thought it was important to take a picture of ourselves at least once a month. In the winter months I took a photo of our Christmas dinner, or Thanksgiving dinner. In the summer I took a lot of Polaroids of our good garden. Nothing against One-Steps, but as the years went by those little slip-out photos kind of faded into a gray-tannish blur. Gina kept the pictures in a blue-padded album. When we divorced, we flipped a coin, she won, and she got to choose her favorite photo, then I got one, et cetera. We ended up with sixty or so apiece. When I'm feeling either really low, or optimistic, I daydream about our getting back together for at least a day, then trading over the photos, like two kids with baseball cards, or old lovers who wore necklaces that held broken pieces of a golden heart.

I said, "Tripod," so he thought that I paid attention.

"This old boy—hey, did you hear about this, Gregg?—this old boy somehow talked himself into one of the gated communities around here. I'm talking places where the minimum square foot has to be four thousand. Four thousand! And each lot's at least three acre! Some the houses are six, eight, ten thousand, and some the lots five, seven, nine acre."

I thought about how maybe I should start forgetting to use plurals, if I wanted to fit in. I needed to button up my shirt and quit using esses. Grgg stood alone, watching softball. He said, "My girlfriend's preacher's brother lives out there, but he didn't get caught up in it all." Grgg looked like he chewed gum, but he didn't have anything in his mouth. He was one of those people, like my cousin Jerry.

I started thinking about how Jerry—my mother's sister's son—turned out. Jerry and I ended up being, for the most part, normal. But I wondered if Jerry's hips hurt like mine did at the moment. I wondered if he'd *know* if his hips hurt. And I wondered if he realized how his father had died. There's something to say about living a life wherein you don't know when people die. I thought about DNA, and that Nature and Nurture thing. I thought about how my mother and her sister Maura rarely talked, and about how my father and Uncle

Willard/Spence often stood at the very back of the lot, feigning to tend a smoker jammed with pig, flicking cigarette butts into the yard, drinking beer. When my mother died, Aunt Maura and Uncle Spence showed up. Maura said, "She was my older sister." Spence said, "It's for the best, Paul."

Geniuses. When my father died six months later, they sent flowers to the funeral, even though the obituary requested none, stating clearly that people should, if they wished, offer donations to Mental Health America.

• • •

Grgg poured more bourbon in my glass and said, "No charge." Lewis said, "Here's how they did it. Somehow they got into this gated community. And they knocked on everyone's door. They said, 'Hey, we're with Google Street View. Tomorrow between nine and noon we're going to be driving around, taking film of this area.' This was on a Monday. They said, 'Are you familiar with Google Street View?' because, you know, people living in such a luxurious setting are old, and maybe don't know the ins and outs of the World Wide Web."

I said, "Right around here?"

He nodded. He thrust his arm off to the east. Lewis said, "And then they pointed at the end of the driveway and said, 'We're going to be coming around with that car. With the camera on top.' Listen, they'd gone so far as to buy one of those magnetic stick-on signs on both sides of the door, you know. If these old people knew anything, they'd've known that Google Street View would use cars with one them advertising situations. You seen those things before, right?"

I thought, Yeah. I nodded. I said, "Car wraps."

Lewis touched that top button on his shirt twice. For a moment I thought he adjusted a tracheotomy. "Well, any these people should've known that a good Google Street View car would be a Prius, not a 1996 Corolla. I'm going to jump ahead and say right now that everyone who got rooked told the police, 'It was a Dodge' or 'It was a Ford' or 'It was a Toyota' or 'It might've been one them Kia, Subaru, Nissan, or Yugo,' because they didn't know anything outside of Mercedes, BMW, and Lexus."

My father kept an old, old Mazda rotary-engine pickup. It's what he used, in the garage, six months after my mother's death.

This guy Lewis knew what he did. Somehow I thought it necessary to say, "I love my Toyota RAV4. It's great."

I don't want to say that I'm a look-ahead-and-see-the-punch-line kind of guy, but I understood where Lewis was going. I almost said, "I know a funny joke about a woman nymphomaniac who tells a bagboy at the grocery store that she has an Itchy Cooter, and the bagboy says she'll have to point it out because all Japanese cars look alike to him." I didn't. If I've learned one thing after almost twenty-five years in the Office of Appraisal and Reassessment, it's that one needs to slowly acclimate to every situation before choosing to tell a bawdy and/or ribald joke. I said instead, "I got you," to Lewis. I said, "I'm right with you." I shifted my weight from one leg to the other. It didn't help. I looked up at the TV and saw that the woman pitching put the thumb of her softball glove up to her left nostril, then blew. ESPN quickly switched cameras to show a young girl in the stands eating cotton candy.

"So next day, same people show up, same car, same fake camera perched on the roof. I'm going to go into the minds of these folks: I figure that they came out to the end of their driveway, dressed, you know, in jodhpurs and such, maybe riding crops in hand, so that when people looked up their address, those people'd see how rich and horsey these millionaires might be. You know, like maybe a old college roommate thinks, Hey, I wonder how Wanda-Marie's doing? Go find that old Christmas card from her; let me take a look at that return address. And then they'd look at Google Earth and see the top of the house, and choose Street View, and see old Wanda-Marie standing there looking fool like she just dismounted Secretariat or one them other studs."

I said, "Jim Beam's not as bad as I remembered. It's pretty good."

I finished off the glass, and Grgg lifted his eyebrows. I said, "One more."

Lewis said, "Don't go anywhere." He said, "I got to take a leak. You're going to want to hear the rest of this story." He got up, telling Grgg that he'd be back.

I said to Grgg, "How long you worked here?"

He said, "I got an ex-girlfriend who used to be a softball player in high school. She now has a girlfriend. Or a wife."

That maybe explained the softball on the TV, but it didn't explain anything else, although maybe it touched on my desire to drive by my ex's house.

I said to Grgg, "This seems like a rather large hotel for a small town. Why are people coming here?"

Grgg turned to one of the Fox channels, stared, and said, "They say that she and her husband sold their souls to the devil. That's why I'm not voting for her. I'd vote for the devil before I'd vote for her. At least the devil's a capitalist, buying souls and whatnot."

I didn't know what to say. I looked at my watch—still thirty minutes before I could check in. If there's one thing I've learned in Appraisal and Reassessment, it's Don't Give a Tip to Someone Who Will Use That Money for Wrongdoing. I thought about calling Aunt Maura down at the KOA, but I'd left my cell phone in the car and didn't want to put my hips through a hundred-yard walk yet. I said, "Do you sell Goody's Powders?"

Grgg kept looking at the news channel. He said, "No."

"BC? Excedrin, Tylenol, Advil?"

"I got some St. Joseph's baby aspirin," Grgg said. "I got a little bottle them."

I shook my head. I didn't ask if he had a roll-on stick of Icy Hot. I thought, Why would a bar have baby aspirin? Did they have a large clientele of babies at Sparks?

Lewis pulled back his stool, sat down, and said, "So these guys showed up with a camera on top of their car, saying they were with Google Street View." Then he got up, pulled out the stool next to mine, and sat down. He slid his drink in front of him. I said, "When you left, you had these people standing around at the ends of their driveways."

"Oh," he said. "Did you check in while I was gone?"

I said, "It's not time yet."

I noticed that Lewis now had a cell phone in his shirt pocket. When I look back, I understand that he went to the bathroom, said, "Toyota RAV4, six hours from here, seven counting the time change." He called someone who knew to look for a car with either Alabama, western Tennessee, or western Kentucky plates. I couldn't have come from Virginia or West Virginia, or central Florida, seeing as it would be the same time zone.

He said, "Okay. So where were we? Did I already mention to you about these guys showing up saying they were from Google Earth?"

I said, "I think you said Street View. Google Street View." To be honest, "Google Street View" meant nothing to me. I had other things to worry about. Like I said, I worried about Gina, and like maybe I never said, I didn't really care for my job, though I felt it necessary to put in another few years so that I could retire, cash in some bonds, later take my social security as early as possible, and cash my pension checks. Working for city government, much like teaching, requires only twenty-eight years of service. I'd done the math, and as long as I didn't ever get a toothache or have to purchase a new car in the next 12.5 years, I would make it.

"As they said it in the paper, all these people came out, waving and whatnot. The supposed Google Street View people urged them to keep standing where they were, that for the operation to work well they'd have to turn around and do a few sweeps of the area. They went back and forth, is what I'm saying, up and down those streets. This particular gated community—what's it called, Gregg?"

"Old Oaks Country Club," Grgg said.

I downed the bourbon and said, "One more."

"Old Oaks has a golf course off to the side, you know, but it's only something like one six-thousand-yard street with nine cul-de-sacs, one them places," Lewis said.

"You want another?" Grgg said to Lewis.

Lewis's phone buzzed in his pocket. He read a text, then shook his head no. He said, "Long story short, the whole while these people posed for their shots, their houses got robbed from the golf course side. I'm talking silverware and jewelry and coin collections. Any wallets laying around. The Google Street View scam artists had a whole network of burglars working with them. I don't know if it's true or not, but I like to think they pretended to play golf—it's a country club, yeah, but people can pay to play the course, I've played there once or twice—then rode their carts right up to back doors, broke in, et cetera."

Grgg said, "Irish Travelers, I'm betting." I noticed that he looked out the window of Sparks, then touched his top button twice, then three times, then one more time. He said, "My girlfriend's boss at Great Clips has a daughter got conned by Irish Travelers saying they'd seal her driveway, but they ended up only painting it black."

Lewis looked at his watch. He said, "Well, anyway, that's what you're missing around here. Hope you have a nice stay! I'm late for a meeting."

And then he left without paying his tab.

• • •

I got up and walked around the empty bar. I picked up one of those triangular cardboard stand-up menus from the middle of one table, advertising jalapeño poppers, potato skins, mozzarella sticks, chili cheese fries, nachos, soft taco sliders, hushpuppies, and fried mushrooms. I looked past Grgg for any kind of kitchen door and saw none. Through the window, though, I saw an Applebee's, which I bet offered the same appetizers. It didn't take much for me to imagine Grgg taking an order, saying, "One minute," then scooting out a back door and telling someone named Tiffany, or Amber, or Tiffani what he needed.

I said to Grgg, "That Lewis guy was something, wasn't he? He one of your regulars?"

Grgg kept looking at the TV. "He's something." I looked up at Fox and watched a clip concerning who the American Hair Stylists Union would back for president. I thought, They have a union? Their spokeswoman looked like one of the Alices on that *Star Trek* episode where Kirk and his comrades got temporarily hijacked by androids on K-Class planet Mudd.

I saw a quarter on the carpet, started to bend down, but couldn't, what with the hips. I thought, I'm not going to be able to retire at twenty-eight years, what with needing hip surgery, plus my RAV4, by that time, will need a timing belt. I thought—and I'm not proud of this—If I find a nice gold or silver collection that Aunt Maura doesn't know about, I'm going to keep it. I thought, Damn, woman, you didn't even come to my father's funeral, and didn't say much about your own sister when she passed away.

"You want one more?" Grgg said.

I thought, I need to call Gina. I can't call her up. The last thing she or I needed was for me to call up one more time drunk, pleading. I couldn't drive over to her neighborhood, explain that I was lost, then have her call that goddamn *HP number she punched one time when I left our house kind of messed up, only to have the highway patrolman turn his blue lights on behind me.

I thought, Fuck it—I ain't going to even check in to this Marriott. I'm going to go sleep at Uncle Spence's house. Who would know? Why would it matter? How long would it take Aunt Maura and dopey Jerry to drive up from Myrtle Beach?

I turned to Grgg and said, "Yeah, why not?" I said, "I ain't got nothing to do besides being here." I said, "Now that that Lewis dude is gone, is there any way we can change some channels? I'd like to watch one of those stock market channels. Jesus. Can we watch maybe something that's not softball?" I said, "There must be a thousand channels about flipping houses, or rehabbing. Something about houses. Can we turn to one of those things?" I heard my voice slur a little. I thought, Concentrate. I thought, It's a good thing you're not home. I said, "That one about buying people's junk. Or that one about hoarders, let's watch that one."

I took little shuffle steps back to my spot at the bar. I realized that if I kept shuffling at twelve-inch increments, I didn't feel the pain. I needed something more than St. Joseph's aspirin, more than Goody's powders. I needed one of the opioids everyone talked so high and mighty about. I needed Lortab, oxycodone, OxyContin, morphine, whatever else they had out on the market.

"One more, and then I'm going to have you pay your tab. We change shifts at four. Alex will be your new bartender," Grgg said.

I thought, No, I better go check in here and regroup. "Sounds good," I said. Grgg handed me a channel changer. I settled on staying—maybe Gina would feel more comfortable coming to the Marriott. It could be like a third honeymoon, I thought.

Grgg handed over my tab. I added 20 percent after he promised not to donate money to an unbalanced candidate, and I told him I'd be right back. "I'm going to go get my room, then come back down. If you're not here, it's been good talking to you."

Maybe I would've seen someone, or caught a license plate of a car burning rubber out of the Marriott, had I not decided to stand behind two couples eager to check in as early as possible. If I'd seen the line, then gone out to my car, maybe I would've caught Lewis or his co-conspirators mid-jimmy, stealing my suitcase, the GPS, my cell phone, the checkbook I shouldn't have left in the glove compartment. I checked in, the desk clerk gave me directions to the elevator, and I walked out into disconcerting sunshine. I, of course, thought, Why did I leave my driver's-side door open? I thought, This isn't my car. I thought, Damn it to hell, one more, one more, one more.

Back inside, we called the police. Two sympathetic officers took notes; one of them said how this happens twice a week and no one's ever caught. They said I happened to be unlucky enough to park outside the security camera's range. I told them all about how I suspected this guy Lewis—and Grgg, for that matter—but didn't go into all the touching-the-top-button codes, and so on.

I couldn't call my ex-wife later with another hard-luck story, I knew. At least I understood that much. Poor Aunt Maura would take the brunt of this—I would scour that house until at least a cache of Peace dollars appeared, and they'd go home with me. To make it up, though—for having to buy new clothes, a new GPS, toothbrush and toothpaste, cell phone—I'd at least have the decency to erase the porn from my uncle's computer history, delete any dabbles of his looking up the whereabouts of ex-girlfriends, get rid of any files holding questionable correspondence. I would write his wife a love letter, then leave it on the dining room table for when she and her special son returned, ready to start another life. I'd leave a sticky note saying, "I found this in his desk drawer." As I figured it—as I *appraised* it—this would place me in some kind of positive column, later. I would have no trouble with the letter. I'd written them often.

EVERYTHING'S WILD

Marvin Freel got to the point where he couldn't remember hands. He'd been part of Thursday Night Poker for more than half a century, there in one of the greenhouses, after hours. Usually Lou, the owner of Foothills Farm and Garden, sat at the head of the swept-off plywood-topped table, at the other end from the window exhaust fan. Sometimes Lou's wife, Starla, sat in, as did Marvin's wife, Lillian, before she succumbed to pancreatic cancer. Summertime college students lost their paychecks to Marvin and Lou, though the two men always found ways to grant overtime or hand over a twenty and say it was tip money from a kindly spinster they, the seasonal workers, helped load a car trunk for earlier in the day. Then there was Pete—Pete Boggs—who claimed to be a distant relative of a famous baseball player. Lou said he only hired the guy because of the sound of his name, arguing that a man with such a moniker couldn't possibly be inadequate when it came to soil amendment or mulching. Full-time employees Jorge and Miguel played, though Marvin didn't like the games they called—games he felt they made up, like Mexican Stud and Cross the River, Nicaraguan Surprise and Five-Card Visa. Jorge's wife, Yolanda—who told the seasonal workers what to do—played on Texas Hold 'Em nights. Over the years there'd been Doug, Jesus, Dave, Roberto, Lee-boy, and others. Walter from the uniform service showed up once a month on average, as did a guy named Looper, the river-rock vendor. Vicki and Treesie from the gift shop played when the other one didn't, and always called Follow the Queen, which everyone else hated. This was always nickel ante, quarter limit, three-raise limit, high-low. Rarely did anyone lose more than fifteen dollars, and only Marvin ever seemed to win more than twenty.

"Think again," Marvin said to Lou on what ended up being the last time they played. "Flush beats a full house."

Lou peered over the rims of his trifocals. He said, "You don't have a straight flush. You got a flush." He pointed with his pinky. "Three, six, nine, jack, queen of hearts."

"Bullshit, Geoff," Marvin said to Lou. "Flush beats a full house. Ask anyone." No one in attendance happened to be named Geoff. Back when Foothills Farm and Garden sold koi, a disastrous year that taught Lou and Marvin they needed to cover outdoor fishponds with chicken wire to deter red-tailed and sharp-shinned hawks, a tropical-fish vendor named Geoff sat in on occasion.

There were six at the table on this night. The youngest, Dave, celebrated his sixtieth birthday on this evening. Starla'd brought a cake. Lou donated a twelve-pack of Modelo. Miguel and Vicki brought chips and dip. Everyone chipped in except for Marvin, who went back to his pickup truck twice looking for pretzels he swore he'd put behind the bench seat. The players' audience consisted of traditional and hybrid pepper plants: jalapeños, habaneros, Thai, Scotch bonnets, cayennes. They shuffled and dealt and bluffed and sighed among Big Black Mamas, ghost peppers, apocalypse scorpions, wrecking balls. The misters had been turned off.

"Who the hell is Geoff?" Lou said.

"I think I know my hands," Marvin said. "Flush beats a full house."

Dave said, "Well, I know that I have the low." He showed his cards. "I got a perfect." He reached into the middle of the table and started dividing up the chips.

Everyone looked at Marvin. He gripped the edge of the table with both hands. No one said, "Funny," or "Come on," or "Miguel's deal." They'd spoken about this particular moment—they'd imagined this time—for six months. Marvin had referred to his dead wife as Nicole, sometimes as Ava. He'd left the Public Entrance unlocked twice overnight when leaving. When landscapers came to buy Leland cypresses, he'd loaded their trucks up with azaleas. He'd left for home, then an hour later called Lou or Starla to say, "I forget where the heck I'm going." He had walked around with glasses atop his head, or keys in his hand, looking for them.

Lou said, "I got a copy of Hoyle's back in the office, Marvin."

Marvin said, "I know. Yeah, I know. I got confused with the game. I was thinking about another game."

Miguel handed over the deck for Marvin to cut. Miguel said, "Okay, this one is called Seven-Card Dominican Baseball. Threes and nines are wild, plus you need to catch the card when I deal it to you, or else you get an error. At the end of the game, whoever has the least errors wins, no matter what. Even if you have a royal flush."

Everyone anted up. Vicki said, "Wait. You're dealing. You won't have to catch a card."

Miguel said, "Sí. I win."

• • •

Marvin graduated with a Bachelor of Science degree in horticulture, fell in love with Lillian, and promised to live back in her hometown although it would not offer any job for which he qualified. Lillian could teach sixth-grade English. Her parents were both in poor health, and she was an only child who needed to take care of them. If pressed, Marvin would've said, "Well, I figured they would die, and then we could move to a real city. I could get a job with the FDA, or at least as an inspector or pest-management supervisor." He even saw himself as possibly working in the field for a year or two—how long would his in-laws live? Then he'd go to graduate school, become one of those professors with enough time to write articles about such things as predatory worms. He saw himself working as a county cooperative extension agent, maybe showing up on public radio once a week to offer tips about aphids and bottom rot.

But Lillian's parents *didn't* die. They weren't close. Marvin took a job with Lou's father—who owned Foothills Farm and Garden at the time—and then stayed on even after Lou, a sociology major, inherited the business nine years later. Anyone in the town of Steepleburg understood that, should they wish to know anything about early blight, late blight, common blight, wilts, club root, downy mildew, galls, blackroot, leaf blister, or smuts needed to talk to Marvin. Lou cared about his clients, and fulfilled a small-town need for customer service, while Marvin took care of pointers and concerns when it came to drought or infestation.

Lillian's parents—her mother taught sixth grade also, twenty years after she could've retired; her father ran an H&R Tax Service outlet in a strip mall until he was seventy-three, exactly Marvin's age when Marvin couldn't remember hands—died in a retirement home down toward Union. By this time it was too late for Lillian to find a new sixth-grade class in a city that offered her husband the kind of job for which he felt qualified. By this time, Lillian and Marvin had grown children who didn't want to come visit their parents even if they moved to Atlanta or Chicago or Denver, seeing as these children lived in Atlanta, Chicago, and Denver. Marvin's children said things like, "Y'all can't move—your grandkids already know big cities. They need to come visit a place like Steepleburg so they can see where meat comes from, and tomatoes."

Marvin talked to one of his three kids—two girls and a boy—at least daily. He kept a journal. His journal read, "A woman asked about ladybugs. Told her they weren't poisonous." It read, "A man asked about hummingbirds. Told him they didn't have rabies." It read, "Told the children that their mother wanted to be cremated, her ashes waved into a garden, as will be mine."

Lillian's parents died one after the other, one month apart. Lillian and Marvin didn't have to wait for Probate Court. They kept what they wanted, which meant a dining room table and a collection of silver dollars. The auctioneer banged his gavel a number of times, including for the two-bedroom house, and Marvin hugged his wife hard sideways, shoulder to shoulder. He said, "I am sorry, Lillian."

She sniffled. She didn't say, "I thought they were supposed to die way back when we first got married, like I told you. Please forgive me for kind of ruining your life, Marvin." She said, "I know."

He said, "How many people live into their nineties? Good god, what a life," and he meant it.

At the funerals—both times—Lillian said, "You have dirt underneath your fingernails."

• • •

"You feeling okay tonight, Marvin? Hey, why don't you get a ginger ale? I found a place that sells both Buffalo Rock *and* Blenheim's. I got them in the fridge," Lou said.

Vicki said, "Okay, this is called Follow the Queen," as if everyone at the table had never heard of this game, as if Vicki—and Treesie, who was married to Vicki's first husband—ever ventured off into a similar ridiculous game, like Indian poker.

Marvin looked past Dave across from him and said, hardly audible, "Three of a kind beats two pair, right?"

Dave said, "I agree. Maybe you ought to go get a ginger ale. Sit out a hand. You don't even like Follow the Queen."

"Straight doesn't really beat much playing with wild cards," Marvin said.

"Straight," said Lou. "No, a straight ain't what it used to be forty years ago."

Marvin got up from the table. No one said anything about how he still wore his Foothills Farm and Garden uniform—khaki pants, short-sleeved blue shirt with a name over one pocket and "Foothills" printed in a hump, like a hill, over the other. The "F" and "n" bled down with roots toward the pocket so that it looked similar to an outline of South Carolina. No one said anything about how it appeared that he'd not brushed his teeth in a couple days, or that his car hadn't seemed to have moved from its parking space in a while.

Vicki dealt out one card each when Marvin wandered off toward the breakroom, which meant he needed to leave the hot-pepper greenhouse, go outside, walk into the main building, cross through the gift shop, and take a left. No one said, "Marvin's gone, and is sitting out this hand." Without a word, and with no confusion, the five remaining players slid their first cards over one spot, and Vicki said, "Pot's right."

"I read an article the other day about this," Starla said. "Marvin's got early-stage dementia. There are things we can do, though."

Vicki dealt second down cards to everyone, then said, "I forgot to say, roll your own." She started dealing a third card down.

"What? Like what?" Dave said. "I think he's just still grieving for Lillian. If you ask me, Marvin's probably not sleeping much, and it's made him a little confused. You know how it gets when we're working our asses off for Valentine's Day, or at Christmas when every goddamn person in Steepleburg thinks they need eighteen poinsettias."

Lou looked at his cards and flipped over a seven. He said, "I don't know. I don't know. Listen, between all of us, Marvin's way beyond retirement age. He's got money. He's screwing up. Miguel, don't you go tell him I said this. I don't tell everyone this, but I spend half the day following him around, fixing what he's fouled."

Miguel said, "No, señor."

Vicki and Starla said, "No."

Dave said, "Seeing as I'm sixty today, I figure I might want to start taking some precautions."

"I don't want to fire him," Lou said. He said, "I don't know if I believe in an afterlife, but if I fired Marvin, and then met my daddy in the afterlife, my daddy would never let it go."

Everyone checked. No one liked Follow the Queen. Even Vicki checked. She started flipping out cards and went, "Ace, four, queen—queen! Next one's a wild card. Queen again! Next one's a wild card—six of diamonds. Sixes are wild!"

They bet nickels. Miguel raised a quarter, which made everyone else believe that he held a six in the hole. Lou, Starla, and Vicki folded. Dave said, "Y'all are fools. It's high-low!" He called the raise. He said, "It's my birthday. I don't care."

Starla said, "I read this article that said dementia can be thwarted by a diet heavily imbued in potassium. We need to make sure that, from now on, Marvin gets a couple bananas with his lunch every day. That's what I read, anyway."

Lou looked at his wife. He smiled. "We've been married for thirty-plus years, and I've never heard you use the word 'imbued.' I'm not sure it's even the right word, but I'm proud for you trying to use it, honey."

Starla said, "Thirty-six years." She said, "Wait a minute. It might not be potassium. It might be ginkgo biloba. Maybe we should start trying to grow that here."

Dave said, "We could put Marvin in charge of that. Maybe it'd rub off on him."

Vicki said, "All bets are in. Two players left." She flipped over another queen.

Dave said, "Son of a bitch. Happy freaking birthday."

Miguel said, "I will go back to Nuevo Laredo if I lose this game."

Vicki dealt an ace to Miguel. She said, "All right. Aces are wild."

Lou's cell phone rang. He picked it up and looked to find "Marvin" on his screen. He said, "Marvin," and slid the answer symbol. He said, "Where are you, buddy?"

Marvin said, "Who is this?"

Lou took his phone away from his face. He said, "Not good." He looked at the pot on the table. Dave went low and Miguel high. Dave had a nine-seven, which wasn't normally good. Miguel had three sixes, which, too, wouldn't normally take a pot. Lou looked back at his cards to see that he had a low flush for a high, or an eight-six for a low. He said into the phone, "Damn it to hell."

"I think I got the wrong number." Marvin hung up.

Lou eased up out of his chair, coughed twice into his right hand, and went to look for him.

• • •

Marvin and Lillian shared a love unmatched by their friends. More often than not Marvin drove over to the elementary school for lunch, just to sit with his wife and eat sloppy joes and canned corn or lima beans, surrounded by her sixth-graders. When she graded tests and made out lesson plans at night, Marvin sat with an open notebook, penciling in ideas for future hybrids. He thumbed through botany textbooks from college, and sketched flora. In their fifty years of marriage, not once did they go to Myrtle Beach. Lillian volunteered to teach summer school or tutor students not prepared for the next grade level. Marvin worked, always exuberant, at the nursery. He took his two-week paid vacation between Thanksgiving and Christmas—between pumpkins and poinsettias—and if Lillian's semester ended early enough, they drove to the mountains of North Carolina and spent a day or two panning for rubies and sapphires. Marvin bought a rock tumbler, experimented with coarse and medium grit, and in time retrieved their gemstones.

Lillian's funeral might've been the largest ever in Steepleburg, a town whose children rarely strayed far off. Past-student mourners aged twelve to sixty attended, plus most members, past and present, of Thursday Night Poker. Even though Marvin specified "in lieu of flowers" in the obituary—Lillian requested donations be sent to either Hospice Care of the Piedmont or the Steepleburg Public Library—Lou sent a four-foot potted magnolia to the funeral home, with instructions that the tree be planted in Lillian's honor somewhere on her school's grounds.

Marvin did not argue with his wife's wish to be cremated, though none of their family or friends had ever chosen such an option. Lillian wrote out, in the notebook in which her husband sketched blackberries, weeping willows, peppers he'd invented—Big Red Nana, Hot Wrinkled Fingers, Flaming Redhead Branding Irons, Endorphins' Revenge—"Spread my ashes, Marvin, in the community garden down by the Farmer's Market. That way I know that you'll come visit me, and seeing as you're there, then maybe you'll buy some vegetables, and take care of your health."

They weren't churchgoers. Neither wished to have a preacher talk at their funerals. Marvin decided that Lillian wouldn't mind her ceramic urn on a stand, in front of the funeral home's sanctuary, while a slide show of photographs appeared behind, on the wall. She'd asked to have a rendition of a bluesy burlesque song called "Night Train," the one by Louis Prima, played over and over, on a loop. Lillian wanted people to laugh. Marvin said to an embalmer named Mr. Harley, "I'd like to get up and say some things about my wife. Then maybe other people could talk."

"That sounds like a fine plan," Mr. Harley said. "We've performed many such a remembrance."

Marvin had said, "Performed."

"That might not be the correct word," Mr. Harley said. "Undergone. We've fully committed ourselves to having what the deceased, and the deceased's family, wishes."

Marvin had to go buy a suit. Six hours after Lillian's last breath he drove down to Steepleburg Haberdashery and bought a black suit off the rack. He went next door to Church City Shoes and bought wingtips.

When the music faded and the last slide turned off—Lillian standing to the left side of her 2001 class—Marvin got up from the pew and approached the lectern. He'd not made notes. He had planned to say, "I fell in love with Lillian ten years before I met her, because I daydreamed, as a little boy, about the perfect woman." He'd planned on saying things about her eyes, smile, and patience. He wanted everyone to know about her abilities as a mother and neighbor, a teacher and citizen. Marvin wished everyone in attendance to leave the funeral parlor thinking, "I will be a better person, because of Lillian Freel."

He gripped the sides of the lectern. He looked out at the audience. Marvin found himself thinking about a professor he had during his first year in college, a professor stuck teaching a lecture hall of a good hundred mostly uninterested students. Marvin thought, No wonder that guy's voice tended to waver. No wonder he didn't make eye contact.

Marvin stood there staring for three minutes. Then he placed his right, callused palm on his dead wife's urn. He didn't say, "Lillian." He unleashed his tie using his left hand. He said, quietly—but people in the front two rows heard him—"Most people take up just enough space on this planet to fill a grave. Some people are less selfish."

He did not cry publicly. Marvin walked off into the office spaces of the mortuary.

• • •

Vicki and Starla played Spades against Dave and Miguel, agreeing that the game would stop the moment Lou and Marvin returned. They played for a penny a point. Vicki said, "It was like turning on the nozzle. One day he was fine, then Lillian died and he went off."

Miguel said, "I had a tía who went loco after my tío died. She lived less than one year."

"Speak American," said Vicki.

"'Loco' means crazy," Dave said.

Starla looked at her hand and said, "I bid two."

Miguel said, "I know where Marvin's gone."

Dave said, "I bid four."

"There are thirteen possible tricks," said Starla.

"He didn't pour his wife's ashes in the community garden. Her ashes are back in the compost heap. I saw him," Miguel said. "I said to Señor Marvin, 'Hey, what are you doing?' and he said to me, 'I get the feeling that Lillian wanted to go on more trips. She wanted to see places.' That's what he told me."

Starla said, "I want to go up to three. I want to bid three. I have a crummy hand, but not that crummy." She said, "I don't get what you're saying, Miguel. I believe you, but I don't get it."

Dave said, "You can't go back and change your bid after I've already bid."

"Me, either," said Miguel.

Vicki said, "Let her change her bid. We're all friends. Plus an amigo."

Miguel said, "He explained it to me. He said, 'If I put my wife in the compost, that compost feeds plants. Plants grow and get sold. People eat the plants. Señora Lillian becomes part of those people. They go on vacations. Señora Lillian goes on vacations."

"Or," said Starla, "we have people buy a plant, then they plant it somewhere far away. Like maybe they take it to a relative in California, or Mississippi. Or they plant it, then dig it up and take it when they move. People do that all the time. I know of a couple who have Carolina jasmine they bought here, then the husband got transferred to Utah, or Arkansas—one of them western states. Well, she said she'd only go if she could take part of their yard with her."

Dave stared at the exhaust fan. He said, "I might have to check the humidity in here. I don't know if it was you mentioning Utah, or if I really think it might be too dry in here."

Vicki looked at her hand. She said, "I'm going nil."

Miguel said, "Señor Lou will find Marvin sitting in front of the compost heap." He said, "The word for zero in Spanish is 'cero.'" He said, "I bid ocho. That means 'eight,' for any of y'all who've not been paying attention to me for all these years."

They threw out their lowest clubs to begin. Vicki's was a five. She took the trick and lost her team a hundred points immediately.

• • •

Lou limped through his nursery, calling Marvin's name. He turned lights on from room to room, greenhouse to greenhouse. He walked into the parking lot to find Marvin's truck still parked in its spot. He noticed a bag of pretzels in the bed of the truck.

Finally, using his cell phone's flashlight, he discovered Marvin, sure enough, knelt down at the bin where employees discarded their coffee grounds and leftover lunch salads, where Miguel and Jesus and Jorge tossed corn husks from their tamales, where Dave threw plants that would never grow fruits or vegetables, where Marvin poured his wife.

Lou said, "It's your deal, buddy."

Marvin looked straight into the eight-by-eight bin. He'd poured Lillian's ashes into the back right corner on purpose, and delegated her bone-pellets a thimble at a time into the regular, black-soiled detritus. Marvin didn't respond to his boss. He said, "And I bet they're not learning state capitals like you used to make them know. Or presidents in order. Or twelve times twelve." He said, "I miss going back there to eat sloppy joes with you."

Lou said, "Come on, Marvin. Get on up and let's finish playing. Later on I'll drive you home."

Marvin turned his head toward Lou. He said, "I don't know what's happening." He held his mouth ajar. His eyes looked at Lou as if to say Who Are You? or Why Are We Here? or I Know I Clipped that Coupon for Buy-One-Get-One-Free. He stepped over the three-foot-high front sliding metal wall of the compost bin, reached in, and took a pinch of his wife's ashes. He placed them in his mouth. He said, "Gritty as ever."

Lou said, "Come on, Marvin. I'll drive you home."

• • •

"I'm going to drive Marvin home," Lou said, holding Marvin above the elbow. They walked side by side into the greenhouse.

Dave yelled out, "Game!" He said, "That's the rules! That's what we said! It's my birthday!" He and Miguel were up by 120 points. He looked back and forth at the women. "Y'all owe us sixty cents each."

Starla looked at her husband. She said, "Is everything all right?"

Lou nodded, but with his eyes he said to Starla, "We might be losing Marvin for the rest of our lives. We might need to hire on someone else. We might need to put an ad out in *Horticulture Times* for a germinologist."

"I don't want to go home just yet," Marvin said. "Come on. We can play another round."

Starla said, "I tell you what. I'm about tired anyway." She looked at Vicki, Miguel, and Dave. "Why don't we call it a night? Next time we can play for an extra hour." The others got up without protest. Starla said to her husband, "I'll see you at home. Take all the time you need."

With everyone gone except Lou, Marvin said, "It's too much, back home. If I go back home, it has to be within about two minutes of my falling asleep. I can't look around at anything."

Lou checked his wristwatch. He said, "We'll be okay here."

When Miguel's muffler could no longer be recognized through the cicadas, peepers, and crickets, Marvin said to his boss, "I know I'm slipping, but it's not the way everyone else slips."

Lou sat down. He said, "You want a beer?"

Marvin shook his head. "It's not like I can't remember anything anymore. It's just that my head's filled up. It's overflowing. I mean, I always had a head full of possible hybrids swirling around, but now I have memories, and guilt pangs, and wishes. If my mind were a grinding wheel, you wouldn't believe the sparks I'm producing nonstop."

Lou picked up one deck of cards and shuffled. He said, "I hate to say it, but I kind of hope that I go before Starla. I know that sounds mean, but I don't know if I could take what you're going through. Women can do it. Hard as it is for a man to admit, a woman can endure heartache a little better. I think that's why most men die before their wives."

"Deal something out," Marvin said. He nodded. He smiled. He said, "Hand me that made deck. I got a new game called Five-Card Draw, Everything's Wild."

Lou handed the cards over. Marvin nudged them back Lou's way for him to cut. Lou said, "That won't work. We'll just bet, raise each other, stay pat, then end up splitting the pot."

Marvin kept smiling. He dealt out five cards. He said, "Remember, everything's wild. This is a high-only game, seeing it's just the two of us." A strand of his hair fell right across his left eye.

Lou said, "This don't make no sense, buddy. We'll both have the same hand."

Marvin dealt. Lou bet a quarter. Marvin called and raised a quarter. Lou called and raised another. Marvin took the last raise. He said, "You want any cards?"

"Is this some kind of trick, Marvin? *Everything's* wild. Is that what you're saying?"

The exhaust fan stopped its whirring inexplicably. Something skittered across the pea gravel off in the corner, a mouse or chipmunk. Marvin breathed deeply, as if it would be his last exposure to the scent of peat moss, soil, and fertilizer. He said, "Don't make me say it again."

Lou turned over his cards—a pair of sevens, a three, eight, and ace. He said, "If they're all wild, then I have five aces."

Marvin craned his neck and inspected his boss's hand. He said, "You got me. I wasn't thinking. I got a royal flush, but five of a kind beats a royal."

Lou didn't say, "You have five aces, also, Marvin." He didn't say, "Tomorrow's Friday. Why don't you take a long weekend?" He didn't scrape the pot over to his side of the table, either. He said, "In all these years, I don't remember our vegetables doing so well. I guess it's because they're all imbued with Lillian."

Marvin leaned over to Lou and whispered, "Do you remember thirty, thirty-five years ago when you had a woman named Greta who worked in the gift shop? She was only here a few months. She played cards with us once."

Lou said, "Yeah," though he couldn't place her.

"That's why I have this grinding wheel going. That's the reason why I'm being challenged such. She got drunk that one night, and said she wouldn't mind me 'freeling' her up. Get it? Because of my last name."

Lou stared at his most valuable employee. He shrugged, then laughed nervously. He said, "Don't beat yourself up, Marvin. Is this what's got you so confused?"

Marvin said, "I almost left Lillian for Greta. I mean, we had a plan and everything, to move down to Florida. Someone with my background can get a good job in Florida. Greta quit here and moved on down. I never followed."

Lou said, "Come on, Marvin," and got up from the table. In his mind he went through the directions to Marvin's house—take a right on 215, drive a mile or thereabouts, left on 221, cross under I-26. He'd not been to the Freels' in a decade. What he remembered was perfect azaleas, a boundary of tea olives, a gravel driveway, and ranch-style brick house. There was no way he could imagine what he'd find inside, helping a sobbing Marvin through the front door, turning on the living room light, and seeing, spelled out in polished rubies and sapphires two feet high across the wall, S-O-R-R-Y. Lou never foresaw Marvin trudging inside the house, walking between two wingback chairs, going straight for the gemstones, and pressing his palms against them, on a lean, as if bracing the wall.

ACKNOWLEDGMENTS

Thank you, with love, to Glenda Guion, again and again and again—a woman with patience, except when it comes to the myopic notion that freedom involves the need for semiautomatic weaponry. Never-ending biscuits to the dogs at my feet, Lily and Mabel and Sally. Thanks to my students and colleagues at Wofford College for putting up with me. Thank you James Long at wonderful LSU Press for believing in this collection, and managing editor Lee Sioles for her faith, and for the stellar copyediting from Susan Murray. Additionally, Erin Rolfs and Catherine Kadair proved to be patient, expert, right-minded, convivial virtuosos. And I couldn't spare living without Barbara Bourgoyne's striking design work. Then there's editor Michael Griffith—Man oh man: Superb genius writer, bon vivant, Best Editor in the Universe, fellow South Carolinian much missed.

Some of these stories originally appeared in slightly different versions in the following magazines, journals, and anthologies, to whose editors grateful acknowledgment is made: "Staff Picks" in *One Story*; "Columbus Day" in *Oxford American*; "Hex Keys" in *Atlantic Monthly*; "Four-Way Stop" in *Georgia Review* and *Pushcart Prize XL*; "Trombones, Not Magic" in *Georgia Review*; "Gloryland" in *Evansville Review*; "Linguistic Fallacies and Facial Tics, Sex Ed and Death" in *Georgia Review*; "Flag Day" in *Shenandoah*; "Resisting Separation" in *Heck*; "Probate" in *Cincinnati Review*; "Eclipse" in *Subtropics*; "Rinse Cycle" in *Goliad Review*; "One More" in *LitMag*; "Everything's Wild" in *South Carolina Review*.